LAURE

the collected writings

LAURE

the collected writings

translated from the french by Jeanine Herman

city lights books
san francisco

This book was originally published as *Ecrits de Laure*

Book Design by Amy Scholder
Cover Design by Rex Ray
Typography by Harvest Graphics

Note from the French publisher: The writings of Laure and her correspondence are presented here in their entirety. However, certain names of people and places have been replaced with imaginary names.

Jean-Jacques Pauvert
Jérôme Peignot

Library of Congress Cataloging-in-Publication Data

Laure.
[Ecrits. English]
Laure : the collected writings / Laure ; translated by Jeanine Herman.
p. cm.
ISBN 0-87286-293-3
1. Laure—Translations into English. 2. Revolutionary poetry, French—Translations into English. 3. Women poets, French—20th century—Correspondence. I. Herman, Jeanine. II. Title.
PQ2672.A7825A24 1995
848'.91209—dc20
94-33144
CIP

City Lights Books are available to bookstores through our primary distributor: Subterranean Company, P.O. Box 160, 265 S. 5th St., Monroe, OR 97456. 503-847-5274. Toll-free orders 800-274-7826. FAX 503-847-6018. Our books are also available through library jobbers and regional distributors. For personal orders and catalogs, please write to City Lights Books, 261 Columbus Avenue, San Francisco, CA 94133.

CITY LIGHTS BOOKS are edited by Lawrence Ferlinghetti and Nancy J. Peters and published at the City Lights Bookstore, 261 Columbus Avenue, San Francisco, CA 94133.

10 9 8 7 6 5 4 3 2 1

Contents

Preface	vii
Story of a Little Girl	1
The Sacred	37
Correspondence	95
New Fragments	163
Political Texts	207
Notes on the Revolution and The Red Note Book	215
Appendixes	233
My Diagonal Mother	275

Translator's Acknowledgments

I would like to thank Lisa Silver for a close reading of *Laure* in English, Meighan Gale, Sabine Guez, Stéphanie Lang, and my editor Amy Scholder.

Preface to the City Lights Edition

Laure (Colette Laure Lucienne Peignot) was born October 8, 1903 in Paris. She came from a wealthy, Catholic family, but denounced her bourgeois and religious upbringing. Writing and dissolution became her revolt. Toward the end of her life, she became the lover of the French writer Georges Bataille. She died at thirty-five of tuberculosis on November 8, 1938 at Bataille's house in Saint-Germain-en-Laye.

Laure's letters to Suzanne, her brother's wife, are written for the most part when Laure is an adolescent. She hates the world, feels depressed, quotes writers who suggest that life should be joyous and intoxicating, calls herself "savage." She likes Rimbaud, has an aversion to the young girls around her, and wants something more, "true life."

Her first love is the writer Jean Bernier.[1] They have a brief affair, but he is involved with another woman, and Laure realizes that he does not love her. She finds a revolver and, in a hotel room, tries to shoot herself in the heart. This attempt at suicide is not successful.

In 1928 she goes to Berlin. It is here that she leads a decadent life with the German sadist Eduard Trautner. He keeps her in dog collars and black silk dresses. Only a page remains from her journal of this time; she burned the rest.

She studies Russian at the prestigious École des Langues Orientales in Paris and goes to the Soviet Union in 1930. She lives with peasants in a remote village but falls sick and has to be brought back to Paris. In 1931 she is involved with Boris Souvarine, one of the founders of the French Communist Party, who later forms Le Cercle Communiste Démocratique. He edits *La Critique sociale*, the leftist journal for which Laure not only works but also finances. She writes

1. See Jean Bernier's *L'Amour de Laure*, Paris, Flammarion, 1978.

small articles on Russian literature under the pseudonym Claude Araxe. Bataille contributes to it as well (some of his most important essays are published here, such as "La notion de dépense"), as does Raymond Queneau, Michel Leiris, and various other dissident surrealists and Marxists. Laure becomes friends with the only other woman to contribute to *La Critique sociale*, the writer and revolutionary Simone Weil, with whom she shares a certain rigor and fervor.

It is not until the summer of 1934 that Laure and Bataille actually begin their affair, the night before her trip to Austria with Souvarine. They correspond, and Bataille follows her to Austria. They meet in Trento in July, and Laure abandons Souvarine. Later Souvarine has Laure committed to a clinic "to rest." She is placed under the care of Dr. Weil, Simone's father.

Laure was said to have been the great love of Bataille's life, but he did not remain faithful to her, and in fact, was "systematically, abundantly" unfaithful to her.[2] Her letters to him are at times outpourings of love, at times bilious and accusatory.

A year later, in 1935, Bataille writes the novel *Blue of Noon* in which two characters, Dirty and Troppmann, correspond, the former writes from Austria, the latter from Spain. Dirty, the object of the narrator's affections, is probably based on Laure. She is the abject character in sumptuous dresses and drunken stupors: "Dirty was stretched out on the bed, still drinking [. . .] drunkenness gave her the forsaken candor of a child, of a little girl" (p. 17).

Later the narrator tells Lazare (the character based on Simone Weil): "Dirty is the one person in the world who has ever compelled my admiration. (In a sense I was lying—she may not have been the only one—but in a deeper sense it was true.)" (p. 37).

2. See Michel Surya's biography *Georges Bataille: La mort à l'oeuvre*, Paris, Éditions Garamont, 1987, p. 207.

Laure is also a bit of Xénie, a character who visits the narrator when he is sick, as Laure did Bataille in January and February of 1934 at Issy-les-Moulineaux.

In 1936, Laure is involved in *Contre-Attaque*, the leftist group which temporarily eases the rift between Bataille and the surrealists through a common goal—revolution through sexual and moral upheaval—but this soon dissolves. Laure sees the Spanish Civil War and the Popular Front as a source of great hope and goes to Spain in May of 1936.

Later that year she is involved in Acéphale, a secret society that strives to recreate dionysian rituals, meeting in the woods and sometimes bordellos. Its symbol is a headless man, representing anarchy, a state without a head. She is its first female member.

Ecrits de Laure was first published in 1977. The material was collected by Laure's nephew Jerome Peignot. His ecstatic essay, ostensibly about Laure, is perhaps less about Laure than about Peignot himself. This is the first translation of *Laure: The Collected Writings* to be published in English. Footnotes, unless otherwise indicated, are from the French edition.

People describe Laure as pure, dissolute, dark, luminous. "I drank, I bathed in her radiant purity" Jean Bernier says. Michel Leiris writes about her lyrically in *Fourbis* and *Frêle Bruit* as "the saint of the chasm." Bataille calls her uncompromising, pure, and sovereign. It is tempting to romanticize Laure in the most sublime and violent sense—as consumptive poet, a fervent revolutionary, Bataille's great love. But if she is radiant and Dirty, she is also insolent. That, it seems, is what saves her.

Jeanine Herman
New York, 1995

Story of a Little Girl

Title of a short story:
Sad Privilege
or
A Fairytale Life
Story of a Little Girl[1]

Title of a novel
As an epigraph: Lautréamont
Evil—Being
"Death seizes living flesh"
Where death . . .
When death . . .
Story of a little girl
Why has already been *explained* enough
in the beginning: autobiography
but continue = seek
all that in "free" life
is confined by the
same dilemma
explain oneself through Christ
death taste *truth*
death taste of the absolute

1. Written in another ink—that of the following fragment—as though the *final title*.

STORY OF A LITTLE GIRL[2]

Sad Privilege
or A Fairy Tale Life

A child's eyes pierce the night.

The sleepwalker, in a long white nightshirt, illuminates the darkened corners where she kneels, mumbling in her sleep before the crucifix and the Virgin Mary. Holy pictures cover the walls, the sleeper submits to all the genuflections and then slips between her sheets. Abandoned to less real phantoms who also have all rights over me, my room once again assumes the heavy immobility of premature nightmare.

Terror rises among four walls like wind on the sea. A very old woman, doubled over, threatens me with her cane, a man made invisible by the famous ring watches me every second, God "who sees all

2. The title chosen from among the others by Georges Bataille and Michel Leiris.

and knows all thoughts" watches me, severe. The white curtain comes loose from the window, hovers in the shadows, approaches, and carries me off: I gently pass through the pane and ascend to the sky . . .

Thousands of luminous points appear in the darkness, dance in circles, move away from the nightlight, swarm toward me. A fine rainbow of dust settles on the objects, drops of color slide onto each other. Liquid and phosphorescent cones, circles, rectangles, pyramids, an alphabet of forms and colors, solar prism, sky of my eyes in tears; the phosphenes dance in circles . . . the bed pitches beneath the swell of dreams.

And the days of these nights were a sordid and fear-ridden childhood, haunted by mortal sin, Good Friday and Ash Wednesday. Childhood crushed beneath heavy veils of mourning—childhood, stealer of children.

No, all has not been said. Criminal hands have gripped the wheel of destiny: many go no further than that, vigorous newborns strangled by the umbilical cord and yet . . . "they ask only to live."

Listen to them, the night is filled with their cries: long wrenching cries interrupted by the noise of a window being brutally shut, harsh and liquid cries stifled by a gag, cries dying between the lips, strident calls, names of men or women cast into the eternal void, vengeful laughter falling from above in a cascade of contempt, vague and diffuse laments, the wail of children with voices like men. All these cries, tangled in the flight of autumn leaves, rise from a garden like the smell of dew, wet soil, and cut hay.

I've found a very Parisian garden to hide in. From behind the spindly trees a pale man has emerged, he bows, shakes a hand in the emptiness, retreats, taking small steps on white pebbles, bows again, clasps a nonexistent hand and sets out again cautiously around the lawn . . . Another man emerges, face ablaze, lips vermilion, he's found my refuge embedded in the wall, hidden by these dreadful clumps of fuchsia. There is a lot of ivy here, soot, begonia blossoms crushed between fingers, and hopscotch marks traced in chalk. The man, obscene gesture, comes closer, but there are many clever detours, and another man sits astride his window, frantic, thrashing the air like a windmill, frothing at the mouth: "they've robbed me the bastards." He is subdued. Now a woman passes by, hands clasped under her chin. She runs, her shapeless body limp and clumsy. The sight elicits from a passerby a half-smile, frozen immediately, because above, a pallid face appears, someone's trying to get through the bars of a cage, trying straight on and then at an angle, but in vain, so that an emaciated white arm passes through them and hangs gently until evening, like linen in the wind.

A lying, smiling mob (parents and doctors) circle the ditch of madmen in the garden of childhood.

Poor fallow beings and their pain that surrenders, having resisted too much, and their pain, defeated, powerless, crushed, idiotic. Listen to them: a b c d I no longer know how to speak, 1 2 3 4 I no longer know how to count.

What do you care about the village idiot or the neighborhood madwoman? Aren't the streets full of bought consciences, broken backs? Still others, destined for a nearer death or a better life, end up at fairs, in ports, in squares, under bridges.

Living wreckage from every shipwreck—misery or despair—find themselves stunned on crumbling docks. Stunned to see each other face to face, man to man, and because glances are exchanged, passwords are exchanged, meaningless and heavy with meaning. Those, alone, who return from far away understand each other speaking *this way* of rain and fair weather. And it seems the earth, responding to the sound of voices, becomes more solid underfoot. The river rolls its oily waters, carries along its heavy stenches. Above the bridges, the city;

beyond the city, the fields. And in the city and in the fields a changing sea of human glances.

There is not one glance that does not hide a secret, a *story,* one that is not an answer, an appeal, an explanation. Glances so clear and pure, their depths muddied with stains and streaks: human algae and detritus. Bulging, blue-green and gummy eyes, voiceless glances, others illuminated, glances that know how to hate and scorn, loving and confiding glances, glances that reveal *one* goal, *one* wish, glances veiled in blood by desire. I saw all these glances through one—insistent and lost in the pallor of a starving man—that seemed to ask for an explanation for all impotence, all human defeat, except his own.

—I inhabited not life but death. As far back as I can remember cadavers rose up before me: "You turn away, hide, renounce in vain . . . you are part of the family and you will join us this evening." They held forth, tender, amiable and sardonic, or else in the image of Christ the eternally humilated one, the insane executioner, they held out their arms.

From east to west, country to country, city to city I walked among graves. Soon the ground, whether grassy or paved, failed me, I floated, suspended between heaven and earth, between ceiling and floor. My eyes, rolled back in pain, presented their fibrous orbs to the world; my hands, mutilated hooks, carried a senseless heritage. I rode the clouds a madwoman or a beggar of friendship. Feeling somewhat of a monster, I no longer recognized the humans I nevertheless liked. Finally, I slowly petrified until I became the perfect ornament.

I have long wandered, crossing the city through and through, top to bottom. I know it well; it is not a city but an octopus. All parallel and diagonal streets converge toward a liquid, swollen center. Each tentacle of the beast has a single line of houses with two façades: one with small windowpanes, the other with heavy curtains. It is there that, from the mouth of Vérax, I heard the good news of Notre-Dame-de-Cléry, there that I saw Violette's beautiful eyes injected with the blackest ink, there finally that Justus and Bételgeuse, Vérax and La Chevelure and all the girls with names like stars were absorbed by the powerful current of magnetic doors. The darkness shot through with invisible rays reveals space in their own image. The only incandescent transparency: the skeleton and the shape of the heart. One by one silent launchings send out flashes of sulphur and acetylene, encircle the automatic bodies in mercury. They see themselves mauve and then green . . .

The hour of attractions having passed, they are ejected into the street by this same complicated machinery. Faces purified, they return to the summits where they think they were born. (The legless man goes around his neighborhood thinking.)

In the daytime, the octopus covered in sand leaves no trace of its stretchings and convulsions, one can head for this sun-drenched beach.

It was on such a beach that I discovered the sky, a huge and cloudless sky in which a kite disappeared. I thought I was following it, I kept my eyes on it, I ran endlessly to reach it. Panting, I threw myself onto the sand: sand slips through your fingers with a warm caress that makes you laugh.

The inevitable procession: these women in black took me back through streets of icy winds toward a "Gothic villa" whose panes reflected a purple sun. It was the first day of my life that I looked, seeing.

Leaving Memories there, the landslides and scaffoldings of a still-born life, the bronze and plaster statues of all civilizations, and relying on an angle of a bluish slate, one fine evening in the middle of Ile de la Cité I took part in the flight of birds. The heavy carrier pigeons landed not far away, on the square where, *devoured by the demon of curiosity,* I blended into a crowd.

We waited for the parade. I saw the standards and flags of frail little boys and knock-kneed old people (canes in hand); I saw the banners and gaudy finery of sweating priests (armpits green and stinking), I saw the scapulars and the grimy rosaries of young girls, trembling children of Mary: "Father I've had bad thoughts." They howled, breath rotten: we are the *hope* of France. Three old women nodding their greasy heads of hair found, between their mustaches, false teeth filled with rancid host.

There you are beneath these flags, insane holiness! Why not smile free of illusion or burst out laughing amused . . . ? But no, I stand there, spitting the blood of my ancestors who resemble you. Won't I soon end up rejecting this heavy ballast? Yes, it was not so long ago that Veronica smiled at me with her handkerchief sweating Christ; the Virgin and her crown as well as the large nails in the wall and the trails of blood were wavering in the incense; the Holy Face was crying its tears of oil behind a red lamp, the only light in the "chapel of the Seven Sufferings." It was retreat, the hour of meditation, I was seven, I was kneeling, trembling. Arms and legs exhausted, I forced myself to invent sins, mine seemed so insignificant, so out of keeping with the gravity of these faces, the severity of these texts and invocations. I made things up . . . The priest received me in a dark room which I entered, terrified, and in which he confessed me on his lap. I was brought back to the carriage. The house was far away: "between Sainte-Anne and La Santé,"[3] my mother explained to the coachman and I kept trembling in the humid, felt upholstery, fearing death at every turn, the streets streaming with rain where the horse's hoof slipped and skidded.

I had to swallow the host, too, and was ashamed of not knowing how, and of asking questions. "Whatever you do, don't let it touch

3. Trans. Sainte-Anne, a psychiatric hospital, La Santé, a prison.

your teeth," my mother told me. What a horrible struggle between my tongue and the Lord, full of saliva! It took so long and was so unsuccessful that I started to doubt that this was . . . God. The idea took hold of me, it was impossible to think of anything else: I sobbed. Seeing my emotion, the priest and relatives congratulated themselves on my extreme piety. I let them talk; could I admit the horror of what was happening? Was I not already in a state of mortal sin? They spoke of fervor . . . For the first time, the adults' blissful smiles and superior airs seemed strange, *questionable*. Yet I was proud to be the only child whose First Communion would take place, as my mother wished, without any material festivities to mar the holiness of the day.

And once again holiness sought refuge in the attic. It was a catchall room filled with trunks and old scrap iron. The window, never opened, was covered by a thick curtain that let the light of a stained-glass window filter through. I stayed there for hours on end, fleeing their ennui, plunging recklessly into my own. One day a jumble of objects was moved aside in order to reach and open the casement-window; it was the only room from which to see, close up, a captive balloon that had fallen into a neighboring garden. You could make out the nacelle from twenty meters, wedged between two walls, the orange envelope half deflated, streaked with thick ropes flopped onto roofs and tree branches. Finally I saw the pilot extracted from this odd heap; the smallness of this being fallen from the sky seemed bizarre and disappointing. This rush of air bursting into my garret was an unparallelled event.

I was friendless. My mother disapproved of everyone for being "too well-off" or "not pious enough." The poor woman was naturally forced to interact with the neighbors or lend them a hand, to let her children play with the others on the sidewalk, to speak to the shopkeepers herself, to know the stories of the neighborhood. But her "situation" allowed her to close herself off in total distrust of anything that was not Family and in complete ignorance of anything that could be cheerful, active, engaging, lively, productive or even simply human. "To have relations" or "to entertain" threw her into a state of solemn panic whose repercussions we suffered. Only my brother pulled us from the malaise with an offhandedness that brought forth those sacriligious bursts of laughter that had to be contained in the drawing room or in church.

The house always looked dismal and unchanged. The mail's arrival thrilled me because of the very rare letters from Africa, America, or China written by a distant uncle. Although there was never anything on the decorated bronze shelf but bills, announcements, and the *Echo de Paris,* I waited each day for this mail of thick envelopes, extraordinary stamps and bizarre handwriting.

Despite her maids, my mother remained obsessed by housework, obsessed to distraction by dust, moth balls, and furniture polish. A day did not pass without a new task absorbing her and causing a commotion. What she referred to as "tidying up" was never finished. Everyone was expected to participate actively in this general upheaval. Children and maids, faces screwed up in the image of one another, came and went, upstairs and down, nothing was spared. Only the catchall room remained unalterable in its stale air and its stained-glass light.

I took refuge there and, straddling an old trunk of imitation leather or squatting on a little bench, I told myself endless stories, especially the one that took place before my birth, about the time I lived in the sky. Or else, I fervently contemplated a sweet white Jesus and a blond Joseph, blue, pink, golden, starry images, wrapped in silk, tied up with ribbons. Or else, I washed my doll and began exploring my own body, which I was ordered to ignore. A child's curiosity about her belly precisely when she knows that God sees all and follows her into this attic. Curiosity and then terror. Life soon managed to oscillate between these two poles: one sacred, venerated, which must be exhibited (my mother's contemplative demeanor after Communion); the other, dirty, shameful, which must not be named. Both more mysterious, more appealing, more intense than a bleak and unchanging life. Thus I would oscillate between the foul and the sublime, in the course of which real life would always be absent.

There were proud working-class women who would go to work, having washed the children, telling them hurriedly, with a coarse tenderness that does not mince words: "blow your nose, wipe your butt, good-for-nothing." At least children could unbutton their pants in front of these women without thinking themselves in hell. Simpering airs or airs of kindness would not work with them. "My dear woman"? They would send you rolling onto the pavement with a wallop.

There were washerwomen who I thought seemed happy to soak their hands in the Seine: "You, with the diapers, have you finished shitting into my handkerchiefs? It just won't do at all for the owner." And laughter exploded and died out in the reeds. At the end of the day, the young washerwomen got up, an acrid sweat on their brows and under their arms, which smelled good, like the cool wood of the washboard and the warm hay of their workboxes, they got up, backs aching, weary of seeing their breasts reflected in the river.

There were cynical prostitutes who roamed from Marseille to Buenos Aires, with a great love in their hearts drowned in absinthe.

These are hard and precarious existences, neither better nor worse than many others, but in these faces I felt an immediate sense of life that took on a singular flavor when I thought of the others, my mother and the women in black who left church, all their lovely sentiments filtered through a sieve. Workers, washerwomen, prostitutes would know how to taste joy if it were given them in other ways than parsimonious leisure poisoned by the next day's anguish. You others, you stand there all reticence and observance, pinning death on all sides, dreading life, wishing for sickness. You stand there, shame and muteness, days filled with duty: "parents' duty toward their children," "superiors' duty toward their inferiors," the sinner's duty toward his creator. You stand there, calm and soft, doleful and severe, killing joy and living from a filtered kindness that ignores humanity.

How simple and sweet Christiane was, our housekeeper's daughter, the one who threw herself out the window because her mother had taken coal from a cellar. This is how it happened: watched for an entire week by her employer who placed, moved, and counted her coal lumps, Mrs. Beuchet had finally been "caught red-handed" and was taken to the police station. Worried not to see her return at the usual hour, the little girl went to look for her and was greeted with these words: "Your mother is a thief and I shall have her put in prison." Christiane waited all night in her room and then, at six o'clock in the morning, seeing no one arrive, threw herself from the seventh floor. I asked for explanations about this drama, but we "weren't supposed" to talk about it. There would be a new housekeeper, that was all. I persisted, and my mother, who sharply blamed the patroness for being "too severe," nevertheless explained that one cannot "tolerate theft in one's home, and, anyway, it is a mortal sin." I was appalled, concluding once again that *mortal* sin makes you *die*.

I met Christiane one Sunday; her mother, charged with taking me to Mass, had brought her. Blond, twelve years old, all in black, she wore rolled around her neck a long white fur that fell in two flaps to her thin ankles. This fur surprised me, so at home I asked questions.

"It is very vulgar and not at all appropriate to wear such conspicuous things, and, besides, you shouldn't talk to Christiane."

And aping the grown-ups, who were always sure of themselves and always omnipotent, I was ashamed to be in the street with Christiane, and I did not speak to her. Of the tragedy, all I learned later was that "the milkmaid found her first." I imagine this milkmaid with her bottles, and then on the ground . . . I saw this long boa of white curls like babies have, and something knotted inside me, mixed with a real hatred for words that could kill. Mrs. Beuchet no longer came to the house.

"Why?"

"Because we must not get mixed up in such affairs."

Yes, these rough and plump hands do things well, they know how to maintain order in a house. They know how to write menus, hold a set of keys, undress children "modestly," clasp in evening prayer, bury a head in false ecstasies, slap a face with their hard bones, write in beautiful handwriting on my catechism notebook: "Resolution."

These fatal Resolutions, which were always a matter of my not getting angry, burst like soap bubbles, opalescent bubbles that occupied me for hours, along with the starch in the laundry room.

I liked the young chambermaid very much. One day, she told me of her hopes for marriage and motherhood:

"When I have a baby, I'll dress it all in white."

"You won't be able to because you're poor."

Her face turned crimson.

"I'm not poor. I work and my fiancé has a job with the metro."

This word *work* did not settle anything at all in my head, on the contrary, and I continued to persuade this young girl that her child could not be well-dressed. She sputtered in jerky sentences that work did not necessarily make one ugly and dirty, that workers, those who have a trade, are not beggars in the street, and, besides, "an employee is not a worker either, and you are a very mean child." Her anger made me despair, I thought about all this with the logic that my upbringing required. First, the employees of the metro were those to whom my mother spoke in a certain voice, those whose hand one did not shake, and those to whom one did not say "Hello, Sir" but a clipped hello followed by graduated silence; secondly, the chambermaid was not like my mother . . . and then, all of a sudden, a whole hierarchy that was too sophisticated for me was established. The poor in the street, the workers, the employees, what did all of that mean? Henriette tried to explain it to me by the degree of dirtiness involved in the different states. I understood all the more since we lived next to a factory and very often I relieved my boredom, seated on the edge of a window, looking at a young cutter who worked copper with a circular saw. We exchanged smiles and small nods. One day he cut his thumb: I learned of the accident immediately. The window was forbidden because I looked out of it too much and this spectacle had thrown me into a terrible anxiety. Henriette explained that this young man was a worker. I didn't want to believe it: "How could he be a worker if I liked him?"

This is what my mother's rigorous catechism came to—the duties of superiors toward their inferiors—and this semblance of kindness that suffocates any grain of generous and spontaneous human sympathy. A child is either repelled by these forced "duties" and does the exact opposite, or skillfully mimics the grownups with disdainful little airs. At eight, I was already no longer a human being.

There was the countryside.

I learned to distinguish shade flowers and water flowers, sunflowers and St.-John's-wort, water lilies and all sorts of reeds. I knew that there were evening birds and night birds, bats, owls, wood owls;

screech owls fallen from their nest and drowned in a bucket haunted my dreams. A weeping willow closed its smooth leaves over me, a grotto welcomed me in its wet coolness with a young blind cat hidden in my dress and sliding down my chest. I was going to disappear and vanish between the wall and the ivy. There I became a spider, a daddy-longlegs, a centipede, a hedgehog, everything imaginable and perhaps even animal to God . . .

I discovered wheat fields, cornfields, fields of red clover, fallow fields full of poppies and cornflowers, fields lined with willows and poplars. Behind the vegetable garden the plain appeared sparkling in the sun, humming with crickets, bumblebees and dirty flies on fertilizer. I went at high noon, my head insufficiently covered, a stiff cambric tie too tight around my neck, my naked limbs pricked by hay. I went, a new taste on my warm lips and the good smell of lavender and tanning skin, to know vertigo and enchantment.

Overseeing all of this, my father, with his bright eyes, happy and so blue, showed me nature. Through him I knew dragonflies, kingfishers and kinglets, mayflies and glowworms, wild ducks, water hens and all the fish. Through him I knew trees and seasons, moss and resin, the river, the forest and fire.

. . . .

Beads, magic boxes where colors flickered, children's fingers caught in the lids, glass beads, enamel beads, necklaces of ivory and coral, the firmament of little girls. White beads, black beads (where was this?), rusted angels, washed-out words . . . My meadow wreaths are now found on the faces of heros; the greenhouse flowers and apple blossoms, in the cemetery: funerary bric-a-brac.

Here again the rough and plump hands do things well. To the ritual of housework, they add the ritual of death, photographs, standards, flags everywhere. These hands take pleasure in cutting good quality crepe and locking the door upon herself: the mourning will be total, absolute, eternal. "Dear Madam, you have drunk the chalice to the dregs." And the afflicted, affecting hands answer on paper edged in thick black: "Blessed be God and the Fatherland." Henceforth, we would live on our revenue and grand sentiment in a climate of stagnant and putrid sorrow.

. . . One of them returned to breathe his last breath in the house, *in my room*. My sister wanted me to see him. This time I sobbed, too, ashamed that fear had made my tears flow in front of everyone, I who usually could only cry in the dark. I climbed the staircase that led me to him and all the weight of my body pulled me back, as though my knees did not work: with all my being I refused to see the dead man and then the sight of him calmed me strangely.

Did I know what to make of all these afflictions? I no longer knew anything. In a procession, at a solemn moment, I thought the damp crepe smelled strange in the sun, or else, I had a terrible fear of bursting out laughing, of smiling without realizing it, unable to stop; I clenched my teeth as much as I could and if a real friend of my father's walked past, a few tears relieved me and then, everything started again: this time, this was it, I burst out laughing, help! Then I forced myself to picture the faces of the cadavers but their names came to me in a song, a very cheerful tune that ended like this:

They are dead, dead, dead
André and Rémi
They are dead, dead, dead
Papa, André and Rémi
They are dead, dead, dead
Papa, André, Lucien and Rémi

It was at one of these moments, resenting myself for not matching the grownups's demonstrative grief, that something atrocious happened. While the coffin was being transferred from the carriage to the ditch, a sheet of water so abundant it seemed endless escaped from the box, a pestilent water flooding the pallbearers who sought to disengage themselves without breaking with the usual ceremony. One of them, beside himself, let out the most vulgar of exclamations while the assistants looked at each other and recoiled, terrified. My head became very heavy. It seemed the ditch would grow large enough to swallow us all into the warm earth, and we would no longer have to stand frightened, beside other graves, in a restricted space devolved to the living, on these little paths of white pebbles, shifting our weight, ill at ease, where we are so cold, where everything hurts so much. I wasn't even eager for it to be over anymore. My head was just heavy, so heavy . . .

Would my child's brain sink in the unending flood of catastrophes in which my mother henceforth found her life?

Tragic announcements, visits of condolence, funerary trips, anniversary masses, a parade of friends of the family, newspaper articles, wearing veils and orders to "The Nun": it was holy bread for a whole lot of pious and idle old maids who came to sniff at the mourning in our house, to feed on heroism in our family's shadow and to tell other dramas, other tragic cases, none of which, it seemed, attained the beauty of what had happened to us. And afterward, like parvenus associating with nobility, they left to peddle our new glories and other mournings. One day, like all of these, but even worse, I thought it would be good to go to school. What had changed? Hadn't we been crying for months and months? Why not go out? But I was reprimanded, ashamed of my act, which was "heartless." So I stayed there with my mother whose sobs redoubled at each visit. I noticed despite myself that she did not wipe her tears or blow her nose; the result was odious and I thought it was so that her face would be "bathed in tears," as in books; I felt bad. One of my aunts, on the contrary, dabbed her nostrils and her eyelids with little pats, careful of her scant rouge, which I also found odd. From my corner I observed the spectacle of pain. From time to time, children were spoken of and my mother called me to her side; the spectacle seemed to turn to comedy as the ladies made little pitying faces at me and there was something overwrought in all of this that did not suit me. I felt ashamed of my dry eyes and then atrocious remorse for not suffering enough, for in the general prostration, I would sometimes follow the flight of a fly and its trajectory on the windowpane and be quite amused if it rubbed its legs or wings, and I would also have a good appetite and want to play. The child embodies life, movement; she is all metamorphoses and sudden transformations . . . but I was not spared Low Mass in the crypt.

And yet there was a ray of sun. There was a blond baby, a two-year-old girl to whom I had suddenly become more attached than any other being in the world. I wove flowers into her hair and her smile enchanted me. One day, she no longer came to the garden. I wanted to see her: "impossible, she is sick." Her sharp cries reached me in the night. I accidently overheard an adult say: "It's going very badly, pus is coming out of her eyes and ears." These words danced in my head. I was not allowed to enter but I caught sight of the little dead girl, all white, covered in roses. Once again a coffin traversed the house, and we left for church. I held one of the ribbons that came out the four corners of a black sculpted wood structure carried by men. At church I kept vigil all alone near the coffin during the "family lunch," waiting to go to the cemetery. I was at the farthest limit of grief and horror. Beneath this accumulation of roses, I thought I smelled an odor. Would the little dead girl's soul go to heaven in a luminous ray by shattering the stained-glass windows of the chapel? No, I was next to her on the prayer-stool, watching . . .

The little box was lowered into the ditch. Then, only then, did I understand death . . . this one and all the others.

The torpor of these long days would eventually engulf me. I, too, was "in danger."

"Will I die?" Where is the very tender sister who leans over and replies:

"No, we no longer fear for your life."

So, they were afraid. That's exactly what I thought. And, in the course of my unlikely relapses, I waited, like that, very simply, for truly my chances of living or dying were equal. One day, a Lourdes medal was slipped under my pillow. I jumped up and threw it in the sister's face saying I had no need for that. The priest came with communion, I begged to be left alone but no, I had to comply with what they all wanted and suffer these complications again, these extraordinary affectations, these cloths and these objects. I tried contemplation but, although still a believer, I was "absent" and the book fell back onto the sheets. During these suffocating nights, I looked at photographs of the dead. Finally I was doing better. A nurse whose two hands had been mutilated and who had become a simple attendant came each day to take me out into the sun. He ran his arms under my aching body, made me roll onto his stumps and held me in his folded forearms. I was horrified by this man, and this moment, and preferred not to leave my bed. I was henceforth transported on a stretcher. I was also a "casualty of war."

Mama's rough hands were swollen. For an entire year they had twisted compresses of boiling water, filled bags with ice, put wood on the fire. These chapped, bleeding hands had given up the thick gold wedding band "for me."

I was told that my godson, a northern boy in the Alpine troops who'd gotten me as a godmother through the mediation of a nun, had been killed. He was the one who at the *beginning* of the war had sent me photographs of army chapels with Joans of Arc all tied up in ribbons and then rings, shell casings. I answered on paper with little flags (child size). When he came on leave, I expected it to be a delight, a distraction, but it was terribly awkward.

"We thought you would tell your little pen pal wonderful stories." But he stood there, mute. I was told to ask questions: I asked "how were the attacks?" At dessert, he refused the cake, a cake with layers of cream and jam, I was dismayed, we insisted, so he stuck his index finger deep into his mouth: he had a toothache and sugar was of no use to him. With our protests of "what do you mean?" we put a piece in his plate, he swallowed a mouthful then left it. Decidedly, nothing would break the ice and there would be no stories of battles. My mother was vexed, as she was the day my brother's friend visited, who, left alone for a moment in the living room, was found sobbing into the cushions. He had apparently said: "It was awful, awful."

"Chin up!" my mother responded, who, while telling us this, added, "a true soldier doesn't cry." A month later he was killed.

The death of my godson left me indifferent: nothing affected me anymore, I no longer knew how to write or walk and preferred not to talk. I was thirteen and looked like a skeleton. Dazed, docile to my mother's injunctions, I had become her new cult, her heroine, cured from an illness from which one doesn't recover, thanks to her care. "Didn't I give you life a second time?"

Soon, sacrilege entered my life and took hold of it through a liberating *ave maria*. "Je vous salue! Marie, merde, Dieu."[4]

No one came to see us except "Monsieur l'Abbé," the only friend, the true friend, the great friend of the family. He had a habit of lur-

4. Trans. "Hail Mary, shit, God"(merde, Dieu) from "Hail Mary, mother of God" (mère de Dieu).

ing my sister into corners, squeezing her chest while saying "be in peace" and touching her behind while pulling her skirt in between her two buttocks, then pulling it out. I found this bizarre, unpleasant. My sister went along with it, apparently finding in this neither pleasure nor disgust, and calling this priest "Dear Father." She was a guileless and very sane person. One day, I went to "Father's" house and found half a dozen young girls sitting in a circle on the floor mending cassocks, socks and underpants. "Since you don't know how to sew, you will unsew"—and I, too, took part in the festivities. It was a great honor for all these girls enchanted by this half-baked Rasputin.

He came to the country to say anniversary Masses. In the morning, he came into our room, said prayer kneeling at the foot of my sister's bed, and slipped his hand between the sheets. Once he came in and my sister was half naked. I was taken aback. This priest situation caused me intolerable embarrassment and disgust, of which I dared speak to no one. What could I say? What words would I use? I felt a great anxiousness about sex that no dictionary could appease; I did not even know "how babies are made," but I did not associate my anxiety with the maneuvers of the priest. One day, taking me into his lap, he took it upon himself to explain marriage to me in medical terms, then he accused my brother of knowing women, praised my "intelligence," which flattered me, and accused my mother of making me unhappy, which was true and which got me to return. Leaving his house, I came across a couple: a young man and woman, arm-in-arm, cheerful, laughing; this vision was a terrible shock for me: "I will never be like them." I went up the street, my back slouched, my shoulders hunched: I would have given anything for this explanation not to have taken place, for this priest not to exist with his shifty maneuvers and his smell. I still said nothing but things slowly took on another aspect: I confessed to him to having bad thoughts without daring to say that he himself provoked them through his behavior with my sister, especially when she stayed in his bedroom until two o'clock in the morning and returned, her nightgown undone, to me, who had not stopped trembling with fear. One day, after catechism, "Father" hid behind a door, caught me by the arm and said, "we can't let anyone see us," then he pressed his lips to mine and ran off. I rubbed my mouth with disgust. He received me at his house without turning on the light, I saw only the sinister glow of a coal fire in the fireplace. He took me in his lap, lifted my skirts, and passed his hand over my thighs under the pretext of "removing all the pimples that we get on our skin," then he said to me, "I do this with your sister," and he drew my legs apart, placed his hand against my sex. I shifted quickly and he pulled back his hand, covered in sweat. He continued to fondle my body for a long time and to squeeze me very tightly in his arms; then he calmed himself. I longed desperately to get out of there, I was suffocating. From then on I studied this man and all his gestures with total loathing and refused to allow myself to watch when he kissed my sister behind doors.

I was surrounded on all sides.

Who could I speak to? What could I say?

My brother, with his gluttonous and easy ways, did not inspire confidence. He took nothing seriously and extracted himself from the familial stronghold through a cheerful and superficial cynicism. After disappearing for days and nights, he would come back, not wanting to notice the tragic atmosphere my mother imposed on us because of him. At table, I noticed his swollen lips and his peculiar face. I still hadn't decided if he was attractive or disgusting. He read Anatole France, he was his God. The Father came to dinner often. He was repulsively gluttonous and had a habit of collecting, with a dry and nervous gesture of his fingertips, the smallest crumbs on the tablecloth. Those meals! Silence interrupted only by grace, then by the maid's slightest lapse in the serving order; one day we heard a sharp, metallic noise: my napkin ring had shattered in my clenched fist. My sister remarked in an acerbic tone that this was "charming" and very telling. They quibbled: "it was old, worn-out silver"; she exclaimed: "It's still metal, she must have been clenching her fist!"

Whom to speak to? My older sister was concerned only with herself, with her unconscious love for the priest, with her quarrels with our mother. My other sister followed suit, and all of them treated me like a child. My poor health excluded all possiblity of friendship: to my mother's great satisfaction, I never left the house. She wasn't aware that I lived in a sort of interior dream that only I knew about! Also at this time, I watched night fall with a dark terror that grew each day. I knew that I would struggle for hours and that after having resisted the temptation, then giving in to it without restraint [. . .] a debauchery of imagination.

One summer afternoon my brother wanted to take me to visit some friends, "an impossible set," we heard at home, where women seek to please, which is criminal, and young girls use the word flirt, which is abominable. There was friction, my brother insisted, and I prepared myself for this foray into "society" as for an extraordinary expedition. I arrived, silent, "aloof," unable to say hello, awkwardly trying to mimic the others, I stared wide-eyed: all these people seemed to be playing a role, playing at life. I detected a whole shifting of words; some very expressive words, said while laughing, made me grind my teeth; others seemed misplaced, too rich in meaning to sound so empty. My brother was exasperated by my attitude, I felt as though I was disappointing him in his sincere desire to "entertain me a little." Returning home, jostled by the bad road in the darkness, he was fresh and bright after a day of sport; I was sullen: I was returning from a ridiculous spectacle in which I could play no role, I was anxious to go back to my books.

We arrived at the family house just before the storm: the terrace was being thrashed by a strange wind, the straw armchairs moved on their own, a very light chair descended the staircase, doors and windows clacked on all sides. We called out in the emptiness. Anybody there?

A neighbor hidden behind a pillar seemed to be watching the far end of the garden intently. I questioned her: where was my mother? She replied: "I don't know what's going on but your sister ran down to the river." Jacques set off, his gait supple (it looked as though he spent all his time on a tennis court while the others moved through the house as though on a carpet leading to the holy altar). My mother came back, then my brother, saying: "I gave her a good slap in the face," a shadow slipped behind the shrubs: Catherine went back up to her room casting us a look of hatred.

My mother was in her element, there was a scene. What had happened? She had had a simple conversation with Catherine and Catherine had banged her head against the wall and plugged her ears, and then wanted to drown herself. My mother found her in the washhouse when Jacques fortunately arrived.

"What have I done to deserve such children? . . . Life is too complicated for me . . ." and my mother went through the rooms with a haggard air, holding her temples; her hair, worn in coils around her head, always smooth, sleek, and impeccable, was lifted up by wind and anger. My brother, motionless, lips set, decided to lock Catherine up, to watch her window and attach a wire to it. Alone with Jacques, I could not hold back a sob this time: "Well! If this is life . . ." "But no," he said, stressing the no, irritated at being caught up in the atmosphere of drama, "and don't start being a nuisance, too." He was hungry, we sat down for dinner. I did not know the object of what had been called "a simple conversation" but I hated them all, mother, brother, sisters, for making me feel constantly like an accomplice of one against the others, and for not finding in any of them an answer to myself. That evening I was ferociously on my sister's side, and I wanted to force open her door: with her, at least, we could fall into each other's arms and cry together without saying anything. This sobbing together always ended with a very simple evocation of memories of our father. We struggled mechanically to say his name as though he were still there, so horrified were we by my mother's tone which really seemed to make him die a second time.

I would sometimes take pity on my mother against my brother and declare it out loud, but if she took my books away from me I immediately felt a great relief when my brother, for his own reasons, made her suffer. I defended Catherine against Jacques for she also profoundly resented everything that hurt me at home and didn't laugh about it, but I sided with him, his gaiety and laughter, when Catherine started to seem like the shadow of the priest. I loved my sister and admired her because of this spirit of contradiction in her that she asserted in all situations. Thus, in the middle of a zeppelin alert, while everyone was in the cellar, she insisted on going up to the roof which resulted in a little well-ordered scene despite the "gravity of the circumstances." But she went up and I, five years younger, divided between my mother's prudence and my sister's exaltation, nevertheless followed my sister, not wanting to admit that the narrow iron stairway, steep and spiraled like the Eiffel Tower's, already made me dizzy. We arrived on the roof "higher than all of Paris" and where the lights crisscrossed above our heads. I loved Catherine for rising up, everyday, in all situations, against my mother, but I felt horribly distant from all of them, capable of unraveling what each of them wanted, incapable of expressing my own reality to anyone in the world.

Soon I lost faith, refused to go to Mass and to give up something for Lent. My brother, sensing that I was the object of general disapproval, told me one day: "you'll see, we'll have a good time together." I remained reticent, wanting "to be nice" and to hide the fact that his words and his tone hurt me. "Well, what do you want?"

One day my brother asked what I thought of the priest. I spoke as it came to me: finally these words were being said, my brother helped me and I was relieved of a thousand-pound weight. I had to speak to my mother; she was sitting at her desk before her account books and the photograph of my father.

"You dare accuse Monsieur l'abbé . . . it's very obvious, you who no longer go to church and Jacques who leads a dissolute life. You've gotten together to recount these horrors"—and a scene like I've never seen ensued. This time I would answer, I would tell all and, in fact, I didn't yield on any point. My mother went from apoplexy to a deathly pallor, I didn't care, and since she was still accusing me of being "vile," repeating that priests are sacred, I would have no pity on her. Finally, she pleaded that we speak in another tone, "when I think of what I've done for you and the way you're speaking to me, you have a heart of stone." Leaning against a dresser, I responded: "No. Marble, it's colder." Then the atmosphere became electrified: my mother invoked her rights to my affection, she who had "given her life and cared so much." I had a strange smile on my face and replied that she could expect no gratitude from me, she could just as well have let me die: "I wish I was never born." She fell back into her armchair, cried that I no longer knew what I was saying, and broke down. I left, merciless, tearless. For once I spoke, I said everything and the final malediction had emptied my body of muscle, blood and bone. I felt a relief that lifted me from the earth, a pure happiness, with no possible repercussions.

So! She only wanted me to be surrounded by the cawing of ravens, the hooting of wood owls, false whispers, the furtive gestures of bats? Well, for once everything became clear and transparent like this summer light. I went to the garden; white butterflies flew above the bank, a cloud of gnats swarmed in my face; stunned to be aware of such simple things, I stayed at the water's edge a long time and there I acquired the certainty that life would yield to my dreams and that I would not fail: I would suffer but I would live.

From this day on, apparently calm, imperturbable, I began to hurl great cries onto paper. These lines summed up my inertia: "Will I ever be able to leave a trace of will *in the real!* As soon as I am no longer alone, I am no longer myself, what to do? Will I always have this immense faculty to suffer things without *changing* them?"

I had started school again, but through a sort of inevitability, I could bear neither teachers nor students. In class as at break, I would suddenly burst into sobs, the suddenness of which nothing could predict. I found my classmates idiotic. The girls listened, horrified, to me reciting Camille's imprecations. I did the "rhythmics dance" and then I found it precious and ridiculous. I climbed the rope in the gymnasium after a thousand tries and thought I was a healthy and vigorous athlete. I took turns playing characters from Montherlant or D'Annunzio. I decided to "make myself independent through a diploma" and started to study again but was unable to concentrate, to finish something and not go out suddenly for no reason when I was supposed to be working. As for friendship, I acted under the impulse of infatuation and then phobia. With the precaution of a criminal I went into a luxury store one day and bought powder and perfume.

One thing was stable, certain, and irrefutable: my irreligion. My mother wanted me to see another priest. I vowed not to shrink from argument even though I did not feel intellectually armed to face a man who was no doubt very educated. I thought, despite myself, "this may be interesting," but at the same time I was seized by mild panic. How would I enter? say hello? begin to explain? Before leaving I sewed onto a very chaste hat of black polished straw an alarming green feather that stuck straight up. It seemed to me that, in case I became paralyzed, the idea of this perfectly ridiculous object would amuse and reassure me and help me regain my composure. I arrived in a cold, damp visiting room, a sort of basement with chairs all along a white wall. The priest entered, he seemed hesitant, I was decided. I thought I had to say something but he did not give me a chance: "My child, God allowed a traitor amongst the apostles, it's possible that there be a traitor amongst his ministers, be merciful"; a whole tirade against "Father" followed, something that resembled a shop quarrel or a struggle for influence of which my mother had been the object. I interrupted. The "betrayal" in question was not entirely in my distancing myself from religion; I was capable of judging things *from a higher vantage point* and from now on I only wanted to live according to my conscience, since I no longer believed.

He did not let me continue: "What? But, my child, you will come back to God, listen, you'll see, I'm sure of it, my dear child, trust is not easy to give . . . obviously . . . but you will see me again, come now, my child, that's certain, isn't it?"

"I don't think so." I got up and, already ironic, said: "Good-bye, Father."

I was out on the street on a late April day, and I met the warm light with intense satisfaction. The plate glass of a shop window reflected my image: the dust-gray coat did not fit my body, the black cotton stockings were sagging, the feather askew. I burst into candid and solitary laughter in the middle of rue Vaugirard, then I bought jonquils and went back to my room where my first task was to unstitch the feather. I was happy to see my brother and to joke with him. The priest had been so pitiful that it was delicious to laugh about it. This went beyond the known bounds of my character, which was rather to feel "a profound respect for all sincere opinions." Respect, which earned me that of others in return, at home.

Deep down I was disappointed. So *these* were the "directors of conscience! . . ." Decidedly they all looked alike with their skittish eyes and their weaselly hands, and I wrote in my notebook: "Religion? A convenient screen against life, death, suffering. Everything is decided ahead of time, like an annuity, an insurance policy. I will live from now on according to *my* conscience, yes, but I will search . . . I will read . . . in any case there is no need to be more knowledgable to see that there is too much hypocrisy on all sides. Decidedly I hate them *all*. I feel dreadfully and magnificently alone."

I was seventeen.[5]

I immersed myself in music, then abruptly turned away from it, writing in my notebook: "No more valid than drugs for drug addicts"; I was quite aware that spending entire weeks going from Bach to Debussy, from Schumann to Ravel, from Rameau to Manuel de Falla, from Mozart to Stravinsky, I was only switching drugs and that nothing in my life was *real*. It was the same with reading. "Will this *reality* ever come?" There had to be a reality in my image, but what was my image? I found so many contradictions in myself; my life would have to "build" like a Bach fugue: a central motif ceaselessly expanded, enriched, that meets, assimilates, rejects, and then remains at once intact and changed. Bach was my sole "morality," Stravinsky, my fever. In painting I liked only the Primitives or Le Douanier Rousseau, Utrillo, some Picassos. But to like painting did not mean to see a painting and then to go on to something else; it was a true source of life for me, but there again I was forced to conclude with a sort of ironic scorn: "No more valid than the drugs of drug addicts."

Aside from that, life was filled with ridiculous people. Survivors, cousins, came to my mother's house. An "art lover" regretted Reims,

5. [Starting here, the typewritten copy, which served as the basis for this text, no longer has the same finished character as what preceeded.]

nevertheless asserting that he would not hesitate to bomb Florence if Italians were Boches and that this war had still been "the most beautiful time" of his life, "you really felt alive." He was one of those people one sees beneath the metro's exquisite green awning, beneath the luster of gilded wood or in "beautifully decorated, very modern interiors." There they are, doing or undoing their housework, wife or mistress dusting, planning, scheming. There they are, nestled in their households, carried along by daily routine and Sunday's cream tart. Too occupied with their virtue, their assurance, the four walls of their lives and what the concierge thinks, they have never seen a human glance, they stop at appearance, dress, "social condition." If only a barrier could be broken down: a scandal in the family, they are in no way moved; only their curiosity, their malevolence is aroused: "I told you so." And they mark a point and huddle and scowl at home. There they build a barrier that encloses them even more, only sometimes they gaze grimly because their thoughts are bolder than their actions. But life is laid out once and for all, the stages are marked, they can ensconce themselves in their "good positions." They are very nice people.

A long time ago, they and their kind lost the sense of life that pushes human beings to the brink, risking everything along with it. There they are, the termites, the households, their imaginations never rising an inch above daily duty, daily obligations and Sunday entertainments. So, a war: what an adventure! The fatherland offers you a target at which to shoot the sour bile of the sedentary; the fatherland offers you an enemy to hate, to despise, a being to whom you are unquestionably superior (we have the right). The fatherland is both a coat of arms for these parvenus to glory and a feeling of security since, too smallminded to understand the universal, they will be generous within the limits of their frontiers, as their women are good within the limits of *their good deeds*. Tomorrow, they will surrender their sons with the same spirit, for their mawkish offspring have also lost the sense of the human, and war, it's true, is an unparalleled opportunity to go beyond oneself. They need tanks and cadavers to feel alive, magnanimous and transcendent. Gray, drab life becomes blood-red, and tomorrow again they will exchange the threadbare suit at the office for an armor of twill with the stripes of a noncommissioned officer.

Yes, why wouldn't this be the most beautiful time of these coddled, fabled lives, where grandparents point out the triumphant way, the path of duty and that of virtue, with some mutilated Victoire, some truncated Liberté far off in the distance, and the child-man follows this straight, marked path, for he sees "Danger" everywhere else.

NOTES
written by Bataille and Leiris for "Story of a Little Girl"

The brevity of this "Story" is natural to someone who did not burden herself with what did not seem essential. These pages recount determinant events in the formation of the exceptional personality that is already perceptible here and that this Parisian "little girl" later asserts. The war of 1914–1918 brought numerous mourning periods to which the wealthy and conservative bourgeois family in which she was raised insisted on conforming strictly.

Looking at her drafts, it becomes clear that this is more than a strictly "literary" task; it is an attempt to objectify some of the profound ties formed in a person both abrupt and sensitive, ties that tighten to the point of suffocation, so that it is a vital necessity to cast them out for the sole purpose of being free of them. In the opening lines, we can follow this harsh and intoxicated search for "true life" (according to the expression Laure borrows from Rimbaud), a merciless exigency that makes her revolt against the Catholic faith early on and does not cease, until her last breath, to beautify and ravage her.

Page 3. *A child's eyes pierce the night.*
On the first page of the handwritten manuscript, one reads the title: "Nights."

P. 4. . . . *a very Parisian garden* . . .
The garden Laure is talking about is that of Sainte-Anne, near her parents' house.

P. 6. *I saw all these glances.*
Among other handwritten corrections, the original typewritten copy bears "I saw" instead of "Laure saw." The woman we call Laure apparently considered representing herself under this name in a narrative distinct from *Story of a Little Girl.* In the poems and texts that we will read further on, there are several texts that correspond with this plan for a novel.

P. 6. *I inhabited not life* . . . until: *a perfect ornament.*
Several versions of this text, sometimes in poem form, are found in Laure's manuscripts. One of them was reproduced at the beginning of the collection *The Sacred.*

P. 6. *I have long wandered* . . .

The character "Vérax" associated with that of "Laure" appears in an erotic text that we will find in *The Sacred*. It seems this erotic text should be linked to the narrative cycle that was to be turned into a novel.

P. 7. *The inevitable procession . . .*
After evoking the city and its enchanted setting—a part of her later life and a theme she has treated at different times with variants—and after briefly recalling a memory of a beach, Laure describes a procession whose route she found herself on by accident while still a child or almost a child.

P. 15. This is not a break placed here by the editors. The typewritten copy that served as the basis for our text in fact has a dotted line.

P. 16. *One of them returned . . .*
Laure is alluding to the death of one of her uncles, who moved into her parents' house in order to die there. During the war of 1914–1918, Laure successively lost her father, whom she loved very much, and several of her uncles, all killed while in the army. A text reproduced in the *The Sacred* (p. 44.) expresses what Laure felt when her father left for the front:

A memory that seems to me to sum up completely my notion of the sacred.

This concerns the faith for which one feels prepared to die. This has to do with my father's departure for the front—a particularly tragic departure due to strange circumstances (to be explained) and that provoked in me a state of total exaltation, made up of certain foreboding, of sacrifice consented to ahead of time and in the very face of the one to be sacrificed. This, at eleven years of age, mingled with the songs of a delirious crowd—songs into which I blend my voice which at times suddenly dies, total physical upheaval.

Incapable of resuming physical life for several days.

I howl the "Marseillaise" and the "Chant du Départ" for entire days.

A classmate I meet in the metro, wearing mourning clothes because she has lost her father, makes me feel ashamed.

P. 18. *And yet there was a ray of sun.*
Laure is speaking here of the child of one of her family's employees who died very young.

P. 19. *The torpor of these long days . . .*

The illness in question here seems to have been the first attack of the illness to which Laure would succumb in November 1938.

P. 20. *No one came to see us except "Monsieur l'abbé."*
"Monsieur l'abbé" was the leader of a Catholic group to which Laure belonged for a time, with her brother and older sister.

P. 23. *At this time* . . . until: *a debauchery of imagination.*
A few illegible words in this paragraph—the handwritten addition to the typewritten copy—have been replaced by brackets [ ].

P. 27. *From this day on* . . . until: *a trace of will in the real.*
The duplicate of the typewritten copy presents the following variant:

From this day on, apparently calm, imperturbable, I began to hurl cries onto paper: I had a coffin for a cradle, and a shroud for a blanket. I had of love a vision of a lecherous priest or cynical jokes . . . I don't know where I'm going but what difference does it make because I know where I am: against everyone, as far from my sister as from my brother but there are four of us and there are four cardinal points, I'm in the east, why? because the sun only rises and then I can see my cold sister so well in the north, my "dissipated" brother in the south and the other finishing before ever having started . . . How idiotic but since I am banal I should be utterly so. Will I ever be capable of leaving a trace of will in the real? [. . .]

In the original typewritten copy, the page corresponding to this passage is missing; in its place is a half sheet of paper with handwriting, representing in all likelihood the definitive reading, the one that we have reproduced.

P. 28. *Deep down I was disappointed* . . . until: *I was seventeen.*
This passage does not appear in the duplicate of the typewritten copy. In the original, page 30 is missing and replaced by a handwritten page beginning with "feather" and ending with "I was seventeen." Then comes page 31, beginning with: "Aside from that, life was filled with ridiculous people."

P. 29. *Aside from that, life was filled with ridiculous people.*
On two pages of the manuscript (rough drafts of this passage relating to "survivors"), one can see traces of the significance music had for Laure during the time she wrote these lines (which, in the duplicate of the typewritten copy, immediately follow the paragraph: "I immersed myself in music . . ." missing from

the original). Each of these two pages have the notes "Re" and "Ut" in the top left-hand corner, written in large letters and underlined. [Trans. ut = first note in the diatonic scale; re = second tone in diatonic scale]

P. 31. *Yes, why wouldn't this be the most beautiful time . . .*
After this passage, slightly different in the corresponding page of the manuscript, this sentence in pencil:

Few know that by turning away entirely they will find the salt of life.

The Sacred

The Sacred

. . . I inhabited not life but death.
As far back as I can remember
cadavers rose up before me:
"You turn away, hide, renounce in vain . . .
You are part of the family and you will join us this evening."
They held forth, tender and sardonic,
or else,
in the image of Christ, the eternally humiliated, the insane
executioner,[1]
they held out their arms.
From East to West
from country to country
from city to city
I walked among graves.
Soon the ground slipped away.
Whether grassy or paved,
I floated,
suspended between heaven and earth,
between ceiling and floor.
My eyes rolled back in pain
presented their fibrous orbs to the world,
my hands, mutilated hooks,
carried a senseless heritage.
I straddled the clouds
with the frenzy of a madwoman
or a beggar of friendship.

1. Laure used this phrase in "Story of a Little Girl" and again in a note, explaining: "In our turn, it is the executioner because the being thinks he is humiliated, needs to be humiliated. To hate him, to scoff at him, and to be substituted for him. To live his life. The stations of the cross, the story of the spit exalts Christ."

Feeling somewhat of a monster,
I no longer recognized the people
I nevertheless liked.
They saw me alight upon
the heaven of Diorama
where chilled to the bone
I slowly petrified
until becoming
a perfect ornament.

What color does the notion of the sacred have for me?

The sacred is the infinitely rare moment in which the "eternal share" that each being carries within enters life, finds itself carried off in the universal movement, integrated into this movement, realized.

It is what I have felt as weighed with death, sealed by death.

This permanence of the threat of death is the intoxicating absolute that carries life away, lifts it outside of itself, hurls forth the depths of my being like a volcano's eruption, a meteor's fall.

The most decisive "steps" in my life have always been accomplished in a state of trance which alone allowed me to act toward and against all obstacles (lucidity, physical weakness, etc. etc.).

It was what I would have given my life for.

If a being cannot or can no longer experience this feeling, her life is as though deprived of meaning, deprived of the *sacred*.

The adjectives to which you attribute a sacred sense, like "prestigious," "extraordinary," "dangerous," "forbidden," seem to me to be terribly laden with meaning and seduction on their own, seduction that gives them this entrancement in which one feels caught, beyond everyday life, this displacement, this feeling that something is happening.

But, for me, this is not the sacred.

When you call the act of defending a friend against deception or rather the act of taking sides loudly and violently for what one loves "sacred," I do not agree with you. This moment, in which the word is as intense as the feeling experienced, is what I would call more simply: the only worthwhile moment in "life with other people."

(I hasten to say that there is no longer *ever* a worthwhile moment in "my life with other people," but this is a superfluous digression that will lead me too far astray.)

At one time, I acknowledged only these "worthwhile moments," and I became totally mute when I was not able to express what mattered completely to me or at least had a meaning fraught with consequences, charged with expression. I could not stand banality in others any more than in myself (speaking but "saying nothing").

This was not a very humane attitude!

I find it again in this fact:

Being extremely delighted to see friends . . . Afterward . . . deeply depressed because you realize that nothing was truly exchanged, that you were beside yourself by force of circumstance or wretched cowardice.

The bullfight has to do with the sacred because there is the threat of death and real death, but it is felt, experienced by others, with others.

Imagine a bullfight for you alone

(to be explained at length).

Everything that has to do with the reason for being is sacred for me, the reason for still being, reason for life, reason for death.

What deprives existence of all possibility of feeling the sacred: maintaining propriety, maintaining exterior circumstances that do not correspond or no longer correspond to the *truth* of being.

Some always prefer that the ground be missing from under their feet—at all risks: death or madness—but that life remain.

The opposite.

Or one arrives at:

pitiful *acting*,

senile infantilism,

lispings,

stammerings, fake puerility, regression, powerlessness

and to an even more base degree:

Cynicism, vulgarity, skepticism, total perversion of the moral being.

Alteration, as the purest spring water is altered by the swamp.

Against those who lead this swampy life, never enough cruelty, never enough intransigence: to be avoided like the plague.

"All poetic emotion is sacred"?

Agree with you because of (for example and to abbreviate) Nerval's suicide. Yes, but Rimbaud's destruction?

The sacred moment, an infinitely rare state of grace.

There are "pre-sacred" states which lack only one element to complete the sacred.

Pre-sacred in my childhood,

for example, at eight or nine.

In a garden, I'm stretched out on a lawn. There is a certain place in the lawn where the ground rises up in a cone shape. I settle myself so that the nape of my neck is exactly on top of it, so that my head is "thrown back" and I can "see the sky" better.

The first time, I'm with my sister—the one I ask the big questions, the one I trust—I say to her: ". . . but behind this sky, is there another?"

She laughs and tells me there are many others. I laugh too and say that "of course, since there's a seventh heaven." She gets serious and explains to me that we are surrounded by sky, that the earth turns, that the sky has no end.

She leaves.

I stay there a very long time, motionless, dreaming of *infinity,* trying to imagine *infinity* physically. A terrible anxiety seizes me, but I do not move and I soon manage to "feel" the earth turning. My head still in this position "was actually and violently turning."

Each evening, when the noises had died down, I returned there to find this feeling of the earth turning and to feel lost in it, carried away in this vertigo.

Of the same order:

In my mother's bathroom, two large mirrors faced each other.

I positioned myself so that only my head was interposed between the two mirrors and I saw *countless* heads.

I tried to count.

It was impossible.

This irritated me, and I tried relentlessly, extraordinarily fatigued and greatly anguished.

Other times I would interpose objects and move them.

It was truly a magical game.

I simply think that, just as in the garden, this first contact with the idea of infinity (with which a child *plays* and which he would not want to be caught in the middle of *for anything in the world*) has something sacred about it, in the sense that the game is accompanied by anxiety, only happens at certain hours, when you know "no one is around," and takes on the appearance of a sort of lively meditation. A state that reemerged as a memory in certain acute moments of my life. The permanence of this sensation calls to mind the collision of an eternal part of oneself with the universe, but it lacks:
1) the notion of death, though present through physical sensation
2) sharing with others

A memory that seems to me to sum up completely my notion of the sacred.

This concerns the faith for which one feels prepared to die. This has to do with my father's departure for the front—a particularly tragic departure due to strange circumstances (to be explained) and that provoked in me a state of total exaltation, consisting of a certain foreboding, of sacrifice consented to ahead of time and in the very face of the person to be sacrificed. This, at eleven years of age, mingled with the songs of a delirious crowd—songs into which I blend my voice which at times suddenly dies, total physical upheaval.

Incapable of resuming physical life for several days.

I howl the "Marseillaise" and the "Chant du Départ" for entire days.

A classmate I meet in the metro, wearing mourning clothes because she has lost her father, makes me feel ashamed.

Going back to the sociologists' notion, the sacred mixed with the social for it to be *sacred*.

For this to *be,* it must in my opinion be experienced by others, in communion with others.

Imagine a bullfight for you alone.

I need an audience.

The poetic work is sacred in that it is the creation of a topical event, "communication" experienced as *nakedness*.—It is self-violation, baring, communication to others of a reason for living, and this reason for living "shifts."[2]

That which affirms me strongly enough to deny others.

2. This fragment was given to Bataille by Laure as she was dying. Through this he discovered the manuscripts that would become "The Sacred." (J.P.F.)

POEMS
before the summer of 1936

From this invisible window
I saw all my friends
divide my life between them
in shreds
they gnawed to the bones
and not wanting to waste such a lovely piece
fought over the carcass

Priests

Priests, all sorts of priests and fake priests
Listen to me:
I have said "no" to piety
and my piety (with the face of an Angel)
my piety, your toothless halo
laughed

It broke into a thousand pieces
Only now the time for sincerity comes
When we look at each other as brothers

"You take the last boat
The one that reaches no land in the world"

So I loaded my life onto my shoulders
and left, my back stronger
This time

How many times already
have you seen me
set off for death?

Beyond a transgressed doorstep
the moon
straddling
clouds like rams
looked at me
Like winged victory

8

I find myself
trapped
as in a circle
which I escape
by this other
which brings me back

Hieratic gestures, vile grimaces mix, merge, disappear, reemerge . . . then vanish entirely. And this "game" will go on a long time.
I thought I was going to heaven (joking aside) just as life again placed its heavy lid over me.
I used all my inherent contradictions living "to be true" all that one carries within "to the end."
I scattered myself to the four winds with the proud certainty of always finding myself at the zenith and then I fell empty, lost, four limbs mutilated.
I went away over high roads, steep paths, rocks flown over by eagles . . .

The infernal 8 came back to lasso me

I climb along its contours
I drift in its meanderings
I jump out of the circle
and fall back into the other
I remain strangled in the middle
my face is there
frozen   eel   dolphin   earthworm

And who, seeing this fateful sign
    would think of discovering me there,
    would want to release me?

"A prisoner escaped by jumping the wall at the very place he was to be executed." *(The newspapers)*

May 8

Archangel or whore
I don't mind
All the roles
are lent to me
The life never recognized

The simple life
that I am still looking for
        Is lying
in the very depths of me
        their sin has killed
        all purity

Life replies—it is not *vain*
one can act
against—for
Life demands
movement
Life is the flow of blood
blood does not stop flowing through veins
I cannot stop myself from living
from loving human beings
like I love plants
from seeing in eyes an answer or an appeal
from probing the eyes like a diver.
But to stay here
between life and death
dissecting ideas
expounding on despair
No
or immediately: the revolver

There are eyes like the bottom of the sea
and I stay there
sometimes I walk and glances are exchanged
all algae and detritus
other times each being is an answer or an appeal

The Crow[3]

It was in the forest
the silence and the secret
of a many-rayed star.
Far off, at the edge of the woods
on the path
that low trees
cover in an arch
a child passed
lost
frightened, astonished to see me
as I saw him
encased in a sphere of snowflakes.

Whirlwinds approached us
as though to deceive us.
A violet inactive sun
and the faint light of a storm
froze us with terror.
The fairies and ogres disputing
our shared anguish
wanted lightning to uproot
a large tree
not far from there
which opened
like a stomach.
I wailed.
The child, bare legs streaked with cold
        and very real cowl (to wring)
reopened his eyes.

3. Dated January 1936.

At the sight of me, he ran away.

Giving up on following him
picking a strange destiny out of the rut
very logical all in all
I turned around and went back
"as though nothing had happened"
but I felt at my shoulder
that heavy and discreet rustle
of a black-winged bird
and examining it with pleasure
I wanted it to accompany me everywhere and
always to precede me
like a herald his knight.

More and more lost
stumbling against rocks
slipping on dead leaves
sinking into the mud of a pond
I came upon an abandoned house
a well of moss and verdigris
a smashed-in doorway
I entered.

The flowered and moldy wallpaper
undulated in waves
toward a rotten floorboard
a gaping fireplace
displayed the still intact vestiges of an extinguished fire
ashes, bones charred by ash and birch
I pushed open doors without hinges
whose fall terrified me
I opened windows without panes

as though I needed air.

Finally, I climbed a ridiculous staircase
The walls, covered in strange graffiti
        never seen
laid my life bare
with my name written out and associated with crimes:
"what right did they have?
the right of the poor."

In this filthy attic
the bird came back to me
with its cry
to thrash the living
with its beak
to dismember the dead
the dark shadow cast over me
seemed to elect a prey

The night found me
strangled deep in the woods
It enveloped me in a halo of moon
and rocked me in mist
a white, shifting, icy mist:
"I know your star
go and follow it
This nameless being
renounced in turn
by night and day
can do nothing against you
and does not resemble you
believe me
When tomorrow at dawn

your head is thrown
into the basket of the guillotined
remember
Murderer
that you alone
have drunk
'all the milk of human kindness'
from my breast."

NOTES

This last poem unquestionably establishes Laure's ties to "Acéphale," the secret society that Bataille created, or, as Leiris suggested, that Laure inspired. The couple was living in Saint-Germain at the time and this forest could be that of the same name. However, in this note found in Laure's papers, another forest is mentioned:

1. Only enter the part of Yveline forest that used to be called "fore Cruye" under conditions that exclude any possibility of conflict with the character of sanctuary this area will have for you.

2. Do not enter the restricted sanctuary to be determined later except during Acéphale meetings.

3. Never say a single word even alluding to the meetings under any pretext to anyone, with exceptions to be determined as the absolute need for them becomes apparent and only after this is determined.

4. What each of us expresses about the meetings will appear in texts devoted to the internal Journal of Acéphale, but these texts will form a private section of this Journal that will only be communicated to those who have accepted to conform to the rules.

5. Observe all restrictions specific to each meeting (not to speak, not to meet with others, not to wander from a path or to leave a spot during a given time, not to unseal the envelope until the appointed time). Rules that might arise will not be the object of any general obligation.

6. These rules may be modified later and made less severe without anything whatsoever changing in terms of the agreement.

7. They will be lifted when necessary by those who have or who will later have the responsibility of organizing the meetings.

As far as the forest's restricted area, each of us must agree on the boundaries of the premises. Acéphale will go at first with one of us or two at the most. This will continue from one to another and be repeated until everyone is aware of the boundaries.

Sulphur is a substance that comes from the earth's interior and is issued only from the mouths of volcanoes. This is clearly significant in relation to the chthonic character of the mythic reality that we are pursuing. It is also significant that the roots of a tree plunge deep into the earth.

[On Acéphale, see Volume II of the *Oeuvres Complètes* of Georges Bataille, page 271 and following, where this text is reproduced. There are two versions, in two scripts.]

André Masson's drawing for Acéphale found in Laure's papers.

TEXTS ON SPAIN
Church Fire

I was beside myself and yet lucid, strangely calm, able to make a chain to prevent the firemen from advancing, or to stoke the fire burning a pile of priests' robes, to see rather terrifying things but to remain standing. The crowd was at once a classroom at recess, an assembly of hysterical women and groups perfectly conscious of doing what they wanted to do and had to do. There was as much vengeful and healthy laughter (which came from a certain depth of popular common sense) as cries of ferocious hatred. Women rushed forward to see victims, the sight of which they could not bear (or at least some could not). What makes me feel good is that I was really *with* them and not a spectator and that for a moment there was no distrust in them nor fear or distrust on my part. Everyone called out to each other or took each other by the arm to persuade, to convince each other. I didn't quite understand, but I understood enough when my arm was seized by a man or a woman's hand to respond, for lack of words, in kind.

Spain . . . is like the wind blowing in your face: you have no choice.

It's Saint Teresa and knitters at every step. Mystical delirium and sacrilege. I think that true life is absent in the sense that I would understand true life if I honestly believed that it could exist someplace in the world . . . except in nonexistent beings. What comforts and relieves and heals is the solidarity and profound hope that arise from these contacts. What could be depressing: the gulf created between the revolutionary capacity of the crowd ready to risk everything and capable of organizing its "excesses" itself and the incapacity and spinelessness of leaders and intellectuals who treat all of this as the sad "excesses" of the "lumpenproletariat" . . .

Outskirts of towns
wastelands
meadows bathed in sky

All the rivers and all the wines
roll in my head
Manzanatès and Mockva
where was this?

The earth opens up.
They are all there
those who miraculously
joyfully share
both hate and joy

A river of blood has drowned the laughter of children.
Shell fire has silenced these adolescent canticles.
Faith hope charity
"have gone to hell."

Beyond atrocious defeats
overturned victories
mutilated freedoms
war screams at death

They are all there
at the bottom of the abyss
laughing at their brothers
the living
these apostles of sorrow
who can only cry in the dust
moan at gravesides.

Skeletons' jaws
crack and stretch
in a single great sardonic laugh
when this lamentation of fleshy shadows
reaches them.

"Shapeless, hybrid beings
would this be your sorrow
that there is room for everyone in the sun
and one can survive that which alone seemed
worthy of being lived?

You will always be outside the game:
you compromise with yourselves
you will never abandon yourselves, dazzled
pupils irradiated, mouths on fire, stomachs burning
to the beneficent carnage.

You have too much to do in the graveyards of history
you have too much to think about
in your poor heavy head
too much to say with your bitter lips
from which every incoherence escapes.

You also have
too many treasures to waste
in your eternally empty hands.
Shapeless . . . hybrid beings
you do not yet know
that the single instant wants to be lived
you prefer to prolong miracles
which you owe only to us.
What remains of existence

slips away like sand between fingers
and you let it
motionless
or else you accelerate your ruin
to the fitful rhythm of mechanical dolls
or else you strenuously insist
with all your clear-sighted reason
with all your pertinent judicious wisdom.

Yes your tears are laughable
If you do not already know how to
"drive your cart and your plow over the bones
        of the dead"
it is because soon
our *hell* will cover the universe:
the sky's fire
fragments of earth
boiling lava
precious gems
will strike your heart
in a sonorous chaos, absurd and brilliant.

Bullfight

to Michel Leiris

Dear friends,
Don't forget your promise of the bullfight account. Do you think this will suffer the same delay as the bibliographies?

Did the bull spew *all* the blood of his lungs as at *my* first bullfight? The smell of blood rose to the highest tiers, to the furthest seats of the arena where I sat between a cattle seller who b——— like a stag and a young girl drowning in tears whose sister had to take her away (a Spanish girl nonetheless). It went on so long. Until it was incomprehensible how the bull was still standing . . . As though he were simply vomiting. He stayed that way until he rocked on his four legs in a very gentle swinging motion . . . then the front legs gave out, he fell to his knees in the pool of blood (he said his prayer) and finally he fell on his side. This wound was apparently very awkward and vile, and the audience proved it or thought so by whistling in unison. At that instant the weather changed, a leaden sky covered this ditch of serpents, and I left just in time with the last ray of sun before the storm.

Really, that day it would have been better to set fire to the arena. Perhaps it was truly "magnificent" the other Sunday?

FRAGMENTS AND OUTLINES OF EROTIC TEXTS
Laure

They passed each other on a street corner one evening. Each turned to see the other "at least from behind" and found themselves face to face.

An exchanged glance: the man compelled her, she wanted to rush to him.

When she was there, without moving he said to her: "I recognized you, daughter, sister, mother, and slut in heat; do what you know without me expecting it." But she slapped him and ran away.

Then a laugh pursued her, one that hung from her neck like a little bell and pulled her back . . . on a leash.

He had not moved, but his sex was now shining in the night and he held it and shook it from right to left, from left to right, nonchalantly at first. She approached: then, with his free hand, he slapped her, sending her rolling onto the pavement. As she got up, he spit in her face, ordering her to stay where she was. "This environment of mud and shit suits you so well; go on, roll in it." He stood above her, very erect, very tall, his sex shone in a ray of light; so she desired him, she wanted him, and in a low and frenetic voice he said to her: "You slut, how dare you want"; he straddled her and ordered her to roll around again between his spread legs, carefully guiding this trollop toward a sewer opening covered with filth. She rolled over, her arms alongside her body: stomach, side, and back and then in the other direction, prey to delirium and to the sight of his restless and triumphant sex controlling the rhythm. Eventually she bumped against the sidewalk in a gurgling of gutter water. Her hair full of excrement, her eyes crazed, her mouth soiled and yellow at the corners but still eager, she raised two hands, white and diaphanous, stretched out toward his sex. She was all prayer, all offering. He spit into her half-parted lips and bit her slender fingers which he turned into a mouthful of tender cartilage. And as he moved away, backward so that she would not lose sight of his monstrous sex, she crawled before him on her stumps and on her knees. He climbed a few steps and, still backing away, went through an immense Roman door, which she entered in turn like a limping dog. He disappeared into a dark building in the shape of a hallway, she dragged her body, gaping with bleeding wounds and filth, over a purple carpet. Climbing still higher, in total darkness, he ordered her to kneel before a low gate which separated them. Arranging a piece of white linen on his wrists, he placed his cock there.

When she had taken communion, and once his come was swallowed, her fingers grew back (her nails polished "Angelus") and her injured body regained full health.

The great organ, of its own accord, celebrated the miracle, and the man and the woman, Vérax and Laure, went very calmly to shit in the fonts of holy water and piss in the ciborium. Then they washed their asses with the communion napkin soaked in holy water before returning to their affairs, to their lives, each hour of which was a joy and a hatred.

The next day she climbed onto the altar and showed her ass to all the churchgoers and the priest, while raising the host, spread her thighs and inserted the host between them, then he licked this divine ass until the choir boy, kneeling in front of him, released his cock from between the lace and gilding, with blows of the censer and he swallowed the Holy Come that spurted into his face. However, Laure, her ass provided with a sacred suppository, freed her belly and her life with wild cries and convulsions, shaking the grand altar to its foundations until it collapsed beneath her.

And finally a silver Christ was seen glittering in the shit.

Another version of the end of this poem:

He backs away and she crawls toward him as he disappears into an abandoned taxi.

Two days later, the whole neighborhood fearing a mystery, disaster or crime, a street sweeper calls a priest who opens the door and floods of come gush into his face. When the car is emptied of sperm, two fish are found between two loose planks, an angelfish and a guppy, dead.

A strident voice yells and prevails:
        We kill children here.
The sound of windows, of a set of keys, a whole artificial
        silence.
Assertion turns against you: everything defeats the purpose.

That basic lived life gives people the possibility for ecstasy.
—decision of the crime: "Her eyes were like stars, you'd have thought you were at church."
—The crime accomplished: vengeance and love, blood and sperm.
— "we are at the summit of the mountain," "the mountain is crushing us."
—the quick pace of a "detective novel," feelings and psychological analysis.
—human beings, *in flesh and blood.*

—go on
yes: it is necessary, for me and the others,
in order to clear up the misunderstanding
to say everything,
a sudden stop, start again
in another form
of retrospective journal.

LIBERTINAGE
the stages of "Laure"

Birth in a barn, in the hay.
She gave birth.
Birth to a monster.

The residence
detailed description of women:
makeup
outfits
bodies

dinner at the countess's
Her friends also invite their valets.
Dinner: description
—The sensational entrance of the pimps.
—A visit to the room of the children-martyrs.
butcher hooks
detailed descriptions
positions limbs
chains
ropes

For sale: women's tears
For sale: oaths on the heads of children
For sale: madness and passion
The uprooted vanish
devoid of reality
voices of ventriloquists
faces of clowns

Return to the little world of sugar candy and stew pots
the basis of material needs
Laughter triumphs

Lie low No, not that
what wood are we burning for heat
what cock are we USING

In the toilets
In the toilets the summits
idealism, the people who climb
a high mountain and *are crushed* by this mountain
In the toilets
In the toilets
the great emotions
the weighty passions
everything capsizes
our mothers are madams
our wives are whores
our daughters raped

—Is this tolerable?

—Tolerable? The storm and dead calm, the rain and sun, tolerable? Like life . . . life such as it *is* and not *different* than it is.

—Me? My dear friend, I am ready to eat a quick meal, but for something coherent, organized, listen I said ready—ever so ready.

—You know, I like them tall.

I have always preferred anything to these hurried and suspicious confidences, to this chatter of hysterical women, to these manic and depressive lies:

—You? It can't be possible.
—And why not?
—Why?
—Pardon me?
—No, I won't.
—How thoughtless!

—Well, I never!

—Ladies and gentlemen, dear friends, I shall unmask virtue, distinction, decorum, moderation, charm, frankness. Frankness—(she shows her ass)—

—Oh!

Frankness, you are a slit and a hole, abyss, you are not a summit.

Note that the whole gathering laughs as one, laughs their head off, a belly laugh, note that this same gathering is openhearted . . . has heart . . . and puts its heart into its work.

—Too easy, my dear, far too easy!

—Alas!

—What malaise in your house!

—Open the window, would you? We're suffocating in here. What malaise!

Do not say it—enter a madman—fresh, sane, intelligent nonetheless.

POEMS AND TEXTS
after the summer of 1936

The slow compunction of the weak
They live the life of cadavers
To put on my door
"You who enter here
abandon all hope
of not being
what you are"
or else "Here you live naked"
naked
naked

Human existence is priceless
with no greater or lesser price than everything that exists
vegetable, mineral, animal
all that shines, howls, wails, moans
the trumpeting of elephants
the lowing of cows.
The donkey brays, the serpent hisses.
There are no bonds so powerful that they can wrest
a being from death. Death triumphs.
Laughter—Happy insolence: "Drive your plow
over the bones of the dead."[4]

4. This proverb of William Blake's is located in the collection entitled *The Marriage of Heaven and Hell*. The text literally reads: "Drive your cart and your plow over the bones of the dead."

It must be quite vexing, this insidious worm consuming the hours
a bitch at bay howls at the moon
the guardian angel
smiles stupidly
Little Jesus I give you my heart
The crumbling manger
Its beams burnt to ashes
the patched walls
slowly sag
and collapse . . .
Beneath vacant eyes
of passersby
the little girl
shakes there
in the hay

To live? No more meaning no more criterion.
A value has to be introduced.
(Self) imposed? You *have* to be *Machiavelli.*
In the name of what values?
One authority must be reestablished.
Accuse weakness with contempt
(decisive contempt that slams like a door).

and if hardship
or extreme hardship
comes it's because it's what I need
to realize myself
to *go farther*
ever *farther*
and they speak of CRIME!

The greatest strength
to commit a crime
with the certainty of denying it
in front of everyone

FRAGMENTS OF A NOTEBOOK written in 1937[5]

Avoid contact with all people in whom there is no possible resonance with what touches you most deeply and toward whom you have obligations of "kindness," of politeness. Since these obligations engage me strongly as soon as I find myself in the presence of such people and engage me through an ill-fated habit of patience and good-will, which in fact becomes will for humiliation (sometimes abject). Imagine a musician in an orchestra playing off-key because his neighbor is doing so, to be nice.

Flee—literally flee—those with whom you can exchange only absurd remarks about others who are just like them and whom you have seen the previous night exchanging the same remarks, or equally vain gossip, about the very person you are talking to.

There are certain people who end up frequenting and even calling *friends* those they denigrate constantly.

I hate "goodness" and "kindness," which have only led me to *humiliation.*

Keep silent as before. It's better.

Contempt for those whose conversation boils down to all that I hate and flee: to a certain spirit of vulgarity and pettiness. *Farce* is what they feel comfortable with.

I cringe before certain laughter and smiles drawn forth on this terrain.

Sometimes a laugh is enough to cause me to have, not aversion toward, but distrust of a human being.

There is a point at which polite distrust is worse than aversion because it is more reserved, but I can't confine myself to this, and everything in me shouts, screams *aversion.*

5. In the notes that follow there are undeniable traces of a rupture.

Lack of reserve and moral propriety shocks me all the time, due to certain nervous (physical) reactions I can neither hold back nor hide.

Those who broaden the horizon, those who narrow it.

How I prefer a true whore.

Do not get stuck where the *essential* is lost, where everything turns vulgar, base, and petty. Through my own fault, through a will for humiliation. A feeling of abjection. "Defeated ahead of time." So from now on "dust to dust" resembles dust. At those moments it is physically impossible to be clear and *frank*. Shame and false shame.

Easy: to accuse others of being superficial = brilliant = alive.

Return to simple beings, to childlike reactions, a difficult return.

Solitude gnaws like a cancer
Break the circle
Tear away this gag

Sadness and Bitterness
gnaw gnaw gnaw
the heart like rats

Shame on you
no doubt?
But not certainly
such a *curious* discrepancy
of words

Whom to defy?
The everyday
The gray the bleak

It is time to assert that the religion of crime poisons us as much as that of virtue.

We hate innocence adorned with the virtues of crime as much as crime with an innocent allure.

If I've suffered, it was through ILLNESS.
A healthy being cannot suffer.
Happiness is accessible to all who have pride in themselves.

Now comes the Time for Contempt, but take care that it be a contempt without hate, even without hostility, a very simple contempt, very calm, very confident and without sardonic or hysterical trappings, without false gaiety, without bitter sadness.

Nothing is lost
since I'm alive
All the rivers
will have risen
All the currents
will have risen
the sea and the waves

Goal: to destroy the Christian spirit and its equivalences, like death instinct, identifications with death, sacrifice, dust, edulcoration.

A taste for repulsion, for being repugnant, resembling dust.
Attractive beings.
What *** taught me.
I have broken with the Christian spirit and its equivalences.
The meaning of a life,
discovered by Nietzsche.
Nietzsche rediscovered and not read in a drone.

The greatest liberation possible
Beyond all vice
virtue

The cannon strikes the hours, because each hour is inseparable, irremissible, irreplaceable, each hour brings its victims. Time reaps heads in the fields. No act is free. Time is not that bearded and slobbering old man, it is a man in full force, he reaps heads.

Sienna, August 1937

Fragment of an unsent letter

Do you know that a theater troupe is "putting on" *A Season in Hell.*

These theater people are incredible; either they assume—conditioned by their jobs—that they can reduce existence to the level of their nasty Parisian vaudeville; or else they have these pretensions. Can you picture this: A Season in Hell! Come back soon, there is so much healthy anger to share together. At times life becomes fiery, intrepid like a bolting horse. A bolting horse does not think of hesitation, any more than the sailor on a frail skiff carried off by wild currents or torrents during tragic floods (the ones that are remembered for several generations); the navigator *knows* that he is approaching an overflowing lock, a great liquid vault, a whirlpool that will engulf him, smash him, but he seems to rush more and more quickly toward this inevitable end. He does not have the time to burn his papers, but he can *shout, scream* into the wind, since the wind carries everything away.

October 1937

Everything that depends only on total integrity.
Nothing that can be "made up for."
Nothing of the child who breaks a window pane "because it will be replaced the next day."
You can die of cold because of a broken window that is *not replaced*.
Some people spend their time replacing broken windows.

Life: is over.
When it becomes a habit—a need to
"continue" yourself—to be "assured."
Permanence:
tendency for immobility
fatigue

Nothing that does not come from a cry of joy (understanding), from pride.
Do away with moaning and everything that does not come from the happy aggression of being fourteen.
Nothing that is not a cry of joy or pride.
Burn everything that does not come from *this*.

Follow *your* path, yours, that of no "other" human being.[6]
Do you know of one destiny similar to yours? NO.
Only I have seen and see how one can see: absolutely and from so faraway.

6. This fragment, placed here by Bataille, was taken by him from "The Red Notebook," dated 1938.

Fragment of an unsent letter

Today.—Only delirious but joyful iconoclasts please me.

What hell to have gotten the picture—yes there it is: wanting terribly to tell you to go to hell the way one throws oneself around the necks of those one loves.

The hell of these ponderous airs for profound things.

No misunderstandings: I like these great priests for their madness.

Absence of literature. Listen:

". . . he is my playmate. There is neither rhyme nor reason in the Universe. Playful! tears and laughter, all the roles in the play. Oh, the entertainment of the world! Schools of children set free, *who* to praise? *Who* to blame? He has no reason. He has no brain. He dupes us with this bit of brain and this bit of reason. But this time, he will not take me in. *I know the name of the game.* Beyond reason and science and all the words, there is love. Fill the cup, and we will be wild."

Iconoclasts, yes, but no imitations, no mincing, mawkishness, pretense. Do you understand all this?

June or July 1938

I too am well-trained . . . from hour to hour.
We are all very clever monkeys.
Laughter—laughter—laughter.
The name of the game.
Careful: will they notice that *black* means *white*, but no, no, never.
It's simple: impossibility of true exchanges—never more.
What a relief: I am never where others think they can find me and *seize* me.
Existence: alkaline and sickly sweet.
Enough—enough—enough.

You should be a bit more "wary"—jingle my words the way you verify your change: the change from your coin piece.

The "normal," childish voice, ferocious irony simmering underneath. But you are so well-trained none of you sense it. Who would think so much could be concealed when one conceals only oneself and not actions, facts, and self-serving, calculated goals.

June or July 1938

LAST POEM

I saw her

I saw her—this time I saw her
where? at the edge of dawn
and darkness

the dawn of the garden
the darkness of the room

with a smile that cracks
an angel's patience
she waits for me
And I know

Then in a distant voice
she tells me
No no
You are not going crazy
Do you hear, you will not act like this,
You will do this and that. She spoke, spoke and I understood
nothing
I followed her despite myself
In a rustling of silk, a dress with a train and lots of flounces
that bounced on each step.
she disappeared
sparkling swishing
up a narrow and crumbling stairway

At the top
was the men's department, thousands of garments
A closed, overheated room
She, the only living presence
she ran through the empty spaces between the mannequins
each wearing its mask

NOTES[7]
by Bataille and Leiris

A few months ago the woman who called herself Laure died. She died at the age of thirty-five, of an illness that, without diminishing her in any way, had pursued her since childhood.

Rebelling early against a bourgeois and Catholic upbringing, she had become, after a prolonged stay in Russia, totally devoted to opposition communism as the solution to give her life meaning. Events having led her to reject political activity as devoid of value, she had to pick herself back up, as she would say, "from this great earthquake that is loss of faith." Without ceasing to know moments of distress—as well as happiness or caprice—she again found "a more total state of consciousness than ever," the highest ambition someone could achieve when *integrity of being* occupied, in the scale of values, the privileged place.

Through every tribulation, the passion Laure brought to the search for her truth was unfailing. William Blake's proverb: "Drive your cart and your plow over the bones of the dead" was the last sentence she would write a few days before her death, to indicate the book she wanted to reread. While lost in herself she said she was "at the bottom of worlds"; she referred to her agony as a "florid bullfight."

The texts gathered here form but a small part of the collection of manuscripts and notes that Laure left, after having burned what she was anxious to destroy (but without having had time to shape, as she had expressed the desire to, the writings with which she was never satisfied). Her closest friends knew of the existence of certain of these writings, as of the collection of her papers, but she did not pass these writings along to any of them. Although such reserve could seem sufficiently motivated by the very nature of most of these texts and by the implacable rigor that Laure demanded from herself as much as from others, one might still see in this the exceptionally solemn—strictly speaking, sacred—meaning that she attached to the act of "communication" itself.

The notes on the "sacred" that remained incomplete—notes she spoke of openly—have formed the basis for this provisional collection, which will be followed by a publication of the whole. To this text dealing with what seems always

6. These notes were written by Georges Bataille and Michel Leiris for the underground edition of *The Sacred.*

to have been one of her vital concerns, however she formulated it, we have added a number of poems and other writings connected in various ways to the crucial question of the sacred, such as Laure saw it.

Is there any need to add that we cannot reduce one of the most vehement existences ever lived, one of the most conflicted, to any definite image? Eager for affection and for disaster, oscillating between extreme audacity and the most dreadful anguish, as inconceivable on a scale of real beings as a mythical being, she tore herself on the thorns with which she surrounded herself until becoming nothing but a wound, never allowing herself to be confined by anything or anyone.

"The Sacred"

The representation of the "sacred" expressed in this text attests to lived experience: it does not oppose the notion that sociologists extract from the study of societies less developed than ours—but it is manifestly distinct from it. It is a matter of what the word evokes—rightly or wrongly—in one's consciousness. Wrongly in this case would mean without relation to the common experience that founded the existence of the sacred.

It seems in fact that this representation leads to a definition that has never been expressed (either by Laure or by others) but that could be deduced from the text itself.

This definition would link the sacred to moments in which the isolation of life in the individual sphere is suddenly broken, moments of communication not only between men but between men and the universe in which they are ordinarily foreigners: communication should be understood here in the sense of a fusion, of a loss of oneself, the integrity of which is achieved only in death and of which erotic fusion is an image. Such a conception differs from that of the French sociological school which considers only communication between men; it tends to identify that which mystical experience apprehends with that which the rites and myths of the community bring into play.

The text published in this collection was written during the summer of 1938, during Laure's last months. But the importance of the sacred in the whole of her life since her childhood is strongly marked by the following passage of "Story of a Little Girl" (an autobiography of her childhood, which will appear in the collection of the whole):

". . . Only the catchall room remained unalterable with its stale air and its stained-glass light.

I took refuge there and, straddling an old trunk of imitation leather or squatting on a little bench, I told myself endless stories, especially the ones about the time before my birth, the time when 'I lived in the sky.' Or else, I fervently contemplated a sweet white Jesus and a blond Joseph, blue, pink, silvery, golden, starry images, wrapped in silk, tied up with ribbons. Or else, I washed my doll and went in search of my own body which I was ordered to ignore before I had even thought about it. A child's curiosity about her belly precisely when it knows that God 'sees' everywhere and follows her into this attic. Curiosity and then terror. Life soon managed to oscillate between these two poles: one sacred, venerated, which must be exhibited, facial expressions at church, sinking into a sacred torpor after Communion, the other unnameable, dirty, shameful which must be hidden, but both of them so much more mysterious, more beautiful, more intense than bleak and unchanged life. Thus she would oscillate between the foul and the sublime, in the course of an existence where true life would always be absent. Hieratic gestures, vile grimaces would mix, merge, disappear, reemerge, then vanish entirely."

The two poles that Laure describes are not exactly the sacred and its opposite, for the one and the other are sacred; they are two contradictory poles within the sacred world, "sacred" signifying at once worthy of horror or disgust and worthy of adoration.

The same ambiguity emerges in another form in the following lines which were no doubt intended for "Story of a Little Girl," but which do not appear there:

"Laure had found God again. He was not a human being, she made him a hero, a saint. In his arms, then, she wanted him to hurt her. She imagined being beaten, thrashed, being wounded, a victim, humiliated, scorned, despised and then once again adored and sanctified." (Cf. p. 188)

The poem entitled "8" (p. 48) takes up the same theme of opposition, and is constructed, we may note, upon the leitmotif sentence: "Hieratic gestures, vile grimaces . . ."

In these contradictory texts we see not only the extreme attraction of the sacred in its abject and venerable forms, but the extreme anguish that it provokes. Laure's existence never ceased to fluctuate between these two vile and sublime poles, and at the same time between the vile, the sublime, and what she called "true life," the simple happiness to which she ceaselessly aspired. That she came to a conception of the sacred, after many detours and particularly toward the end of her life, that in contrast to that of her childhood took on an intoxicating value for her, does not mean that she found a single day of respite.

A page of the manuscript entitled *The Sacred* bears these words:

"Conrad's different themes. Error. Remorse. Redemption." Conrad had been crossed out.

P. 41. *"What color does the notion of the sacred have for me?"* Reference to the last line of "Le sacré dans la vie quotidienne" [*The Sacred in Everyday Life*] by Michel Leiris (N.R.F., July 1938), published in the collection entitled *Pour un Collège de Sociologie,* which opened with a text by Bataille, "L'apprenti sorcier." [Leiris's text was republished in *Change,* No. 7, where Laure's poems were published for the first time—Jean-Pierre Faye.]

P. 41. *This permanence of the threat of death is the intoxicating absolute . . .*
In a letter of July 1934, Laure already had written:

"The idea of death when one follows it to the end . . . until putrefaction, has always relieved me and that day more than ever. I detailed the various forms of 'accidental death' and all seemed enviable and delicious to me. I became calm again and even cheerful."

And in a letter (unsent) of August 1936:

88

"And what if this is death?

Will I lack the courage to love death?"[8]

I am afraid something in me is *broken:* ruptured, to be weak to that extent.

Don't obsessions replace the fear of God? Isn't it intolerable to have come to this?

I want to talk about "loving death" because this alone signifies loving life *without restriction,* loving it that much, death included. Not being *terrified* by death any more than by life. On this condition, I sense myself becoming . . . noble . . . again.

8. "What an old maid I am getting to be, lacking the courage to love death!" (Arthur Rimbaud, *A Season in Hell,* "Bad Blood")

P. 41. . . . *hurls forth the depths of my being.*.

In an earlier version of the same text, Laure had written: "hurls forth the most profound depths of being."

P. 41. *When you call the act of defending a friend . . . sacred . . .*
An allusion to a conversation Laure had had with Michel Leiris, to whom all of these notes on the sacred were destined, although they were not given to him.

P. 43. *There are "pre-sacred" states which lack only one element.*
The following text underlines the importance of these two experiences for Laure:

"What prestige the little girl who fainted during the church procession had in my eyes. How I envied her: passing out, compulsive fainting, it was the extreme degree of piety.

Girls taking their First Communion glimpsed from the stained-glass window.
The mirror and
The lawn . . . seventh heaven
The wet ground   have I ever been more far away?
The crushed, juicy flowers
The massif . . .
My habits
Cremation
The sewer"

Some time before writing these notes on the sacred, Laure tried meditation using the following schema from G. C. Lounsbery's *Buddhist Meditation,* a work whose spirit she detested moreover: "Lying on your back outdoors, look at the sky, the space, the clouds—Space is limitless—Space is everything—Space is in us—Think of the space between the stars, between the cells of your body—everywhere—fill your mind with the idea of space. Make the clouds—the earth—the sky—disappear in order to identify with space. Do not remain conscious of the space." This is apparently the only exercise of this type that Laure practiced.

P. 44. *A memory that seems to me to sum up completely my notion of the sacred.*

A passage in "Story of a Little Girl" should be connected to this memory:

"We waited for the parade. I saw the standards and flags of frail little boys and knock-kneed old people (canes in hand); I saw the banners and gaudy finery of sweating priests (armpits green and stinking), I saw the scapulars and the grimy rosaries of young girls, trembling children of Mary: "Father I've had bad thoughts." They howled, breath rotten: we are the *hope* of France. Three old women nodding their greasy heads of hair found, between their mustaches, false teeth filled with rancid host.

There you are beneath these flags, insane holiness! Why not smile free of illusion or burst out laughing amused . . . But no, I stay there, spitting the blood of my ancestors who resemble you."

The successive deaths of her father and her uncles killed during the war were for Laure heartbreaking and decisive events.

A very rough first draft of the same text begins this way: "I do not feel I have the right to end with anything but a childhood memory, one among many, that seems to me to sum up for me the notion of the sacred."

P. 45. *"Communication" experienced as nakedness . . .*
This sentence has significance for all the texts attached to the notes on the sacred.

P. 59. *Church Fire.*
The rumor having been spread that poisoned candies had intentionally been given to children, a riot occurred on May 3, 1936, in the working-class neighborhood of Quatro Caminos in Madrid, during which the crowd set fire to a church.

P. 60. *Outskirts of towns . . .*
This poem was written after a trip in October 1936 to Catalonia and Barcelona.

P. 62. "drive your cart and your plow over the bones of the dead."
This is one of William Blake's "Proverbs of Hell" which Laure had just read for the first time in Spain in Grolleau's translation *(Le mariage du ciel et de l'enfer).*

P. 63. *Bullfight.*
Fragment of an unsent letter written in September 1937. It was most likely in Barcelona in 1935 that Laure saw her first bullfight, a spectacle she loved passionately.

P. 64. *Laure.*
This text must have been written during a stay in Madrid in May of 1936. The fragments that follow must have been written subsequently.

P. 67. *Start again in another form of retrospective journal.*
The following fragment is most likely the only vestige of the journal that was *destroyed* (different from the autobiography of childhood that is "Story of a Little Girl") to which it alludes:

"I threw myself on a bed the way one throws oneself into the sea. Sensuality seemed separate from my real being, I had invented a hell, a climate in which everything was as far as possible from what I had been able to foresee for myself. No one in the world could ever contact me, look for me, find me. The next day, this man said to me: "You worry far too much, my dear, your role is that of a product of a decomposed society . . . a choice product, of course. Examine this thoroughly, you will be of service to the future. In hastening the disintegration of society . . . You remain the schema that is dear to you, you serve your ideas in a way and then, with your vices—there are not many women who like to be beaten like this—you could earn a lot of money, you know?" One night I ran away. It was too much, a parody of itself. At two o'clock in the morning, I wandered through Berlin, the markets, the Jewish quarter and then at dawn, a bench in the Tiergarten. There, two men approached to ask me the time. I stared at them for a long time before replying that I didn't have a watch. They came closer with strange looks on their faces, then one of them signaled to his companion by glancing sideways. I also turned my head: there was a police officer a hundred meters away from us; their intention had no doubt been to grab my handbag or something like that. How little it mattered to me, and how I would have liked to talk to them. For, all in all, there you are, in total disarray, you walk in the streets carried away by the bustle of the crowd like wreckage on the sea, you think about suicide, but you have a handbag and you notice a rip in your stocking. After a few minutes . . . they went away and soon afterwards it was the policeman who came to question me. What was I doing there? I was getting air. Didn't I have a home? Yes. Where? I gave my address, my very "affluent bourgeois" neighborhood. That rooted him to the spot. He went on: What was I doing there? I was getting air. Where are your papers? Do you need a passport to get air? Then I fell back to sleep."

Laure had spent several months in Berlin around 1928.

P. 78. *It is time to assert that the religion of crime poisons us as much as that of virtue.*

The same protestation is found elsewhere. It is found once in this form:

"The Religion of Evil requires Good. Evil (crime) that gives itself the appearance, adorns itself with the virtues of virtue."

The same idea is expressed once again in an unsent letter written in October 1937, followed this time by a few sentences that seem to indicate all the acuity that this problem had for Laure:

"What is more comical and more odious: crime that adorns itself with the virtues of innocence or innocence that adorns itself with the virtues of crime?

Why when I see my thoughts through to the end do I get the impression of betraying what I love most in the world and of betraying myself without this betrayal being "avoidable." If you sensed all the anguish lived and to be lived with which this *why* is charged, you would try to respond, but there is no possible response. We bear within us the most dangerous opposition."

P. 81. *Everything that depends only on total integrity.*
This text and those that follow were written either slightly before or after March 13, 1938, the date that Laure's illness entered a decisive phase.

From a sanatorium where she stayed for two months, she wrote to her friends:

". . . Know this: I am horrified by pity and—*even now*—I do not in any way feel pitiful and *even now* it is impossible for me to envy any one in the world.

I envy one thing perhaps, a state, health. That, yes. And still! My illness is so profoundly linked to my life that it could not be separated from all that I have experienced. So? Perhaps it is still one of those misfortunes that turn into luck: you will understand later what I mean by that . . ."

P. 82. ". . . he is my playmate . . ."
The text quoted is by Ramakrishna: it appears in *Vie de Ramakrishna* by Romain Rolland; "he" signifies God.

P. 84. *"Last Poem."*
This poem was written by Laure shortly before her death.

In a book Laure had on Theresa of Avila, page 199 was dog-eared, evidently because of her interest in the passage extracted from *Opuscules* by the Carmelite Jeronimo Gracian: "While Mother Theresa was alive never did she think, any more than I, that these books would be published and brought to all those who wanted to read them. We would have wanted to see these books remain in our convents in manuscript form so that they would only be read by wise persons instructed in the matter of prayer. I have sympathy for the Pythagorean rule that required profound and sacred things to be hidden . . ."

A similar preoccupation—to which her anxiety was clearly linked—was often expressed by Laure, speaking in general. Before dying she formally indicated her wish that her testimony not remain uncommunicated, asserting that one must not isolate onself, as only that which exists for others can have meaning. But the misery inherent in all that is literature horrified her: for she had the greatest conceivable concern not to confide what seemed heartrending to her to those who cannot be moved.

Correspondence

Though not always certain of the dates, I have tried to organize these letters chronologically. The notes at the bottom of these letters are mine.

J. Peignot

Letters to Suzanne

Monday, August 1921

The house is quiet once again but for me it is still animated by your presence and those few days that were so unexpected! . . . I would have liked to talk to you at length and Cécile would have spared us the difficult and awkward beginnings of long talks . . . Now it's hard for me to write to you . . . I need your replies, this letter will be incomplete.

Tuesday

Back from Chateau Vaillant, wasting entire days submitting to an average and base life, taking no action, contenting myself with weak people, letting myself be dominated by apathy, banality . . . the vulgarity of others . . . the vulgarity of ideas, void of intelligence, beauty, the strength of love—I can't stand it anymore—and yet I myself remain vague, undecided.

It is all very charming to laugh like a child, to say you are eighteen years old, etc., but I suffer too much from the utter disparity between myself and my actions; the way I act in front of other people makes those I respect despise me.

So I don't think activity is the conventional, normal, practical kind Cécile talks about, but something caused by enthusiasm, sustained only in order to live out what is strong and true in me, to preserve the true ardor of solitude, to struggle against the ordinariness of the days that contrasts with the fever of the night.

Oh, no, the effort of will it would take to experience life with all our might, to the height of our "potential" cannot destroy our "richness to feel."

But where to direct this effort . . . the anxiety I feel cannot be better expressed than in this passage from *Nourritures:*[1] "You do not know, you cannot know the passion that burns my youth. I am enraged by the flight of hours. The necessity of a choice is always intolerable to me; to choose seems to me not so much to select, as to push away that which I do not select . . . I never do anything but *this* or *that.* If I do this, that immediately becomes regrettable and I no longer dare to do anything, desperately, with my arms always open, for fear that if I closed them to hold something I would seize *only one* thing . . . to choose is to renounce all the rest forever . . ." Oh my dear I want you to like everything I've told you . . . but in any case this letter can help us talk more when we see each other again . . . I want to tell you other things, too, that I can't write to you and that have more to do with you—

How are you? Despite my immense desire to see you again, I don't want you to be sad and tired because of us; on Sunday if you have to leave your brother again or get too tired, don't hesitate to tell mama.

I would like to write to Jacques too . . . to tell him how glad I was that he livened up the house those few days—

Give my regards to the Fleurets; they made a very favorable impression I think. I love you so much

Colette

XX *Tuesday, August 1921*

I can finally write you! I've been extremely occupied and mostly preoccupied lately, and when I started my letter in the evening, and soon despaired at not being able to tell you what I wanted, I tore everything up and had a hard time falling asleep! I constantly reread

1. Trans. André Gide, *Les Nourritures terrestres* (1897) (Paris: Éditions Gallimard, 1917-1936), book four, p. 65. In Gide, this passage is in the past tense; Laure quotes it in the present.

and adore all your letters which are so interesting, full of joy, life and affection. It must be so wonderful to be friends with Drieu la Rochelle! I would be extremely happy to see him at your house but terribly nervous—I am anxious to read everything you've suggested. I am starting *Prétextes*[2] and although I don't quite understand everything that is discussed, several general passages interest me very much.

I'm writing to you from Dampierre; coming to Catherine's always overwhelms me but today especially. She is so tired and always in bed—Now that the question of influence is no longer an issue, everything is better between us. Besides the great affection that binds us, we are both interested in each other's different ideas. It's a sort of affinity (this is a little complicated and I'm explaining it badly!)

This area is really beautiful, I think I'm going to like it—

You must be sorry to see such vacations end!

We might be at the Blancheron baptism—I'm so looking forward to seeing you again; I don't think I've ever been this impatient to see you, I absolutely have to talk to you about a thousand things—Thanks for the photo which I love passionately and which never leaves me—

I kiss you with *all* my heart—

Colette

I am very ashamed of my terrible handwriting and the "general appearance" of this letter—I have a dreadful pen.

August 1921

Dearest Suzanne. I am going to Paris tomorrow to reserve my place; what if I didn't come back and left for Marly? Ultimately I'm too much of a coward—I didn't go to mass, I can't stand all those

2. By André Gide.

formalities and all those rigid displays—yesterday was terrible, after a talk we each cried separately in our rooms. All of this means nothing.

Mama was really very much mistaken; I feel in an extraordinary state, ready for anything—I will not diminish this rebellion in me "the rebellion against slavery, the vehement desire to rise to joy, I want to live life in its entirety and not only be a brain"— I have never lived D'Annunzio's thoughts more.

I'm afraid you don't understand me, I can't stand it anymore and I'm eager to be at the seaside.

I love you I think of you constantly and I don't know what I would do without your tenderness

Colette

Now we have to go to Mr. Gaulois's house with the Durains! I hate all these people so much—today they seem like puppets to me, made to distract me

Dammarie, probably 1922

Darling I am horrified by the number of "I's" and "me's" this letter will contain—it has to be the last of this sort that I write to you. I hate and am ashamed of these "moods" and these complicated hesitations.

I have no reason to be pitied (look what I do with my freedom when I get it!)

It's all my fault—I've lived with my books too long, I can't free myself from the exaltation of them, of being sent into raptures, and hate the return to the simple, cheerful level of people around me; I had a long self-imprisonment, detesting what I saw—the young girls I met with their nice little bland and content lives—

And I was reading *Le Feu, Les Nourritures,* I listened to music, I filled my room with flowers, and each instant was new to me and delicious.

And then this waiting was not enough for me anymore . . . It seemed clear to me that life only gives in proportion to what you give to it. Waiting for it and desperately tasting what was accessible was not enough anymore—it seemed impossible that all this sincerity would remain futile, and I wanted to force things, adapt life to my nature and not simply be content to want and accept all it offered without enriching it and embellishing it myself.

And I was confused sometimes when I saw you. Everything seemed simple and easy to you! But how can this effort be made when everything inside oneself is fighting and contradicting itself? . . . After all, maybe I'm just a little girl who's read *Tristan!*

I would like not to be able to think, not to have reflected so much—to be something precise, defined. It seems this will never happen, that nothing will be enough for me.

This summer made everything worse and I now feel a complete disequilibrium with regard to just about everyone—I am not myself with anyone and I suffer horribly (like last Tuesday!) What use is my freedom if this is what I do with it! I know of nothing more unpleasant and disagreeable than myself on these occasions!

Isn't it *shameful,* my dear, to suffer so much over oneself?

Excuse this long letter—I don't know what I would do without you—

Don't pity me anymore, scold me—perhaps I've been too arrogant, but I cannot be content with mediocrity any longer—

I beg you, forget this letter—what a confession!!

Only you can help me—

I love you with all my heart and I don't know how to tell you how touched I am by your patient tenderness for the complicated little girl I am. Darling I adore you.

Colette

(probably July 22, 1923)

My dearest love I knew that day I could see no one *but you,* yet the simple lunch that "reimmersed" me in your cheerful atmosphere, calmer than me, made me so happy you don't know—

Thank you, thank you, for a thousand things. I want to write you tonight just to say that—and to say it to you again constantly, and then there are too many things for you in my heart—

Even though we are just a diverse succession of "moods," states of mind . . . physical states (yes) that are contradictory and fleeting—today I adore you—could it be that tomorrow I will detest you because of the strange dream I had the other night? O listen—one must not be deluded by big words, lulled by lovely phrases . . .

You don't have time to think so selfishly about so many things . . . it seems to me now that, if at thirty years of age one has not fulfilled all the love one carries inside for desire, life, *beauty* (toward and against *everyone*) it is not worth it anymore, do you understand? To have too much inside oneself not to "be aware" and not to suffer but not enough to . . . win the battle of this game which seems cruel—(it seems to me) but do I have the right to such grand words, me, a little girl who merely has intuitions about things and who above all is not a woman yet—How eager I am to be delivered of this state, which is false, unconscious, unreal despite everything—I still want to believe, but this wonderful impulse is only the reflection of love that is placed onto everything—is this why people are so disappointing? You can't make them embody your own ideal, and it seems they are all fiercely determined to destroy the beauty that you hoped existed in them, that you "lent" them at first, with their meanness—

What is the remedy for all this? Waiting . . . marriage—a stroke of good or bad luck that will shape your life around a person that, despite everything, you would not have chosen yourself, because of a too great desire for love—

Then! There are also days when the thought of a dress, a box of powder, a Hermès bag takes up all the time and importance of things and oneself. But that some people reduce life to a question of comfort is something I have not been able to explain to myself, even though you know how much I love luxury and nice things—but for me this is still certainly "beside the point!" And I would love life as much if I were poor—the opposite seems a disturbing bourgeois-ism. If—enough of these stupid things—I am crazy—why send you all of this which makes me so different from you, as different as you being blond and me dark-haired. Pardon me: sometimes I need brutal honesty—I think you will get used to opening my letters like cluttered drawers!—THANK YOU my beloved darling—do you see there are moments when everything crumbles and collapses and when there is nothing but your tender clarity. I send you this letter like I would fling myself into the water.

C.

Hôtel de l'Europe, August 23, 1923

We are leaving for the mountains, but I want to tell you very quickly that I received everything you sent: your last letter and the package just now, thank you, thank you *infinitely*.

How exciting for you, aren't you already in Le Havre? You must be so completely happy and overwhelmed . . . I am so anxious to see you again after three long years, which have no doubt changed and enriched you in a different way.

I can't believe I will see my brother this winter; you talked about him so often it seems I know him only through you, I've changed so much, it's been so long.

We are leaving Barèges on the 30th, and I will come back to Paris around the 3rd through Toulouse.

I don't think I can come to Louveciennes!! I still hope that a half day will go by unnoticed . . . I would like so much to see you.

I quickly send you a kiss with all my tenderness.

Colette

Thanks again for the book, it was so nice of you to send it so swiftly.

April 25, 1924

Suz dear it's me again! I have an astonishing need to write you this evening—Nothing is more hateful than narrow-mindedness and pettiness, which is what reigns at home—I breathe a little being around Catherine—she is broad-minded and extreme—I like that—we talk about books—I like to discuss things with her—Louis is decidedly, indefinitely mute—

There are delightful walks, this picturesque and verdant countryside reminds me of Pierre Brissaud's song illustrations—

We don't know when we're coming back yet—

I lack a bit of spirit and true cheerfulness in all of this, which is natural and obvious—but there are moments when I would like to send all this philosophy to the devil, and I would like more than anything to have fun!

For that, the pictures of Jacques acting like a clown are precious to me this evening! I send both of you a passionate kiss.

Colette

Would you like it or hate it if I called you Suz??

I often wonder which way you're taking to come back—

I'm addressing this letter to Paris (???) I don't know why I'm adding all this—it's ridiculous!!

Dammarie (fall 1924)

This is just a note: the letter I wrote last night that I told you about on the telephone is no longer "in keeping" with my state of "mind" today(!)

So you are coming Thursday! It is incredible and wonderful, my dear, that you have had a son . . . and that this son, my nephew, is coming here to Dammarie, like a little unconscious and adored package with his strange little nose that it seems I haven't seen for centuries.

Are you sure you won't be exhausted by the trip . . . be very careful—make sure Jacques brings his rifle, he's sure to hunt at Thiérard's, his racket, too . . . and perhaps he'll play golf at Fontainebleau

(I absolutely cannot write today)

Dammarie (probably the end of September, 1924)

Dearest love—I was probably so mean this morning and didn't realize it—

Let me write you without logic or sense—

You think this is utter despondency, despondency over what? Don't you know that no pain will ever be able to overcome this infinite thirst in me for life?

One cannot live by literature you told me one day . . . that's probably true. Do you remember: "My soul is filled with lyricism that sharpens my solitude." I often keep to myself, happy, yet anxious, knowing I find contentment in things too easily. One day I'll explain . . . you'll understand better.

Now laugh at me and mock the too complicated little sister who expects too wild a joy.

I will probably come tomorrow, for I will once again be a smiling and facile little girl. I will not come today, I'm afraid you'll scold me and especially Jacques who doesn't know how happy I am about the

Max Jacob![3]

I would like not to have the time to "think" anymore this week, and have fun.

Do you still love me dearest love? Tell me so in three lines and *send this letter back to me.* It would be too painful for me if you kept it.

I love you dear and I hope you are better now.

Colette

Dammarie, September 24, 1924

I fear this evening you may have doubted my profound and utter affection for you, my dear, confronted with my silence and the impassive, cold, and sad face that hides me.

I would like to talk to you indefinitely this evening but you know I cannot.

How can I not tell you, oh darling, I *thought* life was beautiful and today I *know* it.

A wild and delirious joy is invading me now—this evening—

Tell Jean I'll be good (he'll remember . . .) I'm tousling his hair.

Destroy, burn this letter which I am not rereading, do you know how much I love you?

Colette

Dearest love Your little note is so precious to me, so filled with you and all your affection that it leaves me overcome with joy—this month together has brought us closer than ever, I thought my affection for you had filled my heart, but that was nothing—a miracle that constantly recurs being near you—

May I come to lunch at Garches Tuesday and leave around four o'clock? I will call on Monday, tell me if this is possible without being any trouble (I will have my car)—

3. A gouache by Max Jacob given to her as a present.

Thank you for the address—you will read my letter, I can't judge it. I lose myself in a confusion of words—and yet certainty takes hold of me, more obvious each minute, more urgent to express itself—

It would have been just as easy to "say" this to Rendier the other night but a profound helplessness came over me in the course of it, even though the obviousness of it was already crying out in me—my pride did me no good: so despicable and vain to be futile—ignorance or inexperience of everything he had just talked about prevented me from speaking coolly of "opinions," and I was too used to moral propriety to lay bare what I should have, clearly and distinctly, and no, more than myself—I have never so cruelly felt this disparity between my thoughts and my actions, between my pride and my timidity.

What a pleasure to see you Tuesday with Eric—What things you will tell me—In these luminous autumn days, I cannot imagine the atmosphere of the Boeuf[4] and all the people already coming back to the merry-go-round! I truly understand when you talk about the pleasure of the return to oneself—you must be practicing your singing a great deal—I'm so sorry you didn't have the tranquillity to do it here—but so glad that you were happy about your stay, which passed like a flash of lightning as I took pleasure in each minute of your adored presence.

Hurry, the mail is rushing me, and I leave you in order to reread your letter once again. Tell Jacques how much I love him. I kiss you O! how I kiss you

Colette

Dammarie, 8-18-25

You are with Jean, I hope with all my heart he is better, he must be so happy to see you. How could Jacques let you leave by yourself

4. Probably the Boeuf-sur-le-Toit.

. . . and to go to Touquet with Vincent Dubouchet! Provided this long trip has not tired you, give me news of yourself soon—by telephone if you don't have the time to write—And what has Eric been up to? His little sweater is coming along as quickly as possible with lots of thoughts attached to each stitch—here, too—*nothing has changed.* I see familiar things that are reassuring—my little blue-checked bedroom—the noises of the village, the luminous and cheerful garden—the Vinès full of overflowing affection in which I rest. Hernando is playing guitar in the garden! Mr. Victor is approaching with his broad smile, in an alpaca jacket, Madam in slippers. All of this is cheerful and noisy! We're preparing for Ricardo's arrival; the piano has arrived and starting tomorrow, Dammarie will be given over to "the good magician." A long letter from Hélène on Sunday: "my life itself is my prayer" she says to mama about the lack of Mass down there—While arranging flowers I think happily, impatiently, that in ten days these bouquets will be as perfect as possible *for you.*

All of this is unfolding like a film around me, a film in which I no longer have a part—

This letter is simple, which astonishes me—moral propriety is ferociously holding me back.

You will read this letter after a night of love, and the words will not penetrate you—I'm afraid—they will only be sentences and words to you and not the burning life that is finally coming out of me, for the incommunicable in me is being shared—the idea that this letter will speak to you of Rendier seems paradoxical to you—you're right in a certain sense—I do not hide the "little girl" side of my nature and I feel a grotesque awkwardness destroying me all the time—I could not make you (or anyone at all) penetrate to the isolated part of myself that I myself wanted to feel through some kind of achievement before believing in it—Pathetic failed attempts in which I immediately discovered the "inherent" emptiness of what I called reality—

And only in these scrawlings (where I find things he said to me the other night), which in the evening relieve me of the comedy/joke of the day, it seemed I was *living* a little—but this was still just a dream state—making this unrealness take shape without becoming reality, making this unrealness stay unreal—effective, substantial and not vain.

Do you understand that this miracle is embodied in him and also that he justifies the feeling that if everything that wanted to come to life in me, if all latent possibilities found their expression, it would be complete anguish, the height of anxiety—negation in exaltation.

To all my worried letters you say marriage and love "will quench" this thirst for the ideal, but do you see this is not . . . how can I say this to you—this briefly sums it up: "vice bores me *as much as* virtue"—I hate all those people who talk about literature, automobiles, golf, sleeping around, vices and pornography and also the more subtle ones who safeguard their superiority through skeptical irony—

Thank you. It is through you alone that I have been able to assert myself in contradiction. I would like to tell you all of this simply walking with Cécile, like the other day—I have to end this letter, it's too confusing, too long and "full" . . . though you are looking for more information in it, practical information, I will *tell* it to you.

I am writing Cécile a short note. You can tell her about my letter—as you like—I have total confidence in her and such respect for her—

Don't think anything is going on between Rendier and me—we had a simple conversation—maybe he likes me a little, barely—that's all I've wanted from him for a long time—

I hesitate now to send you this letter—it would be atrocious if there were some sort of indiscretion—I am forcing myself to send you these three pages—what will you answer—pardon the too many "I's" and "me's."

I send you a kiss with all my infinite affection. I would like to see you. *I would like to see you.*

See you soon, the 25th.

Colette

Vinès is here. Through his music he is creating a new Dammarie. During the day, we talk and hours go by without us even noticing—he is translating Catalan poems of rare beauty for *Commerce.*[5] We try to find synonyms, and out of this, have varied and lively conversations—I feel acute pleasure in all of this, being near this intellect, so fundamentally masculine and imaginative—then being alone again—you know if you and Jacques could slip out here one day, you would be welcome, bring whomever you want, but telephone me. I don't know how long he is staying—mama is leaving Tuesday to visit the Flaviens—so here I am, "mistress of the house." I forgot two small belts at your house. One is red, the other white—In any case tell me what is happening with you. When are you coming back?

Dammarie, August 25, 1925

No, I did not laugh while reading your letter—I was so eager to find out your thoughts which not only *accepted* and understood mine but also explained them more simply and clearly than I was able to—I was immensely and wildly happy to hear from you, and you cannot know how grateful I am, thank you from the bottom of my heart—(these words are stupid and trite; one must resign oneself to being trapped by them). I had only one desire: to spend a long time with you—(and this evening will be so imperfect) but—I was and still am absorbed in Vinès's music from early morning until late in the evening—it is a total and delirious state of joy . . . There is a sort of "perversion" (!) in this continuous and solitary pleasure that is so per-

5. The review.

fect—I don't know if I should say perversion or sanctification—in any case, it's YOU I miss, so much more worthy and likely to seize all the beauty of it—

The "information" I mentioned to you was exactly the desire to give these tendencies—desire, firm will—concrete expression. I suffer not knowing the *precise* means by which to do this, and I dread making another mistake—I am eager for action which, far from destroying individuality, can only (it seems to me) enrich it while lavishing it—and then, what lovely individuality, this many-faceted personage too in love with everything to be faithful to anything over whom I am wearing myself out in vain—my "nature" is not so far away from "this" dear which will only make blossom what wants to come to life in me because all action is but an act of love and *not of constraint*—I always confuse desire and will—the idea of marriage has never seemed contemptible to me, but you see, too, dear, that I have come to this incredible moment when one must *throw* oneself into life and embrace it with all one's might whereas for others, life is more simply accommodating, easier. But how bland and useless—

You know that you have not disappointed me. You are so generous and understanding—it seems to me a thousand barriers have been erected between us? and then your "unexpected" little note this morning gave me unspeakable joy—a year ago we were all so anxious. I think about it constantly—I'm also sorry that I don't have a proper present yet to celebrate Eric's birthday when he comes on Wednesday—I'm afraid you still don't know the place this little being who is part of both of us occupies in me

—See you Wednesday, what a pleasure it will be to see each other again.—I kiss you with all my tenderness.

Colette

This draft is shapeless. This is the only paper I have left, and I want so much for this note to be sent quickly despite everything.

(beginning of December 1925)

Why is it that I don't write to you when I think of you all the time—where are you? What are you doing? Who are you seeing? How are you?—at this hour, probably in your bathroom where I could reach you quickly by a telephone call, but you would ask me . . . polite questions as always, and I would speak in my cheerful voice that irritates me—

Is Diane's room finished?[6] Is the cradle and everything ready? Certainly I will come to Paris Wednesday or Thursday, if for nothing else but to witness all this and kiss you under the pretext of 10,000 errands to run. Yesterday I was at the tennis courts at Fontainebleau to shake myself up a bit, and the same horrible people are still there wandering around and smiling at each other—the courts are pretty, but it's stupid just to be a spectator—Always!

And you? You play golf all the time, I imagine, with Mr. "so-and-so" or Miss "so-and-so" who tell you such-and-such story about this or that person, etc. etc. etc. and there you are—and all the people will meet again this winter . . .

Don't try to figure out what all this means. It's raining. Life is stupid and so am I—with all my "means without an end," my "ideas without action," and my beautiful *sentences*—isn't that so.

What has become of Monique and Brigitte? I think of them often.

I wrote to Eric one beautiful day. Received a very nice letter from Marie-Anne. How can truly balanced "young girls" exist—

I never touch the piano anymore. Everything I play is so amateurish and vain and all my books stay in their place—For everything, I say: what's the use except to roast in the sun when there is any—while waiting for the energetic and independent man I want for my husband—that's intelligent! and I despise myself.

6. Her future niece.

Good-bye my beloved dear—I'm using a whole new sheet just to kiss you—

I have a picture of you that I adore, but it is not fully developed and I'm not sending it to you—

So I will come Wednesday or Thursday—I will be *alone* both days at Dammarie, Mama will be at Dampierre and so will Hélène probably—Mama is rather well, but I reproach myself all the time for being so hard and mean toward her, in my limitless selfishness and my desire for joy, whereas her life is totally shattered and *never* made easier by us four—What a truly horrible letter, too disorderly for you my sweet darling whom I adore always and all the time.

Colette

Dammarie (probably December 1925)

I don't know where you are living, but you don't have the time to tell me—you are so busy with all the people I'm ferociously jealous of because they benefit from you, vulgarly, basely, unknowingly.

I must see Jacques too so that he will tell me about the Taza region (the climate), for Hélène is probably leaving to be a nurse in Morocco. I'm persuading Mama to let her go while I myself am bowled over—would this news interest Jacques?? In any case far from criticizing Hélène, he can only and should only admire her—she too knows how to live marvelously—this surprises you—yes—According to herself—I have never suffered from such selfish indifference, not only indifference toward me but everyone's toward everyone else—but dear, Friendship, Affection are only *words* when one cannot rise above differing ideas—we say we are "broad-minded" but once out of our sphere (our circle of friends) the heart does not follow—Affection is broader and more subtle than all this pettiness—our poor mama is in a very painful state of physical and moral depression—she disapproves of any expression of life, in any sense whatsoever, in any form, she is scared of it and I'm rebelling against the idea that all the willpower in me is constantly being directed toward restraining myself, that more than ever all my efforts are used to concentrate on keeping quiet—obliteration and not blossoming out.

Why are you so far away, so definitively far away, you too—I'm the one spoiling what was your tenderness with the same atrocious habit I have of destroying what I desire—for once listen to me—I was so good for so long—I don't know how to talk anymore—shameful modesty over this moral undressing—but this evening my heart wants to be one with someone—

—it's like falling into a vice again—you still don't know what a radiant presence you are to me—you are so dear to me so dear and I know I am so selfish and that the most horrible uncertainty is to love selfishly . . . to love because one likes loving—Tell me does one find the self there too? then nothing is worth anything anymore.

Do you understand, do you know that . . .

Sorry. Why am I saying this to you—notes are not worth the same between us and especially this one—please excuse the weakness of sending you this long draft which is taking your time and boring you. I *trust* you

Colette

Dammarie (probably the end of 1925)
Thursday

All I think about are those five days with you . . . I wish the last day had never happened . . . tell me quickly that it was of no importance and that you have forgotten it . . . why is it always "Me among others and me . . . and why so complicated?". . .

This house is terribly large, dear; it would be so good to fill all these empty rooms with friends and cheerfulness, and yet I cannot despair in this silent garden "savoring the great nourishment that only solitude can give us; its brief joys are intense enough to dispel the tedium inseparable from isolation." But I would prefer no longer to think that solitude "so intoxicates us that the most refined frivolities of life in society are henceforth mixed with bitterness for anyone recalling the vigor of sensation he is forgoing by mixing with others." And yet . . . will I ever manage to hate solitude! Help me, my darling. Only you can, only you know everything inside of me and every thing and I eagerly reread your last letter . . . darling I wanted to struggle against the endless waiting that is shattering everything in me and crushing *all* my strength—struggle, enrich myself through Effort, add to all the strength that I feel is possible and certain in me

I ferociously envy all forms of life that I see around me and I *despair* to remain uncertain and powerless, and yet I cannot express to you, this evening, this innner feeling of fullness sweeping over me.

(probably the beginning of 1926)

Congratulations on your golf game! Lucky you, always showing off your extraordinary talents! As for me, I still think I am on the verge of making big decisions, breaking with the monotony and intolerable uselessness of a "young girl's" life, but I am starting to take myself with a certain amount of irony and to see that I am just waiting for a husband or anyone at all, for love, and I wish for this gift all the more because you will love me more than in this "dream" where I am tossing and turning now.

I kiss you, dear, with vast "fraternal" affection, cheerfulness and wild tenderness—why do you make me say so many stupid things and write so badly?

Coco

Give my best wishes to your delicious companion

(Dammarie, probably the beginning of 1926)

Suz dear, how sweet your tenderness is and how much things change and become better near you . . .

Thank you for your lively letter and everything it talks about, and how ashamed I am to have written you another letter full of complaints the other day, to you who always give me everything generously—everything, and your ever more precious and dear tenderness. —I think of Diane often and am surprised that I already love her very much, but she *must* not make you suffer.

Why excuse yourself and stop yourself when talking to me about Jacques? I like it, I love your love affair like joy, sun, fresh air, and both of you are often more dear to me when you are together.

Pardon my last letter, this beautiful weather intoxicated me and overwhelmed me. I would like not to be so savage, so . . . brutal, for a smile not to be a stupid grimace to me, to be made of good, easy, gentle feelings and not rebellious, selfish, and passionate ones; ultimately to be everything that you could love even more and to be able to give it all to you as this evening I give you all my infinite tenderness.

Your little Coco

I received a very nice letter from Eric.

Is Brigitte still in Paris? I think of her often.

I hope to come back Saturday.

Dammarie (beginning April 1926)

I already want to write to you again, but tell me if my letters tire you . . . if you are weary of them—

In spite of myself, savagery pursues me: Françoise found nothing in St-Jean[7] and left Laberdon today; she's heading toward the moun-

[7]. This must be Saint-Jean-de-Luz.

tains and thinking of stopping at the first pleasant spot! Isn't there anything you could suggest to us in this area?—Bonnefont is tempting her, but she wants to be sure not to meet anyone from the group[8] . . .

I'm leaving on the 10th, but I don't know where!

Tell me what you are doing; who is at Louveciennes? You can imagine how much and how often I think of everyone; I would like to talk to you about it this evening, but I have to stop—this letter will no doubt follow you to Clairefontaine.

I love you and I kiss you dearest darling

Colette

Mama's knee is hurting her a lot right now.

Tuesday (April 1926)

I am leaving this evening—it's not Mama I'm leaving, it's *all of you*—you have to know this and understand this—I will leave from Marseilles tomorrow for Corsica.

I have absolutely no idea what my address will be, but I will send it to you soon so that I can hear from you—I spoke to Françoise about this departure today—this will calm Mama down as much as possible, show her that this is not an "impulse" and that it was certainly apart from all of you that I made my decision—

I quickly send you and Jacques and Eric a kiss with all my tenderness

Colette

I think about the two Sophies[9] all the time—send me news—I hope everything is all right with your father.

Hôtel Impérial

8. Of Abbé D.

9. Suzanne gave birth to twins: Jérôme and his sister.

Bastia, Friday (April 23, 1926)

My dear, how are you—aren't you too tired? Please tell me how you are—And your father?

You know through Françoise that my trip went very well—as soon as I was at the station in Paris the spectacle engrossed me so much I forgot to get on the train! In Marseilles I didn't know whether I was embarking for Bastia or Ajaccio, I left it up to my porter (who was very handsome) to decide. After eighteen hours at sea, I arrived here at night, my heart beating.

My room looks out over the port where there is a lot of commotion, as much as the crowdedness of the place will hold. People shout and thrash about a lot—this is the market port, the fishing port is on the other side with all the Bastian houses and people.

The bad weather would upset my plans if I had any.

Down with books: when it rains too much, I open a history book about Corsica—all of this is simple and good—I recommend a similar trip to every young girl from as good a family as mine.

I kiss you with all my very great tenderness.

Colette

When you write me tell me what is going on with Mama.

Wednesday, April 28, 1926
Hôtel des Étrangers, Ajaccio

Nothing from you, and the news I've gotten from Françoise is eight days old. HOW ARE YOU?

Give me news of yourself. Did Paquit tell you to rest, or can you go on with your normal life? And Eric? I dreamt of you and him yesterday in a long complicated dream

It seems you were "upset" by my departure—but no, dear, you must laugh at this and that's all—the weather has been splendid since yesterday afternoon—I took a walk through Ajaccio—soon I hope to take a boat ride with a fisherman and swim at a small nearby beach—

Ajaccio itself is rather unpleasant—it seems I will find no suitable lodgings further south—I'm going to try to go there anyway once I've heard from you—

I kiss you very tenderly, my dear, as well as Jacques and Eric.

Colette

Can you pass on my good news to home because I can't write them through this mail, and there will be no boats for two days. How is your poor Papa?

I kiss you again with all my tenderness.

Colette

Italy (probably 1926)

What a pleasure to see you again the other evening. Everything seems to become simple and easy again when I see you—

Listen, everyone is content with a "petty life" and abandons the ardor of living for fear of suffering. I like this, I don't know where I read it: "Everyone needs an intoxication whether it be passion, heroic action, wine or opium; a work of beauty is always an act of love for life, even if it is in the midst of despair and negation—there is never sin in love; the sinner is the one who abandons the ardor and grandeur of living"—

No, I *cannot* wait, telling myself "that I have everything in me," that everything will come to me.

No, because I am capable of more if I want . . .

You can't imagine what wild joy I feel each second, seeing my strength whole only since this summer, and I would like to exhaust my body in a thousand ways; I hate sleep, and I despair to see that by avoiding it in the morning you succumb to it earlier in the evening

. . . we can break down every barrier, we are still *limited.*

I have many other letters for you that I never sent, my dear. Never speak to me of this one. Do you see, I'm afraid that the solitude I have always lived in is still separating us, or rather, preventing us from understanding each other—I am suffocating from this vastness in me of all the forms of life that I want to possess, that change each day, and I waste my time and this ardor in false activity—

You can't imagine how a thousand things and each minute that are immaterial to you are infinitely palpable to me. Perhaps this is what separates me from everyone else, and I remain stunned and silent and I love solitude and my savage joy—and then at times this will for action no longer exists and I no longer know what to live out, my books . . . music . . . each moment—

I'm afraid to send you this letter. Perhaps it will only point out to you the often "complicated" things about me that you don't like—

Tear all this up, quick. Forget it completely and keep all your affection for me.

Colette

Italy seems awful all of a sudden.

I want to take action, do something and go far away in the meantime—

Why this P.S.? Tear all this up, quick, *please*

Sunday December 6 (probably 1926) Orléans

Suzanne my dear

I really don't know what to say! For so long I foresaw what today is happening to us—This brutal clash between us the day my life became clearer—

I told Catherine the other day: "What melodrama! With Jacques against you, with you against Jacques, while each of you or rather the shape of your lives and your respective circles have done nothing but incite my revolt against everyone."

That didn't surprise her—it is true I never hesitated to speak to her harshly—truly.

Toward you, dear, I have always thought: it would hurt her and it would be useless—but, really just when I trust you most deeply you tell me I am withdrawing my affection for you.

If you saw Françoise, she would tell you that my ferocious propriety is not only toward you—I have stayed the same you see!—my love is very far from being a liaison whose details will amuse anyone at all—but *enough* I think my explanations will only seem ridiculous to you—Nevertheless, I am attempting them to prove my goodwill to you and because I regret not having been able to see you again as I had told you I would before I left—

What is happening at Dampierre? I'm very worried—I telephoned Catherine because it seemed premature to warn Mama right now since I will probably be here alone for a month—perhaps she will only prepare her; I hope Françoise or Catherine will keep you posted so that you will know what to say if she questions you upon her return—

I am very worried about her!

I found a room by chance as soon as I arrived: 11 rue de la République and I am already here today . . .

I kiss you tenderly as well as Jacques and the children.

Colette

Amélie-les-Bains, 12-15-27

Your tender letter touched me very much, and I'm mad at myself for not having answered yet—if I'm silent, don't think I'm being distant. So often it's impossible for me to express anything at all even though my thoughts are very tenderly with my loved ones—

So as not to forget, I am answering your question about Mama: by this same mail, I am proposing a trip to her around December 25 or in the second half of January because plans to rent a place might prevent me from leaving at Christmas—

I would like to leave Régina as soon as possible and find a purer, more invigorating atmosphere than that of Amélie which does not satisfy me—

Perhaps it's very late to be writing to Mama, and I hope my indecision will not have complicated anything for all of you?

I hardly felt I would have the strength to endure this stay until now, so I put off the obligation to decide from one day to the next.

You talked about Danel, I really don't know him well enough to say that I don't like him and to judge him so quickly—it is certain that the rare times I have met him, I felt no affinity toward him whatsoever, which perhaps means nothing at all when you only know someone by sight.

You must be very interested in him right now. He must have seen so many things we can hardly imagine!

I hope my letter will find you still in Paris; do not forget to give me your address.

I kiss you with all my profound affection.

Colette

Practical questions: do you think Martel[10] will send anything to rue du Prieuré? Did he send his bill to your address? In that case, tell me and it will be easier to reimburse you for everything I owe you through the Banque Nationale de Paris into your account at the Comptoir d'Escompte as I have done for myself. I would like to settle this question (which is *very easy* for me right now—I assure you). It must be about three thousand francs.

10. The surgeon who operated on her and saved her after her suicide attempt.

(Probably 1929)

My dear. I'm answering your little note— through Mama I found out more about how you are, which you aren't telling me—she told me about your concert which made me very happy—

I don't know why, when I think of you I see you leaning over me again the day you were called so suddenly, and I feel very moved, and I feel our mutual affection which is indeed unalterable—

Kiss the three little ones I barely know anymore—

Colette

Moscow 2/7/1930

How impatiently I have waited for an answer to my telegram! Finally, nothing serious. Congratulations!

It seems you are still making light of the most dramatic damned ailments. I like the valiance with which you recover from "grave illnesses," pregnancies, accidents, etc.

You won't believe me, but I was all the more worried because I had sinister premonitions about you during my stay in Leningrad, and after a night of bad dreams, I felt I had to send you my address as quickly as possible. Also the fact: no I won't tell you—it would take too long. I am attaching too much importance to these things and then, in general, it's crazy that being far away, never writing, I can find myself close to the people I care about—I don't understand any of this, but that's the way it is: in the streets of Moscow . . . in Red Square, walking quickly, gripped with cold, talking . . . talking and then all of a sudden total absence, you appear, I see you living, I think of you close by—I would like to write, but it's useless after all—In any case it would be very "useful," very nice to receive some news from you—what is happening? Tell me about yourself, about Jacques, and Agneta? Perhaps I'll come back at the end of January,

I'm not sure (haven't decided, would like to stay—but I'm so tired!)

Work on the Review has dragged on longer than it should have—everything will speed up in the next few days—Tell me what Jacques thinks.

I would like to talk to you this evening very, very much—I beg you, write me about yourself. Kiss the kids. Mama tells me the little things I want to know about them but tell me what's "becoming" of them—

I kiss you—Good-bye—Excuse this terrible draft.

Colette

Moscow, end of December 1930

I can no longer remain in this state of uncertainty over you.

What's the matter? Why *nothing* from you, for months. I know: I have hardly written, and also, there are so many misunderstandings between us—but why hold it against me when I can't clear *anything* up from so far away—

Perhaps you're well, there's nothing wrong, and the only thing missing is the desire and time to write. But perhaps also everything is going very badly for you!

I think of you constantly, tenderly, more worried each day. The "news" of you that Mama gives me is old.

Yes, I am coming back soon. It's impossible to fix a date. From now until then *write* or wire me if you don't want to write, but explain yourself—I kiss you with a tenderness that you will never know.

Colette

Postcard to J . . . B . . . 1926[11]

I will come to see you before I leave.

Will be at the little red café at Palais Royal tomorrow, Tuesday at 5 o'clock—I will have a few minutes—I'm sending you the "enclosed" letter because I don't want to keep letters anymore and live in a void, but this has nothing to do with my current state of mind nor does it predict tomorrow's.

Whatever you do *don't answer*—If you're not coming—I'll see that well enough

11. Trans. This was a postcard to Jean Bernier (referred to as Paul Rendier throughout), the writer over whom Laure tried to commit suicide. For more on this relationship, see Bernier's *L'Amour de Laure,* Paris: Flammarion, 1978.

Letters to Madam Adam, B and Other Letters

Draft without a date

Dear Madam Adam,

How have you been since we wandered along the "docks" of Combleux together, you proud and courageous, me in the car?

Since the other Sunday a lot of water has flowed under the bridge, but the Loire with its great majestic airs is no doubt no less swift because of it. It really has a strange way about it, much less determined than other rivers. It doesn't quite know where it's going despite its seeming anxiousness to get there. Its whims of stretching out over the banks or swirling around over itself prove well enough that if it weren't held back by the captivating lines of so purely linear a countryside it would just as well go off in all directions.

But since everything is upside down, since the communists are worse than the fascists, since *L'Humanité* sounds like *L'Écho de Paris*, since Doriot is a new messiah, since the Places where we safeguard Peace are, in fact, deadly insane asylums, since the anarchists (not all of them, fortunately) are more bourgeois than the bourgeois and since the bourgeois (not all of them, unfortunately) are anarchists, I really do not see why the rivers follow their course. This seems a catastrophe to me, it's too natural.

Would you be surprised to read in your newspaper tomorrow: "The Loire veered off its usual course; from now on it will flow into La Gueule du Lion, while the Seine, flowing back toward its source, is flooding central France. The following regions and roads are submerged. In due time, the Popular Front government will take all necessary steps." But the rivers and seas would contribute so much, so well, to the universal absurdity that we would see the earth engulfed by waters again, as it was in the beginning.

Only a few islands of people would float on the surface, islands of childhood and friendship. You could live there on air or else on "clear water and love": truth would always be implausible. The economists would lose their minds over it (they would become reasonable) and soon we would see them, along with the philosophers and mathematicians, sociologists and psychologists, pedagogues and phrenologists, melt like snow in the sun. Then the simple man would be there on his island, between sky and water, traveling along, his two hands in his pockets, relieved of being an enigma and solving problems. Maybe he would go on his way like Charlie Chaplin . . .

I am telling you a lot of nonsense, but this is what is going through my head recalling Combleux and, on these famous islands of my dreams (dreams of childhood and friendship) you never have to turn your tongue around in your mouth seven times *before* speaking but *after*, because the Bible is forgotten.

Dear Madam Adam, if I resort to the typewriter to replace my illegible handwriting it is not at all through offhandedness, as this anecdote will prove to you: As a Russian was congratulating Gorky on his wonderfully clear and precise handwriting, the latter responded: "it is out of respect for man."

I hope the stormy weather down there is not wearing you out too much; here it gets dark at noon, and it makes one think of the end of the world, of some apocalyptic twilight. I kiss you with all my heart.

S., touched by your kind regards, sends you his best wishes.

Colette

Letter to B.

Everything has been said and resaid on the subject of this inevitable and beneficial separation . . . so why not take things *proudly* and never be embarassed in front of "other people."

Shouldn't it be *this way* when two free people make a decision?

There are no culprits, there is no one to blame; we are just taking back our freedom, our total independence.

We could do it with mutual respect and trust, just as we could do it with hatred and wrenching heartbreak.

Trust that each follows his path freely, a path that is his own and not that of others, which you follow while remaining a traitor to yourself. Consciousness of this betrayal poisons existence, makes it useless, unworthy. You can no longer look at what is great; you are out of harmony with the world and life. You grimace, you put on an act.

And above all: refuse to accept *self-doubt,* which will go from "self" to others and give the impression of losing one's footing. Then: you go back into your shell.

A human being cannot doubt himself when he is following his own path. If he doubts, if he lowers his head, it's because an element foreign to strength, to *his* strength *to be spontaneously* is pulling him backward.

Life is only beautiful if, beyond all "tests of fate" and everything you carry within yourself, you can look the entire world in the face. With neither useless, stupid arrogance nor with humility, just like that: simply, gently, proudly. With a calm, clear awareness of being where you have to be: a plant seeks sun and water to grow to maturity and to give all that life expects from it.

You look at other human beings with the calm conviction that if they are neither "brutes" nor "vulgar," their lives, too, are full of heartbreak, of difficulties overcome, and tragedies unconfessed. You look at them, and you like them because, resembling them, you would like to help them and tell them: "Nothing is that bad. Everything happening to you is simply human . . . human with all the beauty and horror that that entails."

Why do human beings refuse to be like plants—they want to be less, much less. They become rust.

I need a white, empty room in a street-level house that would look out over solid ground.

I need to act on my words. For example: what Spain means (to me) right now (?)

I need to travel the road by myself without looking back.

When I get weary, I will lie down on the ground, I will press my ear to the ground, and I will hear the footstep of the man I love.

Draft of a letter to B. 1934

B.

There is nothing to reply to everything you write since you've already *made up your mind.*

If you really think what you say, I do not even see how you can wish for a reply.

I've put an end to a situation that *both of us* deemed intolerable and if *subsequently*—being freed from all ties—I have acted like a free person, no one, not even you, can interfere.

For I still suppose you value as much as I do a certain notion of individual freedom. If two years ago I lost the ability to live, I've found it again today—

What I want, where I am going, is my business alone and I do not see how I can "explain" anything to someone who judges me as you do.

—It is not true that I "talked about you" as you say: I say nothing to anyone who might understand.

You know, and I've told you, that I've never forgotten all that was beautiful and good between us. Let's at least remember that.

Nothing can prevent me any longer from looking the entire world in the face.

The book you speak of (and in which you are *not at all* mentioned) is not being published and will not be published.

Draft of a Letter[12]

For several months your name and your being have imposed themselves on me; I felt as though I absolutely had to get in touch with you. Sometimes I wanted to meet you and speak to you but it was impossible. Too many hesitations came between me and my decision, which then seemed extremely audacious to me, and so I remained totally passive. And then other suspicions interfered, which stopped me from making any move, suspicions that you, I'm afraid, would have been the first to understand and even to share. I know that we can always speak. But to speak the truth, the way people speak German or English, is difficult because of conventions, habits, easy solutions. So I flee into total solitude.

Now I know that I am going to meet you, that I *can* meet you. I also know that these suspicions will fall away by themselves. Perhaps because I will be before you like the fifteen-year-old child who used to read surrealist publications secretly and feverishly, like a starving woman eating a piece of stolen bread. I know that all the decisions in my life have come from this early *complicity* with a few people I didn't know and who didn't know me, a *complicity* that you brought up yesterday in a deeply moving way for me, in a tone of total genuineness and naked sincerity.[13]

12. Paul Éluard's name was written at the top of the page, and scratched out.

13. On the back of this draft Colette added in pencil: "the need to verify through exchange with people who *contradict* me, but only if profoundly and sincerely."

Draft of a Letter to an Unknown Recipient

Just as you understood about Bourénine,[14] you will understand about Georges. I'm trying to find someone to talk to and can't. Imagine the oxygen in the room you live in becoming separate from the nitrogen and creating two rooms, one entirely of oxygen, the other entirely of nitrogen . . . You have to get out, don't you? It's up to me to control things and to lead my life. But nothing. I feel shattered after a week of living together constantly. On top of it, I can't control anything because it's incredibly good and because I turn into something I can't say. I should have been born a praying mantis.

I'm likely to spoil everything. I am writing to you because the other day you said to me "with you hate is so close to love." This is so true I was stunned by it and now I see that you could perhaps become a friend, a true brother, and I'm glad that someone understands. He too understands, he who is my truth and my life, but we are caught in the mesh of the same net.

Circumstances require that this letter be sent off, read, and answered by a living person without my pride suffering. This hate is capable of taking tragic, or vulgar, or such subtle forms that it seeps into him like a depressing uncertainty with which I've infected him.

It reveals itself in order to destroy me and to destroy my happiness. Such happiness that makes me resemble young neighing foals, plants seeking the sun, such happiness that leaves me overcome with gratitude, glorifying to the highest Heavens of my life the person in and through whom I assert myself and take root in the earth. And that is the terrible danger.

14. Trans. Boris Souvarine

Letters to Georges Bataille
1934–1938

Wednesday July 4, 1934

It seems, Georges Bataille, we are going from "coincidence" to "coincidence"—

I have absolutely no desire to talk about the essential

I only want to tell you that as long as I *hope*, my phantoms will vanish.

It is also perfectly superfluous to *say this* to you—I have a feeling you can guess this—

In any case, I would rather not retain this impression of running away—

Besides that's not what it was

since I saw you again at 7:27 and the friend who was with you stared at me without seeing me—(as though I were wearing a "ring that makes you invisible" as when you are a child)

Then you got up, you passed within five feet of me—

None of this is of great importance. I was only painfully surprised that something of this sort could happen to us. So much the better for you—Only it's rather obnoxious, you see. I will not waste my time explaining why, because I think all the things you do in that "little circle of friends" will never amount to more than topics of conversation—Take that as "pretention" if you want! But I want and *I need* to remain silent and unnoticed.

Colette

[July] 1934

If you want to write me—you can do so at Nimley. It will be forwarded—

In my desire to sound simple and calm, I realize I would do better to write you a long letter—

Have a good vacation and I will too—

There is no innuendo in that.

Don't think I am permanently contemptuous of the "little circle"—

I have some very sincere friendships there and a true solidarity—

Colette

Thursday [July] 5, 1934

I will try to explain, but I ought to start with Tuesday evening (when I left you), and that I cannot do—I saw you again, unable to call out to you, I picked up the telephone unable to speak—The thought of you did not leave me. Only the idea that a road accident was possible and even probable freed me from the insurmountable anguish that was you. The idea of death when one follows it to the end, to the point of putrefaction, has always relieved me, and that day more than ever—I thought about various forms of "accidental death" in detail and all of them seemed enviable and delicious to me. I became calm again and even cheerful, but a sort of malicious joy rose up in me against you—I no longer understand why now—

Until now, it was in my power to break all past ties, so that no human being who had known me would be able to recognize me—

and then I understood that whatever I did you would always be there—you would always be able to track me down—you were like the eye that followed I don't know who anymore in a "poem" (!)

So I thought that by drowning myself I had called for help not only from a paralytic but someone who would hit me on the head as needed so that I would sink straight to the bottom—I thought all this and then I felt the need to write you that sentence about "topics of conversation," which, to my mind, was the worst "insult" to level at you—I needed to invent reasons to be wary of you, not believe you—to doubt your love—perhaps even to "make fun" (it's as stupid as that). In this state of mind I sent the letter from Lure, and then once again I was seized by terrible anxiety . . . just like that: seized by the throat by the need for your existence—The feeling that without you I was lost, or rather, that I preferred anything at all to the idea of losing you . . . and maybe even distancing myself from you. You had to know right away, I wanted to telegraph you—but what to say!—The "border" was unbearable to me so I telephoned, and afterwards I was very calm because I was going to get your letter—That's all I can say—

The picturesque and even simple Nature exasperated me. I dreamt of landscapes of cinder and then your note reconciled me with what was beautiful and good in life.

I will end this having told you nothing.

but that doesn't matter.

Above all don't imagine anything about me—I am pathetic and defenseless—and above all don't suffer—I wish these extreme fluctuations (I hate this word, I can't find another) did not exist, either in you or in me—we know what they amount to and what is going on—

I wish only for this absolute faith in one another to remain.

Colette

It doesn't matter that you are leaving for Spain and that I am in Austria

What I feel toward you could never take any recognizable form, or be named, or be something ordinary—

Only signs of life are necessary.

My address remains the same: Poste Restante at Œtz—Austria

I am ashamed of how my letters look, but the difficulties I confront in finding tranquillity, paper, a pen, a pencil are literally *diabolical*—To amuse you: a dream. I was with three blonde girls, one of whom was especially beautiful—they were helping me "escape" (?) we were plotting I don't know what but they disappeared and I found myself sitting next to a Negro—but not the kind that makes you think of noble savages and evil civilized people, a Negro in a red jacket, messed-up like a porter in Montmartre—I was mad at myself for letting the curly-haired, "haughty" blonde woman escape—my fear of conquering the absurd—and I didn't understand anything about the Negro—and then soon, I was very comfortable with him—

I don't know why I told you this was "amusing," this dream was very painful—

Good-bye

Colette

You asked me if doubt pushed me to the other side. No—I notice that when I *doubt,* I exist again—but when I despair, everything that was hateful to me becomes desirable, tempting . . . I might even take great pains to reconstruct something I destroyed furiously the night before and vice versa—and I think this is valid for any *achievement* and along any lines. This is indeed what terrifies me—I can say this only to you—perhaps later you will be able to make me feel at peace with myself without having to sever me—(I wanted to say: without castrating me and then I was ashamed—and I don't want to be ashamed in front of you!)

I have no idea where I am going or where all of this will lead me. I live here in a sort of truce. I hope to hear from you soon, in the meantime your note is precious to me.

Œtz, Austria, Tuesday, July 10, 1934

It makes me very anxious to think my long letter will only reach you tomorrow, maybe after tomorrow. I received your two letters at the same time only last night because I am now in a village high in the mountains where the mail only comes every two days—Georges do not torture yourself—The only coincidence that can happen between us from now on is an exchange of strength . . . or even simple joy, I assure you. Why not think I alone was *guilty* of the most vulgar interpretation possible—and then even about "literature" I, too, could be caught "red-handed" by you. I am no better than the others, I'm not just saying this. Never say you're not worthy of my trust again, and above all don't think it, for then I am seized by shame because I am bitterly aware of my dirty little cowardly acts and weaknesses and that we all have them. We mustn't search so much, or suspect either ourselves or others. By wanting to be honest (you understand what I mean) and avoiding all that seems suspect in ourselves and strangling ourselves, we do ourselves irreparable harm. And I absolutely need your strength, your calmness.

It is a shame (after what has happened between us) that we have not had the time to explain ourselves at greater length. For example: I should know about your book and you about "certain facts" and "my notebook." You can't imagine all the "surrealistic" things that have happened to me daily, completely at random, for the last month or so—but I won't dwell on this—I didn't *want* to admit to myself that you are infinitely dear to me, nor above all admit it to you—stupidly I seized upon anything that might hurt you. I could very well have been in a café, too, drowning myself in noise and insipid conversation—I don't see any mortal sin in that—you must always be calm in front of me, never lose the ability to doubt me and check what I say from the point of view of sound reason, that is, this absolute faith between us of which I spoke to you.

I have not resisted the desire to send you a postcard from where I am. I live a little higher on the mountain, and I come down each day to this marvelous lake where you can swim and row. Also, the house is built entirely of fir which smells very good—it's dazzling with freshness and order. I wonder why on the partition wall (a partition of fir in which you can distinctly see the shape of the trees) there is a large, ornate inscription:

"Streut blumet der Liebe zur Lebenzeit und Bewahret einander vor Herzeleid"[15]

I hope you will not make too much fun of me—I say this laughing *good* naturedly. Perhaps this is even more stupid and "naïvely sentimental" than I think it is. Perhaps it was not translated properly for me.

I would like to laugh like this by your side, and we would be very natural and feel good, and I assure you this is possible without "trying."

Also I want to say this: sometimes it's a great relief to talk. If you are tempted to do this, I would approve of it and not at all resent it. I know that you will, as you get to know the people you see, and Janine and Raymond for example are not really such strangers to me.

If there is important political news tell me about it (no newspapers here) I wonder what meetings you've been to.

I would like to talk to you at length.

Pension Piburgersee—bei Œtz—Austria

Tell me where you are going—

Colette

15. Scattered love blooms over lifetime and preserves one another from heartache.

Œtz—(Austria)—July 10, 1934

I have so much to tell you—I'll never get it all in. Each time I write you I feel I leave out the most essential things. So I feel I never *reply*. At times I would like to take your letters again and strictly answer point by point. Lately I've felt so powerless it seemed to me our correspondence could not continue. Maybe my last letter irritated you and came at a very bad time (I remember it vaguely, for I've spoken to you so often since, I no longer know what is written or not). This is of no importance, that is, even if I were to say or write something that would ruin me in your eyes forever, it would have to be. Everything *true* has to be, and take shape. Why even say it? It's so obvious that, for you, too, life cannot be lived any other way. But above all, you have to know that these contretemps mean nothing because everything in each of us is in flux and we are well aware of it.

This, I think, is what I would have written yesterday before receiving your letter, the one where you talk about mountain springs. Maybe it was because I was waiting for this letter, and I received it, but it gave me a feeling of joy, of deliverance. You seemed less tense and, in fact, closer to me. Yet I am terribly wary of "as though there were no longer two but one," but you understand in what sense I am wary. The best thing would be exchange, not identification, but I'm afraid I may have misunderstood, and I already want to tear up this letter. Also I think each human being has something in him that, in my eyes, *allows* him to pick the most beautiful flowers—

Tuesday I just read the long letter you finished and mailed at the train station on Sunday. Everything is happening at once. I can speak only of the immediate = The day before yesterday, Sunday, I'd fallen asleep on the balcony in the daytime, and I woke up, convinced I was hearing your voice below, and I asked if any French people had arrived. Eight days ago I almost told you I was sorry that "something had happened" because otherwise—I say this because it's true, but it's *absurd* to say it. The reality of my current life (which I do not *want* to talk about) is.[16] Besides I am leaving Austria for Italy (the truth is "we are leaving"). All of this seems totally absurd to me. I will not answer you because I cannot—

When I was waiting for you at the Nationale the other day, I was leaning against the panes, I saw the room through three thicknesses of glass . . . and I thought I saw you coming and that really there was nothing but the walls of glass between you and me. What you say is true for me as well: I hoped I would run into you, and when I did, by chance, I was very happy about it. I have always hated what others say about you; it seemed to me I saw into you through your behavior alone, the slightest nuances of which I caught.

When I do not let myself be taken in by pleasant appearances, when I slip to the very depths of myself with my thoughts, my doubts and the need to throw everything into question, to start everything over, when I am at the very depths of myself, at this moment I find you at my side.

You know one thing: on first reading your letter, I didn't understand what was essential about it. How is it that you know me so well you can point out precisely what, at first, will make me furrow my brows, or make me anxious (but I use this word without gravity)[17] the *religious* for example. You come to me in two ways: on first reading your letter, I doubt my objections, or rather, ideas that cross my mind (generally pure intuitions, I think, but that come to me violently and emphatically) and at the same time I doubt being able to understand and assimilate your thoughts in all their integrity, and already I suffer over it—If at this moment I find beneath your pen that which I did not dare think, that alone shows me at once that I am on the way to

16. You can't understand, I ask you not to imagine anything—I don't know myself where I stand.

17. Added in the margin: "Yes, sometimes this anxiousness is grave."

understanding, truly understanding, and this dissipates what you call "anxieties" (moreover the word is *accurate*). I reread your letter, and this will become absolutely clear I think with you in the fall—

I am tempted to see as tragic the fact that just when we needed so much to see each other—not only did I leave, but now you are far away, and I've started a trip, whose stages I am barely aware of, and during which it would be better to give up trying to write you and receive letters. I will write to you poste restante at Font Romeu. A month goes by very fast; starting August 15th, I will probably be in France in the Aube, but this is not certain—then at the end of August, I will come through Paris—It is sweet to know that you will be with Laurence. If it doesn't bother you, I would like very much for you to tell me how she is. Make sure she doesn't get sunstroke at Font Romeu. I had a bad experience of that sort there. The mountains there are very harsh and very wild—if you can find a place to stay outside of Font Romeu itself, I think you will be fine. I hope so and wish it so much.

July 21, 1934
Postcard from Steinach am Brenner

Tomorrow night I'll be in Botzen, the day after that in Riva—That's where you could write—Only after tomorrow will I know about the plans (Venice, etc.). Very bad health beside me.—I'm writing this card to be sure to write something that will be mailed immediately. Above all go to Iggls and climb to the Top to spend the day in the mountains. Will write tomorrow.

Colette

Botzen Bolzano (?)
Saturday 5:00 (7-21-34)

Perhaps I would have done better not to call—

You probably imagined the best or the worst when it was just simple life—I wanted to ask you if you had slept well. Also I was afraid, rightly, of not being able to write you—

There is a good chance I might see you very soon—I ask you to remain calm and strong until then—You and I have to be stronger in all of this—

This is not the contorted and half-mad person talking, but me as you know me—

Despite my handwriting due to poor materials, it's been a long time since I've been so certain—so assured.

But I beg you here again, do not imagine the best—or the worst—

I will spend some time absolutely *alone*. It is during this time that I will see you. I will write you again tomorrow, and probably call you, because I cannot give you an address, and I don't want you to feel "distraught" because of this.

Be stronger Georges I beg you

C.

I'm not giving you an address because I don't know anything—and I don't know anything because everything depends on something that is in the midst of happening. Something serious.

But nothing tragic. I truly feel that nothing can ever be "tragic" again—

This has nothing to do with you—only with me and B.

I wanted to calm your possible anxiety over this.

Thursday evening (Innsbrück, probably August) 1934

Georges—If I haven't written earlier it's because there were more diabolical little problems = it was impossible to write, then to take the mail but why say this—I sent you a telegram and I felt terrible for making you wait until the last moment before your departure for this reply. All day long I thought of your departure and me leaving into the unknown, when in fact I would have "wanted" and even *desired* to see you. But this is still not what I want to say. Your love enters my life, does not leave me. I would almost like to say: envelopes me—I'm afraid—yes terribly afraid of saying anything at all, of uttering any word. There are so many reasons for this *fear.* I am no doubt beneath you. Otherwise we would have already been on another path.

How can I say this to you and still believe in another absolutely valid, even heartbreaking reality in my life? How is this possible? At times it seems to me that I *have* to do something that will debase me in your eyes. To be more hateful, to make myself more hateful than what you detest most in the world. So today—I won't try to explain.

No, your long letter did not disconcert me. I even think that this is what is most important between us. I feel that this is what prevails over everything. I'm all the more eager to see you so that we can speak freely, so that you can help me understand you absolutely, completely. Until then I don't dare say anything, write anything, I will content myself with rereading you. If I did not put a long letter in the mail this morning it's because I felt it to be so insufficient, full of superfluous things that surprised even me—You see I'm already catching myself in flagrante delicto of being artificial.

Since I've written this letter I'll send it to you. Even this scares me a little—but too bad—

—Above all I would like to tell you that it is not happiness I seek, but a latent, effective, and positive strength—I know I fool people—some think I am already very strong, assured and confident . . . it is not what impresses others that will ever satisfy me—it is what I demand of myself, and I have never attained it. I do not hate happiness, because a certain joy in life makes one stronger, but this joy is made of the very contempt for what others call happiness. I am ashamed to be expressing myself so poorly, but what is important to me is knowing, being sure, that you think this way—in fact, your last letter clarifies this as well—Your last letter clarifies everything, I think. Now let me say something—promise me to forget it later: I don't have the *right* to say it but

I will send you this tomorrow morning first thing—then later in the day a note telling you my address, which I have absolutely no idea of yet—and probably the other letter

—I would like to clarify something. You understand: I know that I will never achieve any "goal" because even if this were to happen, at that moment only one thing would matter to me—to go beyond what would already no longer be a goal but a stage. That's very beautiful, but in life even this cannot yield anything if one has not attained a sort of complete self-possession. I'm certainly far from this. I feel like I've fallen to pieces. I thought it was good to realize *everything* inside oneself . . . and I've arrived at a monstrous cacophony, and if something (your love for example) reminds me of my initial pride, I especially feel my present wretchedness.

None of this interests me as abstract idealism, it's simply that my life can only start here and then go on to the rest (saying this I think of all that is clearly delimited, like work, struggle, and even all that you can knead with your hands, and also human relations and exchanges, that is, what you can feel with your heart)—and

I no longer understand at all why I'm saying all this to you as if it was absolutely essential to say it.

If I often talk about Nature it's because it's a refuge for me from myself, from everything that is excessive, inhuman, "superhuman"—

It's more than a refuge—I can't explain it to you—there are times when I firmly believe I will somehow manage, I don't know how, to live in the country near a forest and a stream. I have looked at mountains and the sky so often, if one day, as you raise your head, you see a little cloud all alone, you can think it's me coming to see you at Font Romeu—

I am terribly annoyed with myself for writing you and not *replying* but this will come later—

Be well—

Colette

About help, I have to admit I felt very ashamed for having spoken to you about this, because I think one really only acquires that which one has conquered by oneself. To "call for help" shows serious weakness, because it creates I don't know what phenomenon of mutual suggestion but nothing valid. I have to manage *alone.* I'm talking in the abstract, but this would be easy to concretize and prove.

probably 1934

You are a person I need to look in the face—

That's all.

I can no longer "explain myself" and if you laugh at me, it won't matter

It's as inevitable as the mysterious ciphers that pursue me

and everything that pushed me,

and everything that happens to me

I will go to Poste Restante office no. 28 and there, whatever happens, I will be silent and Alone

Do you understand that this has nothing to do with what the others . . . with the words and things the others say and see?

No one can understand it's this way: under the mysterious sign where there is only me in front of you, one you . . . even ironic and cruel and distant. But for once I will really look you in the face

I also wanted to turn away from, hide from, renounce the idea of you—I no longer can, I no longer want to—I've understood it this way: by so often thinking "finally when I die—just before—I will be able to say this name"—cry out speak your name—well, it's all the same.

probably 1934

Why am I not facing you right now when I know that at the thought of you only death can overtake me. Your voice delivered me from it, delivered me from death, which takes me by the throat and I remain strangled, in total silence, delivered me from it while it takes me by the head, but my head may well explode: I will no longer grovel in front of the others. Why say this to you, who would like to do I don't know what with your suffering, to you who sees this as ridiculous compared to . . .

Perhaps I'm saying it the way one leans on an arm and then I'm saying it because I am so sure of overcoming all that seems irreconcilable to you with the idea of a *possible* "happiness" between us.

I am sure of it when I think of you *with joy* for then I become strong like a tree, a tree that cannot be uprooted. To write you, to hear you this morning, do you understand it seemed to me that I took root in the earth and that my forehead touched the clouds—I need to say this to you because *I do not want to see you again under the sign of misfortune.*

It seems hard to imagine this piece of paper in your hands and I feel it won't reach you. I live a life that is not here but always elsewhere, as in the foreign city that I mistook for another, always following paths that go in the opposite direction of where I would like to go—so the day has passed this way.

Could you call me this evening or tonight until [ ] or tomorrow morning before 10 o'clock at Odéon 51-40 where I am at 14 rue Cassini: Private Hôtel, and I could see you tomorrow, couldn't I? I am so happy that you are the only one in the world who knows where I actually am. If this letter does not get to you I could still call you tomorrow morning.

Probably 1934

Why did I tell you "I ate" I could just as well have told you "I shat" it would probably have interested you just as much—
Why didn't you say that you didn't "have any money on you"—it was vile all around—I was mad at him—and you, you quietly———— ———— sixty francs—You came at 3 o'clock and he at 6 o'clock—I thought I'd forgotten him————that I'd be wooden—that it was all over—broken on all sides and that it was just as well—
But this man's desire takes my breath away—When desire twists his mouth—in front of other people like that and his eyes turn wild—seeing him—seeing his face would almost be enough for me—But it's impossible, so I arrange a meeting and when the time comes for the meeting———it's over, I'm calm and cerebral—I would have liked to have been very straightforward with you—I couldn't be—because of this mark on your cheek—everything risked turning upside down once again—I wanted, I allowed myself to play with this fire

If only I could scream, roll around at his feet—so that everyone would know, would see me—

Have you seen how I enter the ignoble, vulgar role of a woman who *lies*—never in my life has this happened to me. I've always thought, and I still think, that if I lied *in that way,* exactly *like that,* my life would lose all meaning—I cannot stand lies—

That, no doubt, is what is making me lose sleep and my appetite—It's fine this way—I should even die of it, knowing that *I, too,* can lie ignobly, superbly, triumphantly—

You think "this is not important" but for me everything "is important."

you also said

"You *were* the woman I respect*ed* most and you are the most vile."
a thousand regrets dear friend

I hate you for that sentence

I don't know if you don't understand *anything* or if you understand—*too much*—

For example: I who so like people to help each other and to help them see things more clearly, be better, more efficient, less petty—well, the days

when everything is *turned upside down* and when this upheaval itself burns my stomach

I like to flatter that which displeases me in a man—his vile and petty sides (we all have them don't we).
It's like with children—there is nothing clearer than the look, the voice of a child———and yet you know what I would willingly make of it . . . what I have made of it——like a coward . . . in my head . . . wantonly——I would like to tell you everything—*in detail*——

I am being a bitch again today—
Driver—Take me anywhere: "to the furnace, to the garbage dump, to the whorehouse, to the slaughterhouse." I must be burnt, torn apart, covered in filth, smell like all the fucks, and repel you—and then afterwards————fall asleep on your shoulder—

my life will never be where you think you can find it—too bad for me

D . . . is a very rich country with herds of horses and foals that neigh and come to drink in the river. It is all fields of flowers. There is a bar at the hotel that you would like very much.

I have so much to say to you that I am not writing—everything that is tormenting both of us: I am not surprised it's this way. If it were otherwise we would be okapis with wings. Now the okapi does not have wings and despite its apocalyptic tongue it has strange and tender hooves which stumble in the shadows.

My dear I do not know what color you are in, but I think that we will meet again . . . in the rainbow.

Colette

Fatigue was crushing me. I got over it, grimacing—things are a little better after a bizarre attack of fever.

There are also silvery beech trees.

There are lots of children—Laurence would be happy here too.

"Pontem indignatus Araxes"

Georges, something from me has to reach you immediately and yet perhaps I have nothing to "write you . . ."

In the train I did not really understand why I was leaving you, but we will see each other Sunday won't we? And then you are here near me so gently that I am already completely . . . altered by it.

Also all that you are seems to have the same effect on me as the sound of the drum on Kate. I like this book very much (Plumed Serpent[18]). It goes much farther than I thought. I've finished it. Where are you? Are you happy? We could be so "happy."

Dammarie is very pretty, not at all like last year. There is some very good brandy that I would like to give you. There is a little house with a separate entrance that my mother wants to give me. It's right near

18. Trans. D.H. Lawrence.

the Seine, in the trees. If you liked it, I would come there. Never mind. It is so good to know that the key is under the door. If the weather were nice, I could wait for you in Bois-le-Roi on Saturday or Sunday morning, but it rains all the time, very heavily, so perhaps it would be better for me to go to Paris.

I could also take you to Marlotte on Sunday. You could see Laurence if she is there, and I could wait somewhere else. I will write you again to decide *where* we will see each other Sunday. Perhaps you could write and tell me what you would prefer.

I would like to tell you something in a whisper: I understand that I need you terribly in order to live and this does not make my unbearable pride suffer, you know.

One day someone told me I would never be cured because of this pride. I think that because of it I am recovering , you must understand that better than I.

Am I not better in your arms than "all alone atop a high mountain?"

I would like to know that you are well right now.

Colette

I am counting the hours until Sunday without knowing where such anxiousness regarding you comes from.

Georges,[19] it is so clear now. You think you have enslaved *my existence* forever—you think it's locked away, finite, limited—the limits that you envision, that are known to you, and then you leave . . . to live your true and secret life—or at least you believe that.

As though the true in you could be foreign to me . . . as though your absent presence could give me illusions. Or your drunken return the other day and the atrocious memory that stayed with me afterward.

[19] These fragments of letters addressed to Georges Bataille are preceded neither by a date nor an indication of place. I have placed them here in an order that corresponds approximately to the chronology.

You can believe that this current existence is a reflection of a living reality in me. You can, and I cannot, so that if I feel the need to express myself, it is to other people, in front of other people, that it is *possible* to do so, so that each day life empties itself a little bit more, disintegrates, like a body decomposing before my eyes.

—The most *Christian* time of my life was spent with you.
—the cult of the false victim with no *pride*
—the offhanded way you talked about your vacation as though the six weeks had flown by. The way you changed place, voice, tone—
—WRITE your books, fabricate yourself a novel, this pathetic being that only existed thanks to my JEALOUSY

Georges

You only have one chance left to help me.

It is not sweetness, it is not your desire to "care" for me and that I call you at night: it is your truth and my own.

Georges, do you understand: my life and my death belong to me. Right now I am as close to one as to the other. No person in the world can do anything any longer since I no longer find you *deep down*—where I used to be able to find you. Georges, maybe I "don't love you."

Georges, I know what happened yesterday. I *know*. I hated our life, I often wanted to run away, to go off alone into the mountains (it was to save my life I understand that now). As soon as I had money in my pocket, I thought about it. I was horrified by this crazy pace, by my work, by our nights. You *dared* to insult me by talking about "weakness," you dare it still, you who do not have the strength to spend two hours alone, you who need another person at your side to inspire all your actions, you who cannot *want* what you *want*. I know: she will lead you where she likes, that's been proved.

I believe in our life together the way you still believed in it the first day when you talked about the house. I believe in it the way I believe in everything that brought us together: in the most profound depths of your darkness and of mine. I revealed everything about myself to you. Now that it gives you pleasure to laugh at it, to soil it—this leaves me as far away from anger as it is possible to be.

Scatter, spoil, destroy, throw to the dogs all that you want: you will never affect me again. I will never be where you think you find me, where you think you've finally caught me in a chokehold that makes you come.

Now that, thanks to me, the most banal image has taken the form of dream, desire, drama, passion, now that only the sweetest hilarity will relieve you from all that is burdensome, all in the form and appearance of the *clearest,* most *scheming,* most *selfish,* most pathetic "adultery."

As for me I am beyond words, I have seen too much, known too much, experienced too much for appearance to take on form. You can do anything you want, I will not be hurt.

The tragic ones are such hypocrites: you know this well. This tragedy was so staged—day by day—before my disdainful eyes—or *thanks* to my horrible outbursts which were only a matter of neurosis.

Everything you have been doing, I've known about—*everything*—for more than a year, before and after Sicily, everything that crystallized around a person who took the form of your dream, a shattering dream that knows how to shatter, a dream that is leaving behind the most banal of daily realities that any human being is capable of living: adultery, well-organized, planned out, clever, cunning, burning because secret. Understand me, nothing of this being can affect me. I know—rue de Rennes, the mirror she made you get and in front of which I saw her loll as much as possible, from the first day (the days of "Colette I adore you"), without you even noticing, to her great vexation.

She can do anything she wants except affect me.

Let her feel herself pissing as much as she wants. I would really like you to know what liberation this is: everything has turned to dust.

You can turn my things into playthings, put them at her feet, adore her, never will anything that comes from her affect me. Never, do you understand, will she touch what is between *us*.

I know: she is the one that pleases you "to death" now, to death from pleasure. I know because I know all you have lived. *All* that you *live*.

Down there, you will arrange to meet her when you go for a walk, while I sit here nailed to the spot. If you knew: I would come and help you organize these trysts. I will be perfectly calm and happy, I will show you.

How I managed to adorn this miserable girl with the halo of crime that *excites* you, this girl who was only capable of "laughing" at everything. She studied all my gestures in order to copy them, listened to my words in order to repeat them, she tries to read my books, she tries her best, she exhausts herself to be what I am—it's so *comical* I pity her *with all my heart*.

I have no desire to punish myself—to attach myself just when I *need* to disengage myself.

To be there at the rendezvous in the forest, or in a rented room in Saint-Germain, or at the Saint-Lazare station.

It is with the curiosity of an octopus sticking to everything that she wants to know about all you do and say, all your plans, in order to mix herself up in them, to carry weight. You no longer dare make a decision without her getting *mixed up* in your plans.

Is it even possible to go on this way? *Surely not*.

There can be no compromise in integrity, plenitude . . . life. There can be no compromise in me. It's clear—isn't this how I can live again, by escaping the mediocre, all that is

shameful airs
pretense
language
Good—evil—always these words on one's lips.

To Michel Leiris

I can't cry any more: I vomit. I can't laugh any more: I grind my teeth. How I hated that dry and evil laugh, —that laugh that lived to hear itself when we crossed paths. I saw myself in all senses, in all sentences slipping out, in all the contorted gestures that others think only they understand. But I understand better than you and with a ferocious irony . . . I laugh a long solitary laugh . . . afterwards . . . and then I cry, I grind my teeth and I vomit.

I think I've seen you again, you and the others, only to see him.

It is time to end this comedy, to take my life into my hands and be here, even in a desert of rocks and stones, but be here—me—and not someone else who scarcely resembles me.

Every day of my life—do you understand—he pursues me. I found him again in the red earth and the mud, in the starry sky, in the hatred and in the joy shared by others—that others shared with me *as though by some miracle.*

I found him again in the horror of a "landscape," dreadful and so sweet.[20] It's as simple as geometry, it's like the horizon.

Everything is quite clear, I am not drunk. Only the extreme fatigue of a shadow dragging its life around makes me drunk . . . and shatters me. This shadow (my own) would very much like to leave me on a street corner or else it brings me toward other shadows that I take seriously. But I will not be shattered. I think of my childhood [. . .]

20. A note in Bataille's hand: "This is Rotten Mountain (in the Alps) where Laure went in the winter of 1935." The letter was recopied entirely by Bataille.

separated, cut, they always gather in a single fat brilliant tear—I find him again in the cobblestones and in the leaves, in the solid ground and in the water. Tell him and this time *for real* that I am everything that makes one grind one's teeth, blink one's eyes, everything that makes one turn in horror—no, tell him instead that I am . . . absurd.

One day he will place an ad in the paper: "seeking lost dog."

Perhaps I would only have to say one word for all this is to stop—this ludicrous . . . abject . . . shameful hell. One word which would be a name.

I have often wished I would die "by accident." Then people would repeat "the last word she uttered" and it would be that word, his name.

If I said it now, lightning would strike my head—night would fall in the middle of the day.

Dusk would become dawn.

Streets would become rivers.

I am not drunk. Simply: I am saying what I held back for years—months—days—hours.

I am saying it
perhaps to you because you are real
the others are scum: things one throws overboard.

I have tried everything: to lose myself and to forget, to resemble what did not resemble me, to finish . . . and sometimes I found myself so strangely foreign, it became criminal—but in a very nice way and always this very banal and vulgar voice:

I know your star
go and follow it.

[Twelve crossed-out lines follow which are nevertheless recognizable as the last lines of "The Crow."]

I have tried everything. My life remains in my hands, so do I, *out of politeness!* out of kindness, out of "indulgence," out of human curiosity, I tried to lose my life and it came back. It flashed in the springs, in the stream, in the storm, in the full light of day, triumphant, and it stayed hidden like a dazzling stain and if he laughs: nothing will change, I will simply laugh louder than he.

Another piece of paper much later.

I also think that what is written should be communicated. This letter was written in the spring of last year. I am sure that I must show it to you and not destroy it. The other day was a subterfuge: I wanted to test myself. It had to do with a manuscript! The question was this: is it possible to *communicate* with a human being? To communicate what I am living—if there is time.

Life always goes on—it finds itself—elsewhere—the same. One can have several beings inside oneself and struggle ferociously and even debase oneself (in the eyes of others this does not matter *at all* but for oneself it's atrocious) the days when one breaks one's jaws clenching one's teeth; why say this to you—I could have said this to André[21] as well—I can find life's rhythm again.

I am writing you because of a smile you had—irrepressible: held back as soon as it appeared. Do you know that Don Juan is being put on again this winter with new music. There are already several [. . .] in the springtime.

In connection to this myth, the essential thing is to have the strength of frivolity. And I already talked about this last year. But I stand here as though lost in one of André's drawings or on the slopes of Etna . . . stand here, silent, "as though nothing were the matter," strangled, and deep inside me, I somehow find a magnificent party,

21. Masson.

and then it changes, it's vulgar and intoxicating like a carnival, or else I see with my eyes closed and I am completely covered in a fine rain of sweat and ash.

But I no longer have strength in everyday life—just carelessness, abjection, the powerlessness of conflicting wishes that cancel each other out.

I'm in this room like in a dream where you can't move. I suspend all movement—sometimes I start to howl like a wounded animal. Unless someone kills me or is killed.

This was necessary to cut the being into pieces. The butcher's stall or the bed of a woman who has just given birth could not be more bloody.

The absurd, the blessed insolence that frees, complicity recaptured in a breach of truth.

Infinite tenderness recaptured. This voice: "you are only beginning to love him."

Or the cries of a child outside the game: the game of men and the world *turning*—this vertigo—he sees nothing but decay—he is a total human being, no being in the world can be more *human*—stop him on his path? gently follow his rhythm? Greet him in hatred—I am shattering and falling, in place of calm pride I find only misery and injury, the howls of an *animal*.

An extreme doubt[22]

An extreme certainty of having dug
the furrow alone but an extreme doubt
as to what to sow
Sow? never

There was faith

The period of happy certainty, confident activity. A certain a priori level of confidence

Everything sunk cowardice
Fear
Fatigue
Insoluble tenderness

The straight and firm approach
Everything sunk
The decomposed life—dissolving me
and then profound self-doubt, the death instinct, the need for unhappiness and punishment
= To feel held up to ridicule *to be* held up to ridicule
doubt over the slightest little act [ex.: the communists' tone of voice]
Life is *reconstructed*
Choice—Security—Playing for time
Strength of character is asserted in the ability to play for time

Clear up eliminate *the old ideas of the past*
Look for work
Contact Kojève

22. This page was written on notepaper with the heading "Brasserie Lumina, 76, rue de Rennes, Paris." (Georges Bataille's address at the time is 76 bis rue de Rennes.) Certain fragments on this sheet, covered with writing in all directions, were copied out "neatly" in Bataille's hand.

Caillois
and why not W.
Rougemont
express Anarchy
Christian Socialism
Rougemont—Acéphale
Stop work that is Anti-Christian
that leads to *abjection*
Certainty that to exist *against* is to exist
the need for life for affirmation
for Proof to make a name for oneself
the God Bataille
Bataille—God
The "You will find nothing beyond me"
The easy certainty of *doubt*—Doubt that skims the surface of *everything*
This is not nihilism. This is a sort of skepticism.

★————————→

Practice *this week*— Comings and goings

tragic
hateful
repeated

waste of intelligence
husband
dissoluteness I should have living
together
STUPID comments I should not have
being
beneath
certain laughter to be
choked in certain throats

poor Boris
Socialists because Christian
Rougemont

---

* I was very glad to see you as well
as Esther the other
day. If I do not ask you
where you were going with
her it is because
really
I am not at all thinking of
~~sharing secrets~~
~~It is understood~~
~~that it would never be a question~~
of either you or me
but of what
outside of us
concerned us
in a similar
way
in the course
of different
evolutions
of what
in a word
really
controls
the processes
of an existence.
Pier. Kl., whom [Pierre Klossowski]
(I like very much)
I have great respect for

often came
to my house and we
talked
about Acéphale
that's all
that I
want one
time with
you ~~beyond all else~~
what controls
the processes
of an existence
if it is possible that
~~such a discussion exclude~~
that which
more independent than others
and more detached from all these
You will be surprised to receive a
letter from me addressed
to Grenoble—
1—writing this to you
seems . . .
~~a matter of conscience~~ if I did not hate
the expression I would say: a matter of conscience—
2—I will not ask twice
for your address in Paris
I would like to have a talk
with you it's so simple
that I regret using
this strange
and absurd method

that is too
emphatic
just to suggest
we meet
one ~~afternoon~~
day if you
want to
I suggest the café
des oiseaux
Please do not hope for
any
indiscretion
of any
sort
on my part
I would like
to pass
a certain
text on to you and for
you to be the
first to read it given what you are daring
in terms of
me

New Fragments

Fragments[1]

What does it matter where I am
if I know where I am going
can I know where I am going
without knowing where I am
I can
if I pin myself down
Today
this restless hour
in gray and desolate streets
bus drivers
exhausted by the days
take streets
that spread naked like
women's legs
they've gone back home
to forget
in household duties
that it would be good to live
under the sun.
At each departure
I took the train
There, where acrobats
do somersaults:
beneath the stained-glass arches
of train stations[2]

1. The texts and poems under this heading were found in Laure's manuscripts. Certain passages will be encountered again from text to text, but these repetitions are significant. (J.P.)

2. I am inclined to see this as Laure's reading of Zarathoustra. One might recall what Nietzsche says in the prologue about a certain tightrope walker. (J.P.)

Esmeralda

Esmeralda
Esmeralda
a woman's voice is calling me
off you go   off you go
in the distance the riders
the tightrope walkers can be heard
a moment of danger
the muffled gallop
of a horse
a circus ring
a great black horse . . .
Esmeralda gallops naked
on a wild horse
Esmeralda and her snow-white body
and her long thick
red hair
falling and tangling
in the mane
in the tail
of heavy black horsehair
Esmeralda lies down
rises up
turns around
the long hair and mane
the long hair and tail
longer than the thick
tail of horsehair
with the crack of the whip
Esmeralda is standing on

the horse
gleaming with nakedness
youth
the too-white whiteness
of a redhead
and her heavy breasts
the large corolla blended
into the whiteness
slightly injured whiteness
barely pink and centered
by so tender and so delicate a bud
"Esmeralda" is playing
she leaves
a room hung
lined   veiled with soft green fabrics
she is perfumed
she gets out of her bath
she is playing because
it is time for her
to play   to practice
these exercises more and more skillfully
in the little circus adjacent to her room
Esmeralda is destined for pleasure
          born for pleasure
          and the tender star
she was born under
The men are braced
Esmeralda jumps from the horse
and no longer goes up to her room—she follows
the horse and goes back to the stable
braced braced

Esmeralda
goes back into her box stall
next to
her box stall similar in every way
to the other
The day can be heard like great cracks of a whip
the horse's neighing responds
a cry
Esmeralda—Get up
the chain to the trough
and look at the man
sitting on a little tripod[3]
gold
the knees you spread naked hands on
the thigh
the other holds the whip Standing
Esmeralda—you will be good today
—as always
—Not "as every day"
madwoman
        more than every day
—Esmeralda has understood her eyes
catch fire: there will be a party
he will entertain friends today—
—move aside
put on little airs
—people's success
non—success
—scales of

3. Here the version made out by Bataille and Leiris, and copied out in Bataille's handwriting, ends. The complete text can be found in the red notebook, dated 1938.

trust
and values
—meditation
on the sky
—push aside the curtain
—the childhood memory
on the lawn
through meditation
on creation
—rejecting the "exterior"
—concentration
inhibition
—gestation
creation

[Where do you come from?]

Where do you come from with your heart
torn on thorns along the path
The calloused hands of a stone breaker
and your swollen head
full to bursting?

We are those who cry in the desert
who howl at the moon.

I sense it now: "My duty has been given me." But which one exactly?
It is sometimes so heavy and so hard I would like to run in the country.
Swim in the river
forget everything that was, forget the sordid and timorous childhood.
Good Friday, Ash Wednesday.
the pall cast over childhood by the smell of crepe and mothballs
The gaunt and tortured adolescence.
The hands of an anemic.
Forget the Sublime and the vile
The hieratic gestures
the demonic grimaces.
Forget
All false fervor
All smothered hope
This taste of ashes
Forget that in wanting everything
nothing can be done

To live finally
"Neither tormenting
nor tormented"
Go back upstream
Find mountain springs
women true hard-working men
who give birth
harvesting
To lie down in the meadows
To leave this climate
Its dunes, its sandy moors, this grayness and
its artificial deserts,
This despair of which virtue is made,
This despair that is drunk
sipped at outdoor cafés
displayed . . . and only wants to earn a living
To live finally
Without accusing oneself
or justifying oneself
Victim
or guilty party
How to say it?
An earthquake destroyed me.

Your soul has been bitten
Child!
And these cries and these moans
And this innate weakness
Yes—
And if they have seen my tears
May my head sink
until it touches

the woods
and the earth

beads
hands
the announcement
sister
death
weight
on the
steps
backward
argument
over the
veil
heroine
burial
secular
religious
cremation
our bones the
phosphate
the field
of manure
muck
dung
Let us
bury them under
flowers and
crowns
a sewer
for corpses

a person was
who no longer is
prestige
is the only
certain value
this one
will not fail us
his gnarled
arms
cry of
life
values
and
movement

Who are you
sharp face
hard glinting
blade
slicing the air
cutting into
my dream
whether I am sitting
across from you
or lying down
my head thrown back
you appear to me
escaping gravity
inscribing
a whole precise geometry
in the air
as precise

as this determined angle
where the forced smile
of bitter lips
and mocking creases
is inscribed
A precision of gestures
delimits
the clear
harmonious space
in which you live
The moment
when all falls back
into absurdity
so absurd
that it is better
to talk
and say nothing
to grimace
and
smile

Go further
Further still
Ask for nothing
that has to do
with . . . *your innate weakness*

Help
I thought I was going to heaven
Like a Saint
joking aside
and life again places its heavy lid over me

Some days he helped me: "Dear poor lost soul"
Others he wanted me . . .
Like a glove in a hand
and we rolled endlessly
It was vast and profound
like the sea
turbid and miry

The Centaur

Man is but an illness. An incredible assemblage of two different and incompatible powers, a monstrous Centaur, he senses that he is the result of some unknown infamy, of some detestable mixture that has contaminated man to his innermost essence.

All intelligence is by its very nature the compound and single result of a *perception* that grasps, of a *reason* that asserts and of a *will* that acts. The first two powers are only weakened in man, but the third is crushed and like Tasso's serpent *drags along after itself,* wholly ashamed of its painful impotence.

It is this third power that makes man feel mortally wounded. He does not know what he wants; he wants what he does not want; he does not want what he wants; he *would like to want*. He sees something in him that is not him and that is stronger. The Sage resists and exclaims: *who will free me?*

No vileness, at least not *that*. To know both *where* we are going and what is happening.

Days we can tolerate each other, days we cannot. To be perverse enough, libertine enough so that *nothing matters*.

Man goes along a road and that is *what matters* and not the tender "dear heart," the affectionate moment. And then I recognized that to be strong is to be ALONE, that power is to dare

To have a strong back.

To want in emptiness is nothing
To want? with great powerless cries

Wanting matters little to me, acting, ACHIEVING alone should *count* for me.

And then you hang around like a pitiful child
calling her father or mother.
Work? The highest expression of a human being.

To continue to trust is not what is *essential*
Denounce
All that is impotence and ruin
Denounce
all that is mechanism mania
little acts
little games
Show all the stages of it
Is there pettiness, vulgarity, debauchery?
Denounce all that BACKS AWAY
narrows
dimishes

The moment of great *derision*
has come—derision such that it *empties* all
things, poisons, gangrenes.
Through this bizarre diversion one falls back into the rut—
If a human being wants to *exist* he has no choice but to *lie*—
Even a transparent lie . . . sewn with white thread can be useful.
He thinks he is sheltered, superior, transcendant then. He is almost disarmed by irony. Wonderful secrets, the most vigorous traditions.

I have had a lot
known
seen
met

Solitude = a tonic, a stimulant, *wanting* to read and not debasement, abjection.

The adventure of any human being is not as good as a sinking ship.

I am the salt of the earth. I will not let sugary water flow toward me.

As soon as I have mental reservations,
I will stop this gesture, I will suspend
the act. Better to walk on the tightrope
than on the loose and
battered floorboards whose cracks I know too well

STORY OF DONALD
(Donald as in the second of the three little pigs at the corner dairy)

—To assert yourself as free you need to imagine me as your chains. Then there is something to break, an established order of things to *transgress*. Me, a little girl behaving with you as my mother with me. I must delay your pleasures so that they increase tenfold.

—Do not forget that I have some pretensions, too, and as much right as you to be inspired by Sade. I can still choose the role and interpret it as I wish.

—And you pretend to be inspired by Sade! Stories of family and household will never give me a sense of the sacristy. You are in fact inspired by Catholic priests. Instead of libertinism which could be a sort of powerful and happy impulse *even without Crime* you want bitterness *between* us. You look like a child coming out of the confessional, sure to return.

—Like a priest with nasty habits.

—You act like the dairyman on the corner who also goes to the whorehouse and "doesn't talk about it," swearing people to secrecy.

—Your complete freedom and mine can be preserved more nobly, without even excluding the *burst of laughter.*

Undated Journal and Notes

Something broken, not only with my brother but with everyone—and, at the same time, everyone is very "nice"—a simple question of distance. I am "at the furthest point."

This conviction that no human being can *help* another. Each must follow his own star.

The impression that he is the only one to whom I can speak and the last person to whom I should speak.

I cannot stand the people I have nothing in common with—the contacts through S. make my skin bristle. I cannot stand solitude when it is fruitless.

The time for halos and helping one another is over. More than ever, time for affection. Then to see that this affection itself is but an insoluble suffocation—a deliverance and a prison all at once and certainly for him as well.

Why was the trip to Spain necessary in order to understand and, above all, *to change*—for I have understood this for a long time but my affection undermined me.

The strength to tear oneself away

and for what
toward what

What else is there but emotional ties? Friendship? Love?

—to slide into the sewer of vulgarity where everything gets tangled
—to decide in favor of and against everything: everyday life

(in pencil on a gray envelope)

The utter contempt to which one comes, a contempt so perfect because all that counts is making certain throats suppress certain laughter

It is night
life is
dissolute
everything has been pillaged, wrecked, destroyed,
soiled, spoiled
misjudged

Above all, above all do not accept the presence of what kills, annihilates your strength.
Do not accept what lessens you.

Leave behind what weighs and stifles
Flee the houses where vulgarity leads you to go beyond *vulgarity*
where there is nothing but animosity, gall, and Acting

No true sympathy
The ACTING is so well done
What does that have in common with you?
Somber and awkward
make an outline
detach it
recopy

man and woman, superman?
Every possibility
he goes back into his shell
He arches his back
mimetic and polymorphous
you see it everywhere

going from one to another
from the lion to the kennel
and all of this in the language
of a parrot reading the writing

the servile mind
enslaves itself
and enslaves man
people
bullied all the time

Leap into the void—try it
and return to the infantile life
the one that has not changed
constant disparity—spinelessness
hypocrisy.

The most dangerous opposition is carried within. The kind that forces you to go beyond what was, what is. The kind that negates "tomorrow," the "future." The kind that cannot coexist with a "feeling of security," with "life insurance," with "domestic tranquillity."

The kind that pushes human beings into the open sea like the wind, fills the sails, pulls them from the rock they were clinging to, from the branch they were hanging from yesterday still.

The Seine? It does not seem to me that one can drown oneself in it but only asphyxiate oneself.

This way of playing on velvet
of making up for things on all sides
an invincible pride
and then . . . abjection
or the absurd trust of a little girl in a Confessional

—rays of light

—the glance of the wrinkled, hunchbacked fisherman at the little child
—the embrace of the paper boy and his girlfriend
in the crowd and the obstruction, the rush.

One of the them found a place for himself
in this troop of accredited young poets
They carry their heart
slung across their chest
speak of their mistresses
and Springtime
and good wine . . .

It is high time for me
to leave aside all those
who
calculate
deal
arrive
succeed
plot

it is time
to leave aside
everything that takes away my calm

this calm in the face of destiny

Human ties
weaken you
rein you in.
This great habit:

to make people feel sorry for you
pity you
bemoan you
The blackmail of weakness

All the same
everything has to be cleared up
one day
explained
explain
explain to them

Cult of the dead

Catholics have
the most deceitful cult
incense, shadowy light
arias by Franck, Handel, Beethoven
kneeling, standing
veiling your face
the cremation ceremony
Silence intercut by the noises of a poker in the oven
Cold silence, attitude
Four men carrying a stretcher for a little casket.

Losing sight of things

all of it goes through rites evocations symbols
Memory? more direct but frozen
Stiff because recalled too often
scentless everlasting flowers
neither artificial nor natural
kneelings and mutterings
contemplations

to feel pity their only intoxication

a strong character must emerge from dejection on its own

not through destruction, vivisection

create a diversion } ?
amuse yourself }

No—

Follow the evil to its root

confront the wound

look at it—put your finger on it.

Strength of character is the ability to *play for time*

To note a given situation and then to act "in the long range"

Calmly

not in fits and starts

or "hysterical" reactions

Where is the profound harmony between oneself and *all* the instants of life?

The falsity of so-called "animal" attractions

Harmony between oneself and the slightest act or word

To be nonconformist

Spontaneously . . . naturally

natural strength like a force of nature

touching a chord

maternal = hypocrisy

To the end and constantly?

answer: death

To escape in the negation of oneself: the wish for debasement.

Psychology of little daily occurrences that swallow up an existence.

There are women's clothes that make your head reel, perfumes that you can't help but prefer to the smell of sweat.

What divides me?
Fever
life in revolt
life asserting itself like a prolonged cry for help, a permanent, unbearable cry like the sinister wail of sirens as a ship leaves, unbearable in that it cannot be endured without feeling strangled.

828. The inevitability of this day
The forest.

88. The two 8's of the skis
Rotten Mountain

They are afraid
Few know that in turning away they would find the salt of life
In turning away he is afraid of turning
into a pillar of salt.
Few know that in turning away from the straight path they would find pleasure.

—I believe a man can finally find possession of his soul, as the Buddhists teach, without ceasing to love or even to hate.
We love, we hate; but somewhere beyond love and hatred, we *understand*, we *possess* our souls in patience and in peace . . .
—Yes, Aaron says slowly, as long as you sit there talking about it. But when you can no longer talk about it, when you're forced to live, you no longer possess your soul. Patience is in peace but the first demon that comes along will possess you and do with you what he will while you unravel to the last thread like a worn-out rag.

He knows it he sees it—
I scream with hatred and laugh like a madwoman—
I wake up abruptly *laughing this way*—or else I know . . . I want irreparable evil or else I doubt everything—myself.
He tells me, "don't be cowardly, if you are, I can no longer live, don't flee, you must not *flee*" and this word takes on a meaning so horrible that I stay . . . stay there distraught, not totally crazy not totally mad, since I can see him coming back lying yet *unable* to lie, and true, his whole life crying out.
He wants me to *share* this life. He keeps saying: I'm here because I love you. "If you flee, you betray me."

By understanding everything, doesn't he risk falling into indifference; and doesn't this universal identification, this assimilation, border on alienation and, finally, the loss of his own substance.

Renew the sense of mystical eroticism
Chinese prostitutes
What I thought of
AND HOW to dare it
to carry it out

Michel's intrusion into this dream
because of the graffiti he told me about
Leave behind what weighs and *stifles*
what will become foreign to you
know how not to *accustom* yourself to it
or to strive to be like it

Trees
Parasitical plants mistletoe
ivy

creeper

Man like a fragment of earth
a fragment of this abyss
a layer of amethyst

Laure had found God again. He was not a human being, she made him a hero, a saint, then she wanted him to hurt her, she imagined being beaten, thrashed, being wounded, a victim, humiliated, and then once again adored and sanctified.

A school, a sensible education—through the senses—

War ON DEATH ON RELIGION

Kill them—they will be reborn with a martyr's crown—They rot in the catacombs; they stake their bets on cowardice—

then arrive
in bands
in troops
dip your finger in the holy water and make the sign of the cross
their condemnation
their cowardice
the color of holy water

The blackmail of illness

The little shiver in church—being proper—hiding
youthful flights
on account of SCANDAL

The composure
the "basket"
This evil laugh, contemptuous
ridiculous
The chapel of the 7 sufferings

The priest looks like a pimp, louche
a freezing corridor
a red oil lamp illuminates Saint Veronica
and the face of Christ
fervor, no, overcome by a strange physical problem
difficulty changing position
knees shaking

Once again my life is no longer in my hands
This time I'm the one asking to be here: bound hand and foot.
I am motionless, and he forges ahead.
I feel as though my own freedom is dead since his gestures,
his steps, the sound of his voice, weigh upon me so heavily that life is suffocating in my heart and stopping in my body. Then he sees nothing in front of him but a pale reflection of sorrow.
Herd animals have the teats of breast-feeding women.
On the way back there is the meadow that smells good and there are foals neighing and I think of the Animal Kingdom. We must become everything that roars, croaks, hisses, the screeching of the owl, the trumpeting of the elephant, the chirping of cicadas. We have been turned into people who fear our own voices, who don't know where to step, who want to hide in sinister places while plants stretch toward the sun.

I came across a blind man led by a legless man. There is nothing around me but rock piles and the scaffolding of a stillborn city.

All works of art
Expressions of a sadist?
insofar as asserting oneself
is to struggle against
perhaps
True work in serenity

A detached serenity
No, this is not *possible* either.

To experience all that one carries within?
to cancel oneself out   the best and the worst
cancel each other out.

Conscientious work, ideas that are well established, sensibly ordered, sorted out, examined and developed. A certain amount of *distraction* and play (scenery and costumes). And for the rest: do as the ostrich does. Everything inside of me is contrary. The common experience that we share deserves something besides this conspiracy of silence, this secret complicity that seeps into everything: we mustn't talk about touchy subjects. I want and need terribly to tear away this veil of "discretion," to puncture advertisements for "domestic tranquillity" and to try to see things for what they are, to be defined face to face. Isn't this ferocious moral propriety sordid and cowardly after all? But what person is worth one's being defined face to face and what do I need "exactly"?

Everything in me rebelling: life is not yet a death chamber where an artificial silence is created by holding back even the sound of the sob wrenching your chest. Are you afraid of ghosts? I would rather take the idea by the throat, hold it like this, and look it in the eyes until it dies or I die myself from its putrid breath.

Is it impossible then to see things for what they are and to be able to make allowances, are these only personal reflexes, instincts of hatred and scorn, a source of fatal misunderstandings?

Having "made this allowance" and that of its reflection in my thoughts and my words, things can be seen for what they are. Well, believe me: everything becomes deceptive nevertheless. If you say "Yes," there is as much chance that the person you are speaking to will understand "No" *and will not be mistaken.* This is when you must have the pride to reestablish your thoughts yourself, thoughts full of slips and misprints.

But no, you persist in looking at yourself in a clouded mirror, and between you and your friends there is a mist, a thick fog. So you grope along paths of distraction, smiles and even . . . *a priori* virtue! and you come back to the childlike voice, the one that hasn't changed.

Some, the ones who feel the silences, I love. They exude clearsightedness. Indiscretion is their sweat and their complexion.

In my life, at this moment, everyone is walking on tiptoe . . . This is the fault of all these priests and false priests. There are so many of them, you see them everywhere. I could name them.

It doesn't matter, it would be good to be with friends on a terrain of truth.[4]

4. Trans. Bullfighting term for the arena.

Fragment of a Letter[5]

Imagine, on the train I spent the night with a family, the most French, most bourgeois, most Catholic of families. Father, mother, a fourteen-year-old girl, two boys, nine and eleven. It began like this: they were discussing goatskin "the goatskin of the war" and the father, with an intensely satisfied air, said "yes, I have all my equipment here, or almost" and he settled into a corner pulling at his boots, his boots for the trenches, in fact, and a pair of corduroy pants that could well have been. He was radiant and smiled like someone who finally felt at home. Each of his muscles clung lovingly to his clothes. There was a "warp" over this: things appear to you as though surrounded by a halo. You feel them more than you see them, and yet your eyes are open and you're extremely lucid. I thought I saw, I saw . . . four skeleton heads emerging from beneath the seat and rising up. This man's smile had unleashed that feeling of strangeness I felt so constantly during my "illness." A second later, the four skulls had become more real than the family itself. The act of trying to hide my tears put things back into place. The light was turned off. Across from me in the corner by the door (I was in the corner by the window) the father had his arm encircled around the girl's head. They kissed each other constantly, with little pecks, on the lips, she wasn't sleeping and she stretched out on her father's chest. Once she had fallen asleep, I saw how her father caressed her gently. During my childhood when my mother did everything, I was a prisoner, with no diversions, no friends. An outing with my father had an extraordinary importance.

5. This was a trip that Laure took to a tuberculosis sanatorium where she stayed for several months the year preceding her death. Elsewhere in one of her "notes" speaking of "total revision" which the act of writing must have epitomized for her, Laure states: "in the form of a letter to S., if this seems easier to me." On the same sheet of paper she added "Write about ruptured harmony." Then as a form of mockery she added: "Make up for things by being 'interesting' which finally becomes artificial."

I must have been nine years old. It was an intense joy for me, the youngest one, to go out alone with my father. It was a Sunday, he was freshly shaven and smelled of cologne. He wore gloves of buttercup yellow: I can still see them. I thought that was marvelous and complimented him on it. He was a man, a "wild" joy. We were walking in the street, I know exactly where. This was a memory that long months of psychoanalytical confidences could not make reemerge. This childhood memory came back to me, precise, clear.

Upon my arrival here, I was given treatments that all bore the number 8, in large print and well displayed. This was a blow: you know the "I find myself trapped/as in a circle . . ."

For an instant I didn't know if I was going to defy or deny it. And then I went to the ski slopes in the translucent atmosphere of snow at sunrise. And there I discovered the mountain tops. What was the highest called? Rotten Mountain, apparently. Strange isn't it.

But, you know, I now have a horror of everything that is hopeless, condemned, futile. Cripure[6] is condemned ahead of time; even so and above all he is a *cri pur.*[7] I do not want all of this, I should not attach

6. Louis Guilloux's book *Le Sang noir* (1935) affected Laure greatly. On the scattered sheets of paper that would constitute the "Notebook" of her Journal (the one Bataille speaks of) she referred to this book several times: "All beliefs are suspect to me. I think 'every belief is a fissure' when it isn't hypocrisy . . . One can think of this fissure in nobility, but also in its opposite . . . 'in a sort of lack of integrity, he says, with a disgusted pout, as though eager to cast aside this thought.' This is a book against hatred and scorn. Which is positive (and explained by Etienne Lucien). It is the love of other men, of other human beings.

—Has the Bourgeois ever been better dissected?

—For a long time he was nothing more than a man of means, bound, like the others. It is not likely that he ever attempted an act of liberation. Here nothing encouraged joyous liberating courage: everything encouraged a desperate courage where death coincided with release from custody.

Yes, the title is indeed *Sang noir.* [Black Blood]

—On prostitutes: the fraternal relationship with women.

7. Trans. A pure cry. In Guilloux's novel, Cripure is a philosophy professor working on an "anthology of despair" who ends up committing suicide.

any importance to this, but, in a sense, perhaps I cannot go beyond it if I do not look at it very closely once and for all in order to see it for what it is.

Let's say this is a page of a Journal.

You mustn't think I'm living with my head hidden in the sand or in my life, that there are ghosts that shouldn't be conjured, etc. No. Those misunderstandings may come from this excessive moral propriety that prevents me from saying a word about what affects me most. *But why is it so difficult for me to say a word about what affects me most?*

Life has been hidden from me

Decant
Rave
Life hidden
Bludgeoned
Soiled

The air and my heart have calmed
Breakdowns
In slaver and tears
Torrents of muddy lava
Chemical smells
Painted or withered flowers
Café terraces
Plays of sparkling glass
through all these fake
Convex and concave mirrors
seeking the world and life
Thick fog
Howling winds

Relieved of anguish
Ballasted by a strange peace

And you clever ones, who think of this negation
"What an assertion!"
Know that there were ghosts
yes it's true
from the time I inhabited not life but the edges of death
when my feet did not touch
the ground
you thought I was here stretched out by your side
in fact I was floating
suspended . . . between ceiling and floor
with this propensity always to be
ELSEWHERE
and now life itself
is this elsewhere
here I am on solid ground
once again

It is not a city but an octopus,
all the parallel and diagonal streets
converge toward a liquid, swollen center.
The tentacles of the beast
each have a single line of houses with two façades
one with small windowpanes, the other with heavy curtains.
It was there that one heard from the mouth of Vérax
the good news of Notre-Dame-de-Cléry,
there that one saw Violette's beautiful eyes
injected with the blackest ink
there finally that Justus and Bételgueuse
Vérax and La Chevelure
seeking the world and life

were absorbed by the powerful current of magnetic doors.
The darkness shot through with invisible rays
reveals space to them in their own image
Only incandescent transparency:
the skeleton and the shape of the heart.
One by one silent launchings send out
flashes of sulphur and acetylene
ring the automatic bodies in mercury.
They turn mauve then green . . .
The hour of attractions having passed
they are ejected into the street
by this same complicated machinery.
Faces purified
they go back to the summits
where they think they were born
(the legless man goes around his neighborhood thinking)
At daybreak, the octopus covered in sand
leaves no trace of its stretchings and convulsions.
It is no longer a question of the city,
one can head for this sun-drenched beach.

Faces, nostrils and snouts

Faces of angels
and archangels
Good will
slips slips slips
between your fingers
like an eel

Beads of silver
beads of alabaster
coral

The sheet is smooth
smooth, smooth
one cannot save oneself
on paper
Like a drowning person
clings
to a rock

Paper
is milksop
dried paste
landscapes
scenery
pallid faces
words worn thin

nimal Artists

—you know man adapts to his condition—hence, "mimesis."

—Oh, look, you thought of that yourself. Pleased with yourself, aren't you?

I want to dance, dance

A song and playing on the piano
"C'est mon homme
C'est la troublante volupté"
Lulli's tune "Bois épais redouble ton ombre"

This cadaver drifting with the current
drifting with the hours
Life flows
like a great river
Save your soul
wretched apostle

And still you think
of your family life

A sense of crudeness
possible crudeness

We have talked about this too much—haven't we?

How outdated
quick
Time is
pressing me
onward
everything remains to be done

Ecce Homo Name by which one designates the depiction of J.C. wearing the crown of thorns and dressed in purple as Pilate showed him to the Jews, saying "Ecce Homo"

fig. and fam. = man whose face is pale and gaunt: he is a true Ecce Homo

Encycl. Iconographic face of J.C. crowned with thorns with a reed scepter in his hand. Titian in Madrid.

To André Masson

The greatest strength?

to commit a crime certain of denying it in front of everyone. A few questions to ask.

Sylvain Maréchal

Preliminary speech in the dictionary VIII

"He bowed only to the author of his days" XXIV

"He walked the earth, his head high
his foot steady, the equal of all others,
with no explanations to give to anyone
but his conscience."

His life is full like nature

The deist and every other sectarian
who acknowledges a religion could be designated under
the vulgar expression: Ecce Homo

"Only the sage has the right to be an atheist"
To link to the idea of Conrad's sailor
The sage = he alone is able to stand alone.
His work. See Conrad's sailor.

The stoic = always to suppose that a part of oneself is castrated is no more valid than scorned religion. The stoic *stops himself*
he no longer forges ahead (my burnt journal)

words that sound like
strangers in the street
and see each other but don't
recognize each other

With all
the ANARCHISTS
old
friends too
one can
set fire to
very long hair.
Life conceived without
danger, joy that life
is closing in on all
sides logical joy
Take the parallel again
ecce homo
before this or that given situation
such and such act to accomplish
or not accomplish

such and such behavior
such and such interpretation

Moral solitude

---

the criminal's weakness if he finds someone
stronger than he

Do not *believe*
feel a poignant interest, words have a
strange sonority

---

words without sonority
pass like strangers

Go on even senseless later it
will be more unified and coherent
The theme of Christ . . . Machiavelli . . . God

The God—Bataille

BATAILLE

To replace God

The God

Machiavelli

by

Machiavelli

joining forces
to have the force of cynicism

[Machiavelli
God
Neurosis

Man—God vis-à-vis woman

Liberation?

The expression

The impossibility of . . . .
two existences that *resemble* each other

One { crushes / suppresses / kills / asphyxiates } the other

BATAILLE

to be

God

to be

Machiavelli

to join

forces

Political Texts

The same siren wails at war and slavery.

In the stifling, throbbing, dusty, evil-smelling factory, I saw women chained as in a penal colony. Can they dream of escaping? They have even stopped thinking about it. There they are, without light as without will. Six o'clock, the rush home, backs bent over housework. And through this strange imitation by a person of his human, proletarian condition, they will return tomorrow as today, the color of grime and dust. On the wharf, dockers the color of brick and coal: a curious spectacle for other human beings whose unconsciousness, contempt, and haughtiness are assured by charm, grace, and costly beauty, and an entire "ensemble" chosen to match their dogs' coats. Unconsciousness and contempt? Not even. There are *two* worlds (these worlds do not enter each other except through distorted images) and rare are those who, in one world, are truly aware of the daily reality of the other. There is life. The habitats of each, and the hours, and what they bring to each existence. There are lives that have no hours: the dawn of the desperate, the waiting of the unemployed . . . too many men, these, fever seizes them and makes them understand what is happening and this "intolerable" in which their own lives are knotted takes them by the throat, demands a response.

Then we are surprised that there are not incidents more often . . . every day . . . ; yes, outbursts of anger, in the middle of Paris, on rue Royale, on the Champs-Élysées. But no, fear of tomorrow cancels out the day itself. So half of life is just apprehension, anxiety, or else parsimonious, cautious leisure. And then there are those so adapted to office life, more feverish than home life, who instead of rebelling, share their employer's interests. Everything is a question of FEVER, you start to hope the anger will stay hidden away in working-class neighborhoods, confine itself there the better to arm itself, to spring forth under control.

And soon everything gets confused. It is the time of gray, deserted streets, when bus drivers, exhausted by the day, full of hate and fury, take streets that spread naked like women's legs. In torrents they crush the pavement; they have had enough of transporting a whole traveling aviary, squawking, jabbering, chattering, jostling, and leering at one another. I leave, the idea of them weighing heavy over life like an overcast sky.

What is an unproven conviction? A certainty that is not based in fact? A verbal solidarity? Doubt has crept in like a worm eating away at my heart. To be so far from everyone, from each of them and from myself, this self, riveted to them all the same! My thoughts return to them constantly. It is just as intolerable as coming back to hazy Paris after two weeks in the sun. Everything I have is stolen. Something is weighing, weighing. The streets are empty. They are at home, termites, ponderous and parsimonious, hidden deep within their fireless homes. One sees them beneath the exquisite green awning of the metro or the luster of gilded wood. One sees them doing or undoing their housework, but always ruminating, calculating, scheming: wife or mistress? Why this mental limitation? Why must your acts not be *all of us?* Our assertions turn against us. Everything defeats the purpose. Thought hinders gesture, and we stand there, stuck. Thought? No: facts, history, men and their backward language. So these ideas are shaken up as in a game of jacks? But one cannot save oneself on paper like a drowning person clings to a rock: the sheet is smooth, smooth, smooth and good will slips through your fingers like an eel. Paper is milksop, dried paste with words worn thin. Adhesion, abdication, this is easy to say. But all this is life without your being able to get out of it. Go on, then, see thought through to the end, see it through in all its consequences. But you speak in a low voice as in a house of the dead. It matters little to me where I am if I know where I am going. Perhaps the moment will come when it will be enough to know what one is against. If I were a factory worker or even a shop girl, I would not think as much about the final ends of *action.* I would defend my bread, my tomorrow against the "unconscious," who live a fairy-tale life.

I did not know that "history repeats itself," that leaders are incapable, masked by their criminal phraseology: "our glorious working martyrs," all the while doubting there is an end better than the starting point.

And this is because there are nevertheless thousands defending their right to exist, cent by cent, thousands safeguarding this minimum right of the ant, there is an impulse that is a defense and a hatred, a fear and a warning.

The value of life can only be resistance and revolt expressed with all the energy of despair. And this despair itself is a great love of life, of true human values and great instinctive forces, of all that we experience.

One cannot judge the value of anything unless it is in relation to the working class or to the efforts toward the emancipation of this class. This is what "situates all things . . . it is the great mainspring to which we refer." We know how much this class is currently menaced. We also know what limited horizons it opens to the mind and to the human heart. We must materialize and concretize solidarity with this class in daily struggle. The same traps, the same material obstacles this class faces are in fact found within ourselves.

These beings oscillate in turn between their pride and their poverty. Thinking they have escaped the "rotten" world, they reform a cosmos for themselves made of different habits that are ultimately copied, acquired little by little; a universe where we understand each other thanks to words that have become passwords.

Are we forever prisoners of the world that has made us? Or prisoners who escape successively from all our prisons of glass? Sad exercises. The days flow by dull and bland precisely because we feel them to be worthless. Come to terms with one's own failing.

Something to lean on: love. The loved one is our last hope.

Saying all this we know that prisoners are in fact those who always see themselves in convex or concave mirrors and have never bent over the clear water of a stream. It seems there is, nevertheless, nature.

Different tones, different motifs. Life conceived of as a symphony, as a fugue. —To live it.

To express that something bears it: a sparkling proof, a confirmation.

What if Nietzsche did more for the liberation of man than Lenin?

The rich or poor man constructs his own greatness in his heart, his faculty to resist what exists, to not compromise life as it is intended: soiled and ruined by millions of people. To exist *against* and not *with*.

This does not suppress joy but exalts it, it is not despair but immense hope.

Notes on the Revolution
and
The Red Notebook

Considerations

To see that the set goal is only a stage
that the support sought is only a springboard from which one
cannot leap toward action but from which thought prohibiting
action
must take new flight
thought has limitations, restrictions
"that it is up to the proletariat to take its fate into its own hands"
action is arrested by thought
Take action "so that the victory of this or that proletariat is a victory for the French as well" Portela
Gestures: useless "heroism," go beyond, find more idealism.

Some go to lose themselves in it, some to find themselves. Exaltation of the individual. This is not the rational Levelling—Marxist thought in favor of the community
regression
Our possibilities. Our perspectives.
The Second and Third International.
An era in which words had a meaning behind the words, the meaning of reality, "Going to the people."
Utopic
Scientific Socialism

Slogan read in *Pravda*

Our youth must be made to forget [ ]—it must not know such examples. Just as in individual psychology, if a human being marks out a course of action, something *different,* of a different quality, issues from him. He cannot deny himself by himself. His organism is more "complex," more "twofold," more "tragic" than he would like—

His traced line is sinuous with all the curves of his doubts, scruples, reservations, not to mention lapses, false moves. Likewise the press is the pulse of a country. Pravda let this enormous confession slip—

In all its aspects

from all its sides everything entailed in words of adhesion and abdication

What certainty it was not to fall into vague hopes

Man abandons himself to a part of him that can destroy him as a social being—as surely as the scythe cuts the wheat, so true is it that the *human* being is *social*

Vera Figner in her memoirs tells us at the end: I was no longer struggling for anything "but honor."

How many times have we heard—We are struggling because we cannot *not struggle*

Jeliabov[1] doubted—the question arises: is [ ] beyond all suspicion?

Did he act because they could not let the others die without him?

the rational—

the irrational.

An absolutely erroneous interpretation.

What T. [Trotsky] presents as the success of the socialist sector over the private sector is not a success at all, since it is obtained "by force" and not by the natural predominance of quality, of quantity—If one systematically closes down private enterprise, does this prove in favor of the "collectivized" sector—This doesn't prove anything—

Trotsky called this State socialism

Lenin State capitalism

what is *socialist* about this mixed economy?

1. Jeliabov: Russian revolutionary of the "nihilist" years. In cyrillic letters in the manuscript.

On the tenth anniversary, artisanal thus private production formed one-third of the general production—(an enormous proportion—Naked Russia)

One cannot be a dictator or Government leader without having a complete contempt for mankind.

A Laval: [followed by his electors in the worst contradictions of his own line]

This story of collectivization in Russia—A peasant is arrested, everything in his home is taken, he says nothing.

His wife with a child in her arms, cries, yells; grain is found hidden in the dung heap; he does not flinch. Finally the cow is taken away despite the wife's pleas—Then the peasant rushes toward the child and smashes its head against the wall. The militia men kill the father, the mother throws herself on them; they kill her as well.

This story in its extreme logic and its horrible simplicity is similar to those told by Babel.[2]

How can one pretend to ignore that this was how it was—The leader of the Ukraine's G. P. U. says 8 million died in the collectivization.
B. follows all of this closely—that such facts are
humanly possible.
[Tseretelli for a Federal Rep. of Georgia
Jordania for an autonomous Republic. How J. speaks of the people—His hopes in "the people"— "The bourgeoisie" will do nothing, everything will come from the people.]
Are we condemned to being emigrants who adapt to their new situation?

The proletariat pays the costs
pays for the mistakes the tactical errors or the absolute lack of tactics. The leaders can leave.

2. Trans. Isaak Babel, Russian writer (1894–1941).

The worker parties content themselves with high-flown language.
"Our heroic martyrs"

the experience of the Commune
then the Vienna Commune

newspaper clipping
discipline that bodes well
discipline of the working masses struggling for tomorrow's bread—
the machinery of young, enlisted bourgeois.

No acknowledgment of a strategy to take up. Always these flowery phrases that, if not dealing with the life and death of heroic men, emerge from the worst clichés.

Yes, Jeanne, I'm writing to you. Surprising, isn't it? Don't furrow your brow and triple your chin in distrust. Just listen to me. In spite of all the "resistance" and all the "distrust" that I sense between you and me, and which are perhaps less insurmountable than both of us think, I really cannot keep myself from talking to you about what I think about so often: Spain and the events.

(Perhaps your Mama has told you that the announcement of Quinet's election was met with joy by everyone here. I hope with all my heart this works out.)

Whatever total pessimists say, the defeats are not universal and the entire world is not yet ripe for flogging. Whatever grave mistakes weigh upon Largo C.,[3] one cannot erase socialism in Spain from his papers or from his mind. Why? Because of the upsurge that is like a force of nature, a force acting toward the revolt of the oppressed. I am there, but constantly in thought . . . in Spain where there are people who are neither civilized nor glossed over by an entire false civilization which, here, horrifies me.

This is not a passing impression that will fade, there is something down there that I loved in Russia. This very simple, very spontaneous human brotherhood.

Moreover I will be very absorbed, as I am here, by personal work.

Unlike Boris, I am horrified, you see, by the malaise that the unexpressed creates. Well, whatever our respective positions regarding each other, I think and I am certain that we can meet each other without adopting those bellicose attitudes that express what words silence, and without a whole scaffolding of useless complications, but in utter frankness and simplicity. I will never accept that we cannot confront the most contradictory opinions or absolutely contrary attitudes in the face of people and things.

3. Largo Caballero, prime minister of the Spanish Republic in 1936.

So you do not like the lack of "civilization" of the Spanish people—and that is exactly what attracts me.

When we have a firmly rooted conviction, it cannot be stopped any more than the flow of our own blood. If we are suicidal, we must kill ourselves, but if we live, we must act . . . as we breathe, otherwise history will never advance. In contemplating despair, we lose contact with vigorous realities and may be tempted to realize what is decomposed inside us and similar to [   ] of which we are (choice) products.

We cannot make up for the Past, the Archives, the Papers. Boris is the first to understand my erostratic tendencies when I laughingly announce that we should "burn down the library." For in fact this only signifies that he is bitter and sad to be losing contact with the reality of living militants and workers.

I assure you that it "changes" life not to think constantly "there is nothing to be done," or else "the end will be worse than the starting point." I find that the value of life in current society can only exist in a spirit of resistance and revolt and in the active expression of this resistance and this revolt.

I also think that all the socialist vocabulary should be reworked, that ever since the Russian revolution we have been using a language full of antinomy and illusory expressions. Can't we imagine an autonomous experience freed of our Russo-Soviet pessimism? Don't the conditions in Spain allow for such a position? And then, down there, there is a treasure of energetic and spontaneous human resources.

It should be stated out loud that total pessimism has no place in Spain and that the entire world is not ripe for flogging. It should also be stated that the leftist parties here, despite all the mediocrities and petty politics of people not up to their tasks, are uncontestably standing up against the right wing which has nothing to be proud of, and seems rather deflated and seized by fear since the attack on Blum, the huge demonstration, and Sarraut's speech.

These are only immediate impressions but they are worth something as a "sign." We have to realize that without these leftists (detested for a thousand and one reasons . . .) fascism would infiltrate here as elsewhere.

Then?

Enough of despair. If I am alive, I hope—the rest is a mind game. This vital flow, this blood circulating in my veins won't stop; life wants to express itself, to act; in order to express yourself, to love, you have to know how to hate. Instincts of force and defense reclaim their right—. There are moments when, in order to live, in order to hope, it is necessary to know how to KILL, teach this to [ ]

I don't give a damn about the old papers and history; all of that may as well burn.

One can suppress this life
                    or soil it
All rights
                    I have them
                    I am taking them

A whole generation is preoccupied only with the past under the pretext of purity—under the pretext that the present is vile.

During the elections when the façade of the local [ ] was entirely covered with a giant billboard depicting Gil Robles, a crowd came, swore, spit . . . and chanted: "Oh, oh, the big, bad wolf" to the tune of "The three little pigs." One might say, here as in Russia: what a wonderful childhood.

By chance I witnessed a Communist demonstration: the return of Russian exiles (!) (No one knows what that means anymore!) For more than an hour the main roads were covered with people, or rather with a long moving column that obstructed traffic. A committee of women displayed a flag embroidered like a chasuble, carried by two pregnant women.

Quite a few women voted not for the left but for this or that cousin, nephew, or imprisoned godson. When questioned they replied, "No, I did not vote for 129 A, I voted for Pablo" (or some other name from their family). As soon as the elections were over, they went en masse to the prison (which here is called *carcel del abanico* because it is shaped like a fan) thinking that there would be an immediate, magical opening of the doors.

I am really expecting a lot from the issue on Nietzsche—I mean: a lot of clarifications—Wouldn't I do better not to try to follow him *in his thought*?

It's much more a poetic expression—His thought like a force.

No interior game, and I even think: no system of logic—

a lot of paradoxes that cancel each other out, negate each other, kill each other yet a sparkling affirmation of a person who stands alone in the world—

As for me: never doubt my own reaction, never doubt attraction and repulsion when intellectual judgment fails me.

A terrible need to read all of Nietzsche and to get through it on my own, without help, that is, without preconceived or agreed upon opinions—

Quotations

"The critique of religion is the root of all critique."

"The man who, in the fantastic reality of the sky where he sought a Superman, found only his own reflection will no longer be tempted to find only his own appearance, the Superman he is seeking is forced to seek *his true reality*."

"Religion is in reality the conscience and sentiment of a man who has either not found himself yet, or else has already lost himself again."

". . . This State, this Society create religion, the false consciousness of the world, because they themselves constitute a false world."

"Religion is the general theory of this world . . . its popular logic, its spiritualist point of honor . . .

"It is the fantastic realization of the human essence, because the human essence has no true reality."

"It is the spirit of a spiritless era."

Questions

The man enters through a small low door, takes several steps and finds himself in a room. He is free of all hindrances

then he emerges his face smooth as though purged, he leaves by another door, another street, he goes to the Communist meeting—he will be speaking

he who has just bought women, taken part in the monstrous and vile comedy just like that, quite bluntly with perfect contempt. Did he come to these ideas through love or hate? How can these people who respect human rights, respect proletarians, see a prostitute as an instrument of their pleasure? They do not see the woman, the human being, who comes from who knows where? oppressed by what or by whom to have come to this point?

They stand before a mechanical erotic love instrument

(Rimbaud?)

Eroticism as the depths of despair but absolutely incompatible with active, strong life. Playing the worst games of man's disintegration.

Withdraw

To live facing one's interior struggle.

Form of suicide

To experience everything = to cancel oneself out

"My dear Jean"

You have the good fortune to be receiving this text by Rimbaud which I've copied especially for you at the *Exposition du symbolisme* (a pile of nonsense, between you and me, since there's a full-length Henri de Régnier and André Gide on horseback . . .) But there are two or three exhibits that are delicate and precious—I don't know if you've read Carlyle's *The Heroes* and whether you've also "thought a lot about it" but anyway, I'm sending you these few lines: this is to cure depression the day it hits you in the guts.

As for me, I'm not depressed. I've found a formula; I don't know if it's algebra but it's full of nice round numbers that are pleasant and good.

I went to the local Anarchists'—there was a conference on Spain with these fellows who, like me, had returned from Madrid. We got along wonderfully and they taught me a lot of interesting things that I really want to tell you about. I have to say that I am now an anarchist. The others disgust me too much.

I don't know if you've read in the papers that there is a Popular Front government here as well. It seems serious with admirable intentions along the lines of Roosevelt's brain trust, and best of all, magnificent strikes. There are still bastards who ruin everything and let the chance escape. Still, life is better when it goes against expectations and when human beings surge like the ocean.

I guess you haven't heard about any of this because you've been too busy at the whorehouse, so I'm telling you.

The other day I chatted with an old peasant who looked like his trees: a magnificent face, knotty and mossy. If I can't carry out certain specific projects (I'm serious) I will go to this village where there is a bistro and very "pleasant" people.

If you are sad in your artificial desert, I recommend a Pernod and a nice, hot, slow pipe.

I'm feeling much better here than in Castille, and I am making big decisions very simply and very amicably.

I hope the same goes for you and that you are in good health and that everything around you is going well! whether in Paris, Berlin, or Madrid.

THE RED NOTEBOOK

[Written in a red diary in 1938; Laure was probably confined to bed.]

Make yourself scarce   miss an appointment and arrange to see him again two days later only in the presence of one of his friends so that the others can be witnesses—to his agitation
What she would experience alone would not count
she needs to show it, immediately, even to the most vulgar people
especially to the most vulgar

—Find life once again in its entirety
                    in its totality

—The boredom that falls between two people
                                        landscapes

—Moral authority
the emphasis on "self"
—a matador's fugue
—To think of one's life is to DESTROY it, to make it sterile
—Why would two human beings live together?
because they need each other with all their guts
—money
  gift
  sexuality
Enter the world of *fiction* where you will play a role before me in which you will assign me a role, a delimited place
—the life of a hermit while exchange occurs   and friendly
you will live it in Paris   no, not that
—something
      is overflowing

the locks
are cracking
pain
no more pain
the Rebirth *of life*
—Nothing left
this ardent passion
and this horrible anxiety
and him
No = nothing
pain
no pain
immobility
the silence your whole body
Silence No more pain
at all
in you
And then one day MOVEMENT
restricted
then
free
Physical life
the body as
the plant
the plant the
tree
As though it were planting itself in the earth
through
movement
finding
the force of gravity

a body detached from all laws of physics
from all impressions

is this water
boiling or
freezing
What should I tell you?
no more cries of pain
Pour the boiling water and then lay down the
ice
I don't feel
anything anything
push your thorns into my flesh
—*where* is my leg?
Perhaps perched in the branches
of that tree—there—
where pigeons
are making love

---

your body is
your Law
everything else comes AFTER
Nothing is more *fortunate* than this rebirth
in your body
more *serious*
more *important*
what matters to you

You cannot imagine what a joy
a somewhat malicious joy
this is for me
in the past = all links have been
broken = what can they understand of this

my life, those who pretend
to have a hand in all the plots
to discover dark inflections
to laugh throatily as in the standing gallery
of farces
the throaty
held back laughter of

Appendixes

GEORGES BATAILLE
Laure's Life[1]

As I begin to write Laure's life, she has been dead for four years. Beginning to write, I cannot know who will read these pages, and since on the surface they are no different from others where the author invents, I must state that there is not a word of this book where the author has not wanted scrupulously to limit himself to what he knows.

This story picks up where "Story of a Little Girl," Laure's own account of her childhood, left off. To this story I will add only these details. Laure was born in Paris on October 6, 1903. She belonged to a wealthy family, but not old bourgeoisie; her father's family had risen from the artisan class to wealth. Laure's parents' house was next to Sainte-Anne.[2]

Nor will I elaborate much on the period of Laure's life from adolescence to the time when I met her. Essentially I will tell of my life with her; however, I will say of what came before that which she herself was able to tell me about it. Laure's life had a dissolute quality, but not at first. Around 1926–27, she sometimes met people at her brother's house, where she got to know Crevel, saw Aragon, Picasso. At that time she also met Luis Buñuel. At her brother's she was to meet Paul Rendier[3] with whom she had her first affair. Her father died in WWI (as did her three uncles; a street in Paris bears the name *Quatres frères* . . .), she disposed of her fortune: she brutally broke with her family and left for Corsica to be with Rendier. This decision was one of the most difficult in her life. She got along rather badly with Rendier. I do not know how long their affair lasted. In 1928 or '29, she found

1. Thanks to Mrs. Diane Bataille as well as Editions J.-J. Pauvert and Éditions Gallimard for permission to publish these texts by Bataille, which have their natural place here.

2. Trans. A psychiatric hospital.

3. Trans. Jean Bernier

herself in Berlin where she lived for about a year with a German doctor, Ludwig Wartberg,[4] author of a small book entitled *Gott, Gegenwart und Kokain* [God, the Present, and Cocaine].

What she herself wrote about her life with Wartberg (I did not know him, and I do not know if he is still alive) is reproduced on page 92. of *The Sacred*. I repeat it here:

"I flung myself on a bed the way one flings oneself into the sea. Sexuality[5] seemed separate from my real being, I had invented a hell, a climate in which everything was as far away as possible from what I had been able to foresee for myself. No one in the world could ever contact me, look for me, find me. The next day, this man said to me: You worry far too much, my dear, your role is that of a product of a rotting society . . . a choice product, of course. Live this out to the end, you will serve the future. By hastening society's disintegration . . . You remain within the schema that is dear to you; you serve your ideas in a way, and then, with your vices—there are not many women who like to be beaten like this—you could earn a lot of money, you know? One night I ran away. It was too much, a parody of itself. At two o'clock in the morning, I wandered through Berlin, the market-places, the Jewish quarter and then at dawn, a bench in the Tiergarten. There, two men approached to ask me the time. I stared at them for a long time before replying that I didn't have a watch. They came closer with strange looks in their eyes, then one of them signaled to his companion by glancing sideways. I also turned my head: there was a police officer a hundred meters away from us; their intention, no doubt, had been to grab my handbag or something of the sort. How little it mattered to me, and how I would have liked to talk to them. For, all in all, there you are, in total disarray, you walk in the streets carried away by the bustle of the crowd like wreckage on

4. Trans. Eduard Trautner

5. Trans. In Bataille's footnote to *The Sacred,* this is "sensuality."

the sea, you think about suicide, but you have a handbag and you notice a rip in your stocking. A few minutes later . . . they went away and soon afterwards it was the policeman who came to question me. What was I doing here? I was getting air. Didn't I have a home? Yes. Where? I gave my address, my very "affluent bourgeois" neighborhood. That rooted him to the spot. He went on: What was I doing here? I was getting air. Where are your papers? Do you need a passport to get air? Then I went back to sleep."

I should explain myself before going on: I decided to write this book several months ago but put off doing so, when just now, having found a photograph of Laure among my papers, her face suddenly responded to my anguish over human beings justifying life. The anguish to justify life is so great in me that very little time passed, scarcely fifteen minutes, before I started to write this book. Laure's beauty appeared only to those who divined it. No one has ever seemed to me as uncompromising and pure as she, or more decidedly "sovereign," and yet everything in her was devoted to darkness. Nothing came to light.

During her Berlin period, she dressed immaculately . . . black stockings, perfumes and silk dresses by the great couturiers. She lived with Wartberg, never went out, never saw anyone, stretched out on a divan. Wartberg brought her dog collars; he put her on a leash on all fours and lashed her with a whip like a dog. He had the face of a convict; he was a relatively older man, vigorous, refined. Once, he gave her a sandwich smeared with his shit.

At first, surrealism attracted Laure, but the "inquiry on sexuality" repelled her: she concluded from it the insignificance of the characters. She had read Sade, not without exaltation, yet in her boldness there remained terror, femininity itself. What dominated her was the need to give herself completely, and honestly. She wanted to become a militant revolutionary, yet her agitation was vain and feverish.

She learned Russian at the École des Langues Orientales and left for Russia. She lived there at first in poverty and solitude, eating in miserable restaurants and only rarely setting foot in the opulent hotels for foreigners. Then she met writers. She was the mistress of Boris Pilniak, of whom she kept bad memories, but whom she nevertheless saw again later in Paris. She stayed in Leningrad but mostly in Moscow. Weary of everything, she wanted to get to know and even share the life of Russian peasants. In the middle of winter, she insisted on being taken to a familly of poor mujiks in an isolated village. She withstood this excessively harsh trial poorly. She was hospitalized in Moscow, gravely ill. Her brother came to fetch her and brought her back in a sleeping car.

She returned to Paris: she lived on rue Blomet at the time. Disgusted, she would sometimes seduce vulgar men and make love to them, even in the bathroom of a train. But she did not take pleasure in it.

She then made friends with Léon Bourénine,[6] who tried to save her, treated her like an invalid, like a child, was more a father to her than a lover.

She met me a short time afterward. Her name made me think of her brother's Parisian orgies, of which I had been told several times. But she was obviously purity, pride itself, reserved.

I saw her for the first time at Brasserie Lipp dining with Bourénine: I was having dinner with Sylvia at the table across from hers. I was astonished to see Bourénine (as unappealing as can be) with such an attractive woman. She had just moved to rue du Dragon where I ran into Bourénine one evening. I hardly spoke to him. This must have been 1931. From the first day, I felt a complete clarity between her and me. From the beginning she inspired unreserved trust in me. But I never thought about it.

6. Trans. Boris Souvarine

At that time, my existence had more meaning for her than hers for me. I was the author of *Story of the Eye,* which Bourénine had read, but considered harmful reading for her and refused to lend to her. We liked to meet with each other to talk seriously about serious issues. I have never had more respect for a woman. Moreover, she seemed different to me from what she was: solid, capable, when she was only fragility, distraction. At the time she reflected something of Bourénine's industrious character.

In January or February of 1934, I was sick, confined to bed. She came to see me once or twice. We spoke only of politics. In the month of May, I believe, Bourénine, she, Sylvia and I spent two or three days at a friend's country house (in Ruel). I realized then that her relationship with Bourénine was poisoned. During this time, Bourénine happened to contradict me at the table in an almost unbearably aggressive way. There was a tacit complicity between Laure and me. During a walk, she talked to me about life this time, not politics. In a vague and sad way. I think we were alone together as often as possible. Bourénine no doubt understood what was obscurely going on between us, and, guessing the inevitable, gave free course to his intolerant nature.[7]

(from Oeuvres Complètes, *Volume V, Éditions Gallimard.)*

7. "Laure's Life" breaks off at about the time Laure and Bataille begin to live together, as though the essential had been incorporated into the novels Bataille wrote starting from that date—novels in the background of which Laure is unquestionably found. Bataille's "Laure" was only taken up again in the form of sparse notes that I found in the edition of his complete works and that I have placed here, page 246 and following.

MARCEL MORÉ[8]
Georges Bataille and the Death of Laure

We came into contact through Michel Leiris around 1935. I was a fervent Catholic at the time; but, nourished on Bloy's work since my adolescence, my Christianity was, if I may say so, an "absolute" Catholicism, which attached more importance to the "sacred" world than to that of "morals." Although Bataille (who at eighteen, unless I'm mistaken, had had himself baptized) had already taken a violent position against the Church for several years, my Bloyian Catholicism did not seem to displease him. Never in our conversations did I hear him attack my religious life. All in all there was a certain camaraderie between us, when a dramatic event, which happened in the autumn of 1938, not long after Munich, deeply strengthened our friendship.

Long before Bataille, I had known a woman who would later live with him in Saint-Germain-en-Laye. I had known her in a Catholic milieu, a rather exclusive group of about twenty young men and women gathered under the direction of a priest, now dead. But, as a result of circumstances and at a date I no longer remember, she had broken abruptly not only with the priest but also with Christianity. And I lost sight of her. I should say that at the same time she had distanced herself from her mother and her older sister, both devoutly Catholic. Her mother complained one day that she had a heart of stone. "No," she replied. "My heart is made of marble."

One afternoon, it was probably in 1935 or 1936—she knew Bataille then, but not yet very intimately[9]—Michel Leiris and I sat down outside "Deux Magots." She was at the next table. Michel Leiris wanted to introduce me to her. "There's no need for that," she told him, "I've known Moré for a long time." But she was very uncom-

[8] This text is a transcription of Marcel Moré's radio broadcast in Brussels last December.

[9] Trans. Laure knew Bataille intimately, it would seem, in the summer of 1934.

fortable: she explained to me that, given her current clearly antireligious position, she had sworn to herself never again to see her old friends from the Catholic Group—and there I was before her. She was all the more uncomfortable because she soon realized that we had several friends in common and that, consequently, we would have occasion to see each other often. And we did. But contrary to my expectations, she soon bore my presence very well. We even had frequent conversations, alone, tête-à-tête. Soon I was almost a confidant.

She had been living with Bataille in Saint-Germain for some time already when, in the fall of 1938, she fell gravely ill. I went to see her rather often. She even asked me one day to lend her an issue of *Nouvelle Revue Française* which contained a translation of William Blake's *The Marriage of Heaven and Hell.*

But death was rapidly approaching, and it was impossible not to warn her mother. Since I knew the family, I was charged with the task.

A death is always dramatic, but this one occurred in the midst of circumstances that were particularly so. In the dying woman's room, her mother and older sister remained seated on one side of the bed, and Bataille and two or three of his friends on the other. They stared at and examined each other. The dying woman could no longer speak, and the two parties, obviously of different minds, sought to see whether by some gesture, the sign of the cross, for instance, she would let it be known that with the approach of death she had refound her faith. She died without having given the proof that her mother and sister awaited. I remember the date: it was November 7, 1938.

And immediately the question of the funeral arose. The two parties, although constantly together, never exchanged the slightest word. Several days beforehand, her mother had had me ask Bataille for permission to bring a priest to the house, and he had replied that as long as it was his house a priest would never cross the threshold. Her daughter having breathed her last breath, the mother said to me:

"Once she is out of the house, her body belongs to me, since they were not united in marriage." And she insisted on a religious service. When I relayed this to Bataille, he again dispatched me with a reply: "If anyone had the audacity to celebrate a mass, he would shoot the priest at the altar!" Knowing Bataille as I knew him, I would have been rather surprised if he had carried this out, for, despite his theories about "crime," I have always thought that there was nothing, absolutely nothing, criminal about him. But it seemed necessary to seek appeasement, and I managed to convince Laure's mother to abandon her plans.

Nevertheless, the body still had to be placed in a coffin. I can still see the room: the coffin in the center; in one corner, two women veiled in black crepe; in the opposite corner, Bataille and his friends, in light-colored clothing with pink and sky-blue ties. The silence was broken only by the funeral director's assistants. As they were about to close the coffin, Bataille took several steps forward and placed "The Marriage of Heaven and Hell" on the dead woman's body, pages of which he had torn from the N.R.F. issue. Then he went back to his place. The mother then signaled to me to come and speak to her: "I would like to kiss Bataille," she told me. "Could you ask him?" I relayed the message. "Certainly," he replied. Then these two people who for the past several days had been looking at each other like earthenware dogs, almost with hatred, approached one another and, the funeral parlor assistants having moved aside, kissed each other above the coffin.

A few days later, Laure's mother confided to me that one of her great regrets was that they had not been married. "Oh! Georges Bataille," she told me, "how happy I would have been to have him for a son-in-law!"

I do not think I have ever experienced moments as upsetting as these. I had seen two "sacred" worlds coincide. I saw that hate could bring two enemies closer. And this explained Bataille to me much more than any of his writings.

I have not reread his work recently; and then, the questions that his philosophy and his thought raise are quite complex. I do not like to talk about things that are not clearly outlined in my mind. Yet I would like to say a few words, not about books or articles that Bataille published, but about two "discussions" in which he participated and which are not widely known.

I will talk about the more recent first, a colloquium on "anguish" that took place about ten years ago in Geneva. In transcriptions of the sessions, one can pick out several of Bataille's remarks that are worthy of emphasis. He said:

"In principle, I am an atheist; generally I think that I am an atheist. I am not sure of being an existentialist, but I am even less sure of being an atheist." Couldn't this sort of dialectic be described as the "sincerity of ambiguity"? And in a certain way doesn't it somehow shed light on the scenes I have just described?

He also said: "Anguish seems to me like an illness from which, personally, I would like to recover." And again: "It is with confidence that I would like to make heard for a moment the voice of someone who takes pleasure in the anguish of a God that would be neither reason nor anger, but anguish . . . What I would like to assert essentially is the fact that I take pleasure, at least at times, in anguish . . . I mean that I drown in it, abandon myself to it without reservation, and this, in short, is the reason I can talk about it with complete irony." Bottomless anguish! Wasn't this ultimately what his glacial bearing concealed by the coffin, faced with a mother to whom, forty-eight hours earlier, he had refused the celebration of a funeral mass?

The other "discussion" that I will mention briefly in closing took place in 1944. During the occupation, there were periodical meetings at my house where religious questions, Protestants, the orthodox, as well as non-Christian philosophers were discussed. At the end of 1943, Bataille informed me that he would be interested in leading one of the discussions, if I were willing to have it be devoted to "sin." It took place on March 5th of the following year. Bataille incorporated the subsequent presentation, with some modifications, in his book on Nietzsche published in 1945. But the same year, the debate, to which Fabre-Luce alluded in his *Journal de la France* (pp. 586-87), was reproduced in its entirety in issue 4 of *Dieu vivant*. This issue presents the reader with a long discussion with and about Bataille. It is of particuliar interest because among those who took part in this discussion were Father Daniélou, Pierre Klossowski, Pierre Burgelin, Jean Hippolyte, Louis Massignon, and Sartre. Of the fourteen theses set forward by Bataille by means of the Hegelian dialectic of being and nothingness, I must content myself with saying—at the risk of betraying his thought by summing it up in such a brief and cursory way—that they revolved around the idea of a mystical, inaccessible summit toward which one nevertheless must strive in a completely disinterested fashion "by plunging oneself into evil," whereas morals only allow "bringing into play a useful cause as an end." To which I will add a final remark.

We know the place that "eroticism" holds in his work, and we could expect this word to come to his lips often. In fact, he rarely used it. The term he employed far more frequently was "sin." That is quite natural, one might say, since that was the title of the discussion. But he chose that title, and isn't that already telling? The notion of "sin" is specifically Judeo-Christian, and it has fostered and developed anguish in the Western world over the course of twenty centuries of Christianity. It differs from the simple notion of "misdeed" because sin requires not the punishment of men but the wrath of an all-powerful God. Now that I myself have abandoned Christianity, precisely because I could no longer accept the idea of the vengeful God of the

Old Testament and the Apocalypse (*Juste judex ultionis* is still sung over a coffin today in the *Dies Irae* liturgy), when I reread Bataille's various remarks made during the discussion of 1944, I am struck to note that, still attached to this notion of sin, he had in no way liberated himself from the Church. His is not an isolated case. Bataille, in short, was the living symbol of a humanity that, having renounced Christian faith, still remains, in large part, a prisoner of the anguish of sin. But, in some, anguish is sometimes creative.

GEORGES BATAILLE
Le Coupable: Found fragments on Laure

Is God a man who views death, or rather reflection on death, as a tremendous amusement?

An improper thing to say? No doubt.

A reason to laugh, rather. But laughter and words (I mean words without traps that do not shy away from *all* of the consequences of words) couldn't they, in the end, agree?

This book is the sly, all the more lively, burst of laughter of a man who tried in favorable circumstances (it was painstaking, and on the whole fruitless) to close himself off in the perspective of death (life took him over immediately, the most acute, but sometimes the most heartrent life).

These circumstances (independent of the author's personal life) have to do with the declaration of war in 1939. Pratically speaking, the author based this book on the "journal" he kept, the product of an uncontrollable impulse the day the war broke out. Never had the author, then forty-two years old, kept a journal. But soon, finding himself in front of written pages, he realized he had never written anything to which he was attached in the same way, which expressed him so fully. He simply had to delete passages that spoke of a third party (in particular the dead woman[10] to whom his friend, Michel Leiris, alludes in *La Règle du jeu*). This book is violently dominated by tears; it is violently dominated by death.

Today the author is struck by the fact that *Le Coupable* [Guilty] is dominated, at the same time as by tears and death, by the representation of God. [. . .]

10. Laure.

September 14 [1939].

Yesterday I went to Laure's grave, and as soon as I stepped out my door the night was so black I wondered whether it would be possible for me to find my way; so black that my throat was seized, and I was unable to think of anything else. It was therefore impossible for me to enter the state of half-ecstasy that began each time I set out on this path. After a long time, halfway up the hill, feeling more and more lost, the memory of Mount Etna came back to me and overwhelmed me: everything was as black and as charged with insidious terror as the night Laure and I climbed the slopes of Etna (climbing Etna had extreme meaning for us; we decided not to go to Greece to go there—we had to get reimbursed for a crossing already paid for in part; arriving at dawn at the crest of the immense and bottomless crater—we were exhausted and, in a way, swelling with a too strange, too disastrous solitude: this was the harrowing moment we leaned over the gaping wound, the rupture in the planet where we stood breathing. André's[11] painting of ashes and flames, inspired by our account, was next to Laure when she died; it is still in my bedroom. In the middle of our journey, upon entering an infernal region, we saw the crater of the volcano in the distance, at the end of a long valley of lava, and it was impossible to imagine any place where the horrible instability of things was more evident. Laure was suddenly seized by such anguish that she started running madly straight ahead: the terror and desolation we had entered had made her distraught). Yesterday I continued climbing the slope of the hill where her grave is, overcome by a memory so charged with nocturnal terror (but at the same time with subterranean glory, this nocturnal glory, already shattered, to which real men do not come but only shadows trembling with cold). When I entered the cemetery, I was so overcome I

11. André Masson.

thought I would lose my head. I was scared of her, and it seemed that if she appeared to me, I would have no choice but to scream in terror. Despite the extreme darkness, it was possible to make out the tombstones, crosses, and slabs of stone (they rose up, blurred, whitish shapes); I also made out two glowworms. But Laure's grave, covered with vegetation, formed, I do not know why, the only absolutely black expanse. Arriving in front of it, I held myself in my own arms in grief, no longer aware of anything, and, at that moment, it was as if I had split in two in some obscure way, and I was holding *her* in my arms. My hands disappeared around myself, and it seemed to me I was touching her and breathing her. A terrible sweetness seized me, just as when we would suddenly find one other, as when the barriers separating two people have vanished. Then, at the idea that I would become myself once again, bound to my ponderous needs, I began to moan and ask her for forgiveness. I cried bitterly and no longer knew what to do, because I knew I would lose her once again. I was gripped by unbearable shame at the thought of what I was to become: the person I am as I write, for example, and worse still. I had only one certainty (but an intoxicating certainty): that the experience of lost beings, when detached from the usual objects of activity, is in no sense limited.

What I felt yesterday was neither less burning nor less true, nor less fraught with meaning concerning people's destiny, than the encounter of the *unintelligible* in other, more vague or more impersonal, forms. A being burns from being to being through the darkness, and it burns even more when love has been able to knock down the walls that imprison each person. But what can be vaster than the gap through which two beings recognize each other, escaping the vulgarity and platitude of the infinite? The one who loves if only beyond the grave (he has thus escaped the vulgarity of daily relations, but bonds that are too constricting were never shattered more than by Laure—pain, terror, tears, delirium, orgy, fever, then death were the daily bread that Laure shared with me, and this bread leaves me the memory of a formidable but immense sweetness; it was a love eager to exceed the limits of things; and yet, how many times did we attain moments of unrealizable happiness together, starry nights, flowing streams; in the forest of [Lyons], at nightfall, she walked by my side in silence. I looked at her without her seeing me; had I ever been more certain of what life provides in answer to the most unfathomable movements of the heart? I saw my destiny move forward in the darkness next to me; it is impossible for a sentence to express the extent to which I recognized it; nor can I express the extent to which Laure was beautiful, her imperfect beauty the mobile image of an ardent and uncertain destiny. The blinding transparency of similar nights is equally inexpressible). At the very least, he who loves beyond the grave has the right to free the love in him from its human limits and not hesitate to give as much meaning to it as anything else that seems conceivable to him.

I would like to transcribe a passage from Laure's letter to Jean Grémillon in September (or October) of 1937, upon our return from Italy:

"Georges and I climbed Etna. It is rather terrifying. I would like to talk to you about it, I cannot think about it without distress, and I connect all my actions since to this vision. So it is easier to clench my teeth . . . so hard—until I break my jaw."

I am transcribing these sentences, but I no longer really understand the truth they contain. I no longer even seek it, for I can only seek it by setting out to attain that which is almost inaccessible, and this can only be attempted rarely.

September 19 [1939]

I did not experience this feeling alone. A nervousness, with no other outlet besides a cataclysm, already existed a month ago . . .

September 20

. . . but now there is a new nervous upheaval: since September 17 it has gotten bad. I am eluding it this morning. This morning I am returning to myself, in an angelic harmony with the most . . . reality . . . This morning in this room I will soon have to abandon, where everything happened. All the shutters have been opened wide. The sky is slightly hazy, but cloudless. The linden tree in front of the window is hardly moving. This house, amidst large trees, the only one where Laure found a brief respite before dying, the nearby forest, her grave, the crow and the desert . . . so much malediction, so much miraculous obscurity, but this morning, a sun softened by a luminous mist, and soon, the definitive departure. The transparent secret of light, of disorder and death, all the majesty of a life ending, my felicitous sensuality, my perversion; I will not abandon what I am, which mingles with the immense sweetness of this ruptured world—ruptured by spite, by the sordid rages of mobs, by miseries full of horror for chance; how I love what I am! but I have remained faithful to death (like a lover) [. . .]

The presence of L., sweet like the flash of an ax in the night, appears suddenly "like a thief" and brings a cool embrace as deep, as soft as the night's breath. But it is also *necessary* to *escape* this presence through sheer will: this very presence, with sheer will, demands it. [. . .]

What also terrified me: Laure's face had an obscure resemblance to the vacant and half-crazy face of Oedipus, this man so dreadfully tragic. In the course of her agony, while fever gnawed at her, the resemblance grew, particularly, perhaps, during her terrible fits of anger and attacks of hatred against me. I tried to flee what I encountered then: I fled my father (twenty-five years ago, I abandoned him to his fate during the German invasion, escaping with my mother. He remained alone in Reims, left in the hands of a cleaning woman. He was blind and paralyzed and crying in pain almost constantly); I fled Laure (I fled her morally, terrorized; often I faced her; I helped her until the end, and it would have been inconceivable for me not to do so, as far as my strength would allow, but as she approached death, I took refuge in a sickly torpor; sometimes I drank . . . , sometimes, too, I was absent) [. . .].

The natural condition of simplicity is action. Yet action requires a cruel imperative pushing aside apparent contradictions. How would it be possible for me to act unless tortured by imperatives other than: Laure's sudden panic and agony; the night, echoing with cries of pain, in which my father appeared before me [. . .]

September 30 and October 1

Among the writings I have submitted to various reviews, the one I entitled *The Sacred,* published by *Cahiers d'Art,* is in my eyes the only one where the resoluteness that drives me appears with a certain clarity. This text is perhaps distant; "communication" is no less awkwardly remote or less difficult there than in most of my other published writings. The argument nevertheless touched some of those I was really addressing. I think the ignorance or uncertainty that remains matters little; and now hope can no longer be limited. For men whose life is necessarily identical to a long storm—relieved only by lightning—that which is awaited can be no less delirious than the sacred.

If an essential change occurs, it should not be attributed to writing. If sentences have a meaning, they are only linking that which was being sought. The ones that cry out freely die of their own brilliance. It is necessary to erase a piece of writing by placing it in the shadow of the reality it expresses. This honesty could not be more crucial than it is to me as far as this article is concerned.

[*Crossed out:* I wrote it last year, from August to November, having agreed to do it with Duthuit,[12] in charge of the issue of *Cahiers d'Art* in which it was published. And concerning the circumstances of this, I should mention a detail here that is essent . . .]

Essentially I would like to mention here one of the circumstances in which I wrote it. During the last days of Laure's illness, the afternoon of November 2, I had come to the passage where I express the similarity between our quest for the "grail" and the object of religion. I ended it with this sentence: "Christianity has *substantialized* the sacred, but the nature of the sacred, in which we recognize today the burning existence of religion, is perhaps what is most elusive among men, the sacred being only a privileged moment of communal unity, a moment of convulsive communication of what ordinarily is stifled." I immediately added in the margin to indicate clearly, at least to myself, the meaning of the last lines: "identical to love."[13]

I remember that at about that moment, there was a brief, dazzlingly beautiful ray of sun on the trees, which were then a reddish brown and formed a very tall row a hundred steps from my window. I tried again to begin the next passage, but I had difficulty drafting two sentences. The moment came when I was able to rejoin Laure in her room. I approached her, and I immediately noticed that she was much worse. I tried to talk to her, but she no longer responded to anything. She uttered disjointed sentences, lost in a boundless delirium; she no longer saw me, no longer recognized me. I understood that it was all ending, and that I could never speak to her again, that she was going to die in this way in a few hours and that we would never again speak to each other. The nurse whispered in my ear that

12. Trans. Georges Duthuit, a member of the College of Sociology.

13. Bataille's note: I had written these words in the margin, as I often do, with the intention of coming back to them later. I did not. I had, moreover, read Laure's manuscripts when I continued to write.

this was the end. I burst into tears; she no longer understood me. The world crumbled pitilessly. My powerlessness was so great that I could no longer even prevent her mother and sisters from invading the house and her room.

She agonized for four days. For four days she remained distracted, speaking to someone or another according to unforeseeable whim, suddenly ardent and just as soon exhausted; not a word reached her any longer. In brief moments of respite, her sentences became intelligible. She asked me to look in her purse and in her papers for something it was absolutely necessary to find; I showed her everything that was there, but I could not find what she wanted. Only at that moment did I see a small, white, paper folder that bore the title: The Sacred, and I showed it to her. The hope came to me that when I read the papers she was leaving, she would speak to me again, beyond death. I knew that she had written a lot, but she had not given me any of it to read, and I never thought I would find, in what she was abandoning, an answer to the specific question hiding in me like a starving animal.

I had to give up trying to find what she wanted. "Time" was ready to "reap her head"[14] and it reaped it and I stood there in front of what was happening, full of life, but incapable of grasping anything but her death. I will not say now how her death happened, though the need to say it exists in me in the most "terrible" way.

When everything was over, I found myself before her papers, and I was able to read the pages I had discovered as she was dying. Reading all her writings, which were entirely unknown to me, provoked without a doubt one of the most violent emotions of my life, but nothing struck me and wrenched me more than the last sentence

14. Trans. A reference to the line: "Time reaps heads in the fields." ("The Sacred," p. 79)

of the text in which she speaks of the Sacred. I had never been able to express to her the paradoxical idea that the sacred is *communication.* I had only arrived at this idea at the very moment I expressed it, a few minutes before noticing that Laure had entered the throes of death. I can say with utter precision that nothing I had ever expressed to her could even have approached this idea. I am certain of this because the question had already been of such great importance to me. Moreover, we almost never had "intellectual conversations" (she even reproached me for it at times; she was inclined to see this as contempt; in actual fact, I had contempt only for the inevitable insolence of "intellectual conversations").

At the end of Laure's text, I managed with difficulty to decipher these few scrawled sentences:

"The poetic work is sacred in that it is the creation of a topical event, 'communication' experienced as *nakedness.* It is self-violation, baring, communication to others of a reason for living, and this reason for living 'shifts.' " This does not differ at all from the last lines that I quoted from my own text. (The idea of "communal unity" is itself essential to what Laure expressed.)

I am interrupting this long account to write down this image, a captivating vision—almost an ecstatic cry—that I have just had: "a distant angel, as imperceptible as a point, piercing the nebulous depths of the night but never appearing except as a strangely internal gleam—like the elusive flickering of a flash of lightning—this angel raises a crystal sword that shatters in the silence." [. . .]

October 2 [1939].

This angel is perhaps only "the movement of worlds."

To love her like an angel, nor like a recognizable divinity, the representation of shattering crystal frees this love crying out inside of me that is a longing for death.

I know that such a longing for death is situated at the impossible extremes of being but I cannot talk about anything else after having set forth the two sentences that link Laure's life and mine through the earth that covers her coffin. Indeed, these sentences themselves can only be situated at the same point.

Laure and I often thought the barrier separating us was crumbling. The same words, the same desires crossed our minds at the same moment, and it troubled us all the more because its cause could be heartrending. Laure was even revolted by what she sometimes felt as an overwhelming loss of herself. My memory has retained nothing of these coincidences, but none of them was as extreme as the sentences on "communication."

I find it very difficult to say what I think about the meaning of the two identical sentences. It is necessary for me to show what they establish, but to begin I would have to talk about all that comes into play in what they express. [*Crossed out:* Today, I will content myself with adding that the almost simultaneous publication of the texts obliged me, for the benefit of those who might suffer the same thirst as Laure and me, to say that]

When I began to write at the start of this war, I wanted to come to the point that I am at now. It was impossible for me to arrive at this point any other way. And this I have known for a long time. I decided to do what I am doing now several weeks before a war broke out. But I have not finished. I have hardly begun, and faced with what I still want to say, my "tongue is tied."

(Moreover, what is happening to me today is as inexpressible and at the same time as extraneous to the conditions of the real as a dream. Without an animal austerity, nothing of me would come through this fairy tale: so fragile an illusion would disappear at the least worry, at the least slackening of *inattention*.

I have never felt, except with Laure, such easy purity, such silent simplicity. Yet, this time, it is only a matter of glitterings in a void, as though a moth, unaware of its magical beauty, had come to land on the head of a sleeping man.)

October 3 [1939].

Going on is becoming difficult for me. I will have to enter the "kingdom" that kings themselves enter defeated. But not only will I have to do this. I will have to speak of this "kingdom" without treachery. Even more, I will have to find the words that reach the heart of it. The conquest required of me is the furthest thing possible from the obscure need for self-obliteration. In this "desert" where I move forward, there exists a total solitude, which Laure, dead, makes more deserted.

Almost a year ago now, I found, on the threshold of this "desert," an enchanted ray of sun. Just barely piercing the November mist, through rotten vegetation and magical ruins, this ray of sun illuminated before me an old pane of glass in the window of an abandoned house. At that moment I was in a state of ecstactic distraction—at the furthest extreme of human things. I had just crossed through a forest after having abandoned Laure's coffin to the gravediggers. I saw this pane of glass, covered in almost a century of dust, from outside (I had slipped along a wide projection of stonework to a moldy window). If some vision of rot and decay had appeared to me in this abandoned place given over to the slow ravages of death, I would have looked at it like a faithful image of my own sorrow. I wandered, myself deserted. I waited, I waited endlessly for the world of my desolation to open before me, wondrous perhaps, but unbearable. I waited, and I trembled. What I saw through the window to which aberration had led me was, on the contrary, the image of life and its most cheerful vagaries. Within my reach, behind the pane, was a brightly-colored collection of exotic birds. I could not have imagined anything sweeter beneath the dust, behind the dead branches and crumbling stone than these silent birds left behind by the departed master of this house (clearly nothing had been touched since a death very long ago; beneath the dust, papers were arranged in half-disorder on a desk, as though someone were going to return). At the same time, not far from the pane, I saw the photograph of this master of the house: a white-haired man whose eyes left me the impression of angelic benevolence and nobility; he was wearing the clothes of a bourgeois, or no doubt more precisely, a scholar of the Second Empire.

At this moment, from the depths of my extreme misery, it seemed to me that Laure had not abandoned me and that her incredible sweetness would continue to show through in death as it had shown through in her life even in her most hateful acts of violence (the ones I cannot remember without horror).

October 4 [1939].

Today is the first real day, cold and gray, of autumn or winter. And so I suddenly return to the deserted world of last autumn. I am once again frozen and numb, as far away from every shore and no less foreign to myself than some lost point in the middle of seas. Once again a sort of dull and vacant ecstasy takes hold of me, my teeth clenched in the same way as last year. Thus, suddenly, the distance has melted away between my life and Laure's death.

Walking in the streets, I discover a truth that does not leave me in peace. This sort of painful contraction of my whole life which is linked for me to Laure's death and to the stripped sadness of autumn is the only way to "crucify" myself.

I wrote on September 28: "I see that in order to renounce my erotic habits, I would have to invent a new way of crucifying myself. This method would also have to be as intoxicating as alcohol." What I am envisioning now could be frightening [. . .].

[October 11]

During Laure's agony, I found in the garden, then in a state of dilapidation, amidst dead leaves and withered plants, one of the loveliest flowers I have seen: a rose, "the color of autumn," hardly open. Despite my mental distraction, I plucked it and brought it to Laure. Laure was then lost in herself, lost in an indefinable delirium. But when I gave her the rose, she came out of her strange state, smiled at me and uttered one of her last intelligible sentences: "It's ravishing," she said to me. Then she brought the flower to her lips and kissed it with an extravagant passion as though she had wanted to hold on to everything that was escaping her. But this lasted only an instant. She threw aside the rose the same way children throw aside their toys and again became alien to anything that came near her, breathing convulsively.

October 12.

Yesterday, in a colleague's office, while he was making a telephone call, I felt anguished, and without being aware of it, became lost in myself, my eyes fixed on Laure's deathbed (the one I now sleep in every night). This bed and Laure were found in the very space of my heart or more precisely my heart *was* Laure stretched out on this bed—in the darkness of the rib cage—Laure died the moment she lifted one of the roses that had just been laid out before her. With a furious gesture, she raised it before her and she cried out in an almost absent and infinitely painful voice: "The rose!" (I believe these were her last words.) In the office and for part of the evening the lifted rose and the cry remained *in my heart* for a long time. Perhaps Laure's voice was not *painful*, perhaps it was simply *heartrending*. At the same instant I recalled what I had felt that very morning: "to take a flower and look at it until harmony . . . ." This was a *vision*, an *interior vision* maintained by a necessity undergone in silence; this was not a free thought [. . .]

October 21.

Sent a letter yesterday severing ties with those I was wrong to count on (I have all too often had the mental reservation that I was wrong; [*Crossed out:* I often contradicted Laure's violent imprecations, but I tried to endure them, attaching myself to this misery as to a possibility for life. Today, seeing everything that I encountered and that I love, I know that I would have lost everything without my inexplicable patience. But those who have managed to finish off this patience can no longer destroy what I started with them]) [. . .].

What exists around me today could vanish in a few hours; at least I could be detached corporally from this place of dream. But the need to move about in a world charged with secret meanings, where a window, a tree, a cupboard door cannot be looked at without anguish, a need as *beautiful* was inscribed in me, as it was inscribed in Laure's destiny. Neither she nor I did anything (or so little) for this world to form around us. It simply appeared as the mist cleared, little by little. There was an element no less of disaster than of dream in it. For never would a man who desired beauty for what it is enter such a world. Madness, asceticism, hatred, anguish and the domination of fear are necessary, and love must be so great that death on the threshold would appear laughable. A window, a tree, a cupboard door are nothing if they do not reveal movement and heartbreaking destruction [. . .].

November 7.

A year ago today Laure died.

I am transcribing this letter from Leiris that I received on Sunday. He has never expressed himself this way:

Colomb-Béchar, October 29, 1939.

Dear Georges,

Here we are close to the time of year when we could look back and consider with dread all that has happened in a year . . .

I don't want to say anything in particular to you (anything in particular here would be a sacrilege), simply that there are certain memories to which I automatically refer when I am depressed and that, all in all, they are more reasons to hope than to despair.

It is impossible for everything that unites us to certain people not to be the only humanly worthwhile thing, capable of surviving any vicissitude.

I am using very solemn language here—far removed from my habits—language that makes me somewhat ashamed, for reasons of propriety, or fear of the judgment of others (to conform once again to my habit of reducing everything). I think that you will pardon me and will detect in my words everything that I would like to say to you that would be as spontaneous as a fit of tears or a burst of laughter . . .

Michel

[. . .]

I've just come out of the Helder where I saw *Wuthering Heights:* Heathcliff living with Cathy's ghost—how I wanted to live with Laure's ghost . . . At La Vaissenet, on Saturday, I thought of *Wuthering Heights.* I even thought of Ferluc. I suppose this peregrination through mountain houses was necessary to make me forget my disgust for "comedies." But I'm only supposing. After all, more and more, I am ignorant.

With effort, I have stopped remembering Laure. The thought of Denise, *alive,* possesses me entirely. Amidst the chaos, I remain *alive,* drunk with the weighty purity of Denise, more beautiful than I could have dreamed (beautiful, it seems to me, like an animal). Not to love Denise this way, to the point of feeling this malaise of a death-chilled heart, would seem to me to betray everything. It is as inconceivable as for a plant to cease budding and growing [. . .].

In December of '37, Maurice Heine took Laure and me, as we had asked him to, to the place that Sade had chosen as a burial site. "He will be sown among the acorns . . ." Eaten by the roots of oak trees, crushed in the soil of a thicket . . . It was snowing that day, and our car got lost in the forest. There was a savage wind over the Beauce. Upon our return, having left Maurice Heine, Laure and I arranged a supper. We were expecting Ivanov and Odoïevstova. As had been planned, the supper was no less savage than the wind. Odoïevstova, naked, began to vomit.

In March of '38, we returned to the same place with Michel Leiris and Zette. Maurice Heine did not accompany us. On this occasion, Laure saw her last films at Epernon. *One Way Passage*[15] was being shown; she had not seen it. In the day, she walked along as though death was not eating away at her, and in the bright sun, we came to the edge of the pond that Sade had indicated. The Germans had just entered Vienna, and the air was already heavy with the smell of war. The evening we returned, Laure longed to lead Zette and Leiris down the path we liked. Laure and I deliberately bought the supper at the same place we had ordered supper for the Ivanovs. But we had only just returned when Laure felt the first attack of the illness that would kill her. She had a high fever and took to her bed, not knowing that she would never leave it. Since having revisited Sade's "grave," Laure went out only one day, at the end of the month of August. I took her in the car to the house at Saint-Germain in the forest. She got out once: in front of the tree struck by lightning. On the way we crossed the Montaigu plain where she was intoxicated by the beauty of the hills and fields. But having barely entered the forest, she saw to her left two dead *crows*, hanging from the branches of a tree in a thicket . . .

I wanted it to accompany me always
and precede me
like a herald his knight[16]

15. A film by Tay Garnett (1932).
16. Laure's poem, "The Crow."

We were not far from the "house." Several days later, passing the same place, I saw the two crows. When I told her this, she shuddered and her voice caught in her throat, scaring me. I understood only after her death that she had seen the encounter with the dead birds as a sign. Laure was only a lifeless body then. I had just gone through her manuscripts and what I read from the first pages was "The Crow."

June 3 [1940].

Paris has just been bombed [*crossed out:* and I was told that a bomb had fallen on the clinic on rue Boileau where Laure spent two months before going with me, on July 15, 1938, to the house in Saint-Germain where she died. I do not know which building of the clinic is destroyed. Will the house in Saint-German crumble in turn? In a letter intended for the Leirises, Laure herself had written that the house she contemptuously called "the nun" would end in disaster. I am writing this today now that everything has gone through the "sonorous chaos, absurd and violent"[17] to which she saw the world doomed].

I will add: on the threshold of *glory,* I found *death* in the guise of nakedness, adorned with garters and long black stockings. Who approached a more human being, who bore more horrible fury: this fury has led me by the hand to my hell.

I have just told my life story: *death* has taken the name of Laure.

(from *Oeuvres Complètes,* Volume V, Éditions Gallimard.)

I am a provocation to those I love. I cannot bear to see them neglect the chance they would have *if they gambled.*

L. gambled once. With L. I gambled. I can no longer rest for I won. I can only gamble again, revive this truly wild luck . . .

17. Trans. Bataille's quotation of Laure's poem [p. 60] is slightly different here: she says ". . . absurd and brilliant." Bataille writes, absurd and violent.

L. played and won. L. died.
Soon, said L., the ground gave out under me.

On Nietzsche

On the manuscript of what was to be published under the title Le Coupable [Guilty]—*and which in some ways is the implicit journal of Laure's death, begun a year later—all the fragments that mention her name are crossed out or omitted.*

A singular deletion or caesura interrupts each thought having to do with this death. The arrangement of this cutting in the narrative marks a central place in the relationship that unites Bataille with Laure.

Jean Pierre Faye

Imagine an incomparably beautiful and dead woman: she is not a being, she is nothing tangible. No one is in the room. God is not in the room. And the room is empty.

. . . How does one *recognize* chance, without loving it *secretly*?

An insane love creates it, pouncing in silence. It fell from the sky, like lightning, and it was me! A droplet shattered by lightning, a brief instant more brilliant than the sun.[18]

(from *Le coupable, Oeuvres Complètes,* Volume V, Éditions Gallimard.)

Only *in darkness* have I been able to define what I call the *sovereign operation*. I described the play of complex elements, ambiguous movements, and *sovereign moments* are external to my efforts. These moments are relatively ordinary: a bit of ardor and abandon suffice (a bit of cowardice moreover comes from it, and a moment later, we ramble on). Laughing until you cry, coming until you cry out, noth-

18. Trans. My translation. Cf. *Guilty* (Venice: The Lapis Press, 1988, p. 80).

ing, of course, is more common (the strangest part is our servility afterwards, talking about serious matters *as though nothing had happened*). Ecstasy itself is close to us: imagine the provocative enchantment of poetry, the intensity of a laughing fit, a vertiginous feeling of *absence,* but with these elements simplified, reduced to a geometric point, indistinct. At night, I still see the apparition, at the window of an isolated house, of a dead woman's beloved but terrible face. Suddenly, under this blow, night changes to day, cold trembling to a madman's smile *as though nothing had happened*—for acute rapture scarcely differs from any other state.

Méthode de méditation, La nudité

"I am staring at a point before me, and I imagine this point as the geometric locus of all existence and all unity, of all separation and all anguish, of all unsatisfied desire and all death.

I adhere to this point and a deep love of what is in this point burns me until refusing to exist except for what is there, for this point, which, being both the life and the death of a loved one, has the brilliance of a cataract.

"The practice of joy in the face of death," *Acéphale*, June 5, 1939. (Reprinted in *L'Expérience intérieure*, id.)

The Rose Window[20]

June

Wed	20	
Thurs	21	L and B are coming to my house then Lacan etc.
Fri	22	beautiful star
Sat	23	
Sun	24	
Mon	25	Bergery. met B. twice then L
Tues	26	
Wed	27	
Thurs	28	L. called morning see her Univ. Evening at Lacan's.
Fri	29	L at the exit of B.N.[21] (the transpar. panes) Select. I don't know where. Edith at Wiessee sees Roehm.
Sat	30	S. called at 8:00.

July

Sun	1	I am going to rue d'O at 3:00.
Mon	2	I am writing to L. who called at 8:00. Limbour is coming to Paris.
Tues	3	I am seeing L at Dauph. in the morning. 1st letter from L. L. and Q. at 2M.[22]
Wed	4	L. writes from Lure. I am going to rue de Ptes Ec.
Thurs	5	L. called Janine who is coming B.N. I am going to Francis's then Doriot met Br.
Fri	6	I receive the letter from Lure.
Sat	7	
Sun	8	
Mon	9	

20. This page covered in Bataille's neat handwriting, like a rose window, was given to Jérôme Peignot with Laure's unpublished manuscripts by Thadée Klossowski. It clearly belongs to the body of documents through which Bataille tried to decipher Laure's writing and life. (We have added the months of the year, 1934.)

21. Trans. Bibliothèque Nationale.

22. Trans. Deux Magots café.

Tues	10	Leiris and S.K. are going to the B.N. then Whisky Union then to 2M a little after 7:00 . . . Br.
Wed	11	sadistic intentions. I receive the letter from Œtz a note from
Thurs	12	in the morning letter from Piburg.
Fri	13	
Sat	14	
Sun	15	went to the gare de l'Est propose going to Austria.
Mon	16	
Tues	17	
Wed	18	I am seeing Breton then Janine then Queneau
Thurs	19	called Œtz leave for Innsbruck. Sylvia and
Fri	20	at Innsbruck Hotel Victoria. L from 1:00 to 5:00.
Sat	21	L. called me when I entered the lobby. I receive the postcard. called Hefelakagipfel.
Sun	22	received letter Bolzano.
Mon	23	around 11:00 L. called is giving a d. Mezzo Corona tomorrow 6:00 then 1:45 another call when I enter the lobby. departure 5:00 sleeping car Bolzano Hotel Victoria
Tues	24	arrive at M.C. find L. at 8:00 leave for 30 arrive at Trento around 11:00 walk along the Adige return hotel. Bologna. telephone
Wed	25	very early in the morning then decide L. to stay parcel called around noon. depart. L Molveno auto. lunch. Molveno. arr. Andalo walk. edges lav. lots of lizards
Thurs	26	went Molvano
Fri	27	climbed toward the Dolomites
Sat	28	telephone call. S. the man from Andalo. went Molveno route
Sun	29	depart. 30. drank wine train station Mezzo Corona. buffet 30 the statue of Dante. dinner at Paon. pastries and choc. cake. le petit is moving along.[23] Stavisky.

23. Trans. Possibly a reference to Bataille's book *Le petit*, written in 1934 (but not published until 1943), for which he used the pseudonym Louis Trente. Bataille apparently followed Laure's itinerary as she travelled through Austria with Boris Souvarine. Laure abandoned Souvarine to be with Bataille in Trento.

Mon	30	bath in the morning on tel. decide L. to telegraph. the sacrifices and the 2 burials. dinner at Paon. a walk and went home early.
Tues	31	lunch Innsbruck. arrival silver train station. black banners.

August

Wed	1	machine guns in the sea
Thurs	2	called J. L. after sinister walk toward hospital
Fri	3	a walk along the Inn. in the morning called W. then S. then Ch. telegrams and letters. appeasement
Sat	4	received money and letters S. W. hairdresser. departure sleeping Zurich telephone
Sun	5	Paris Bâle slept Hotel Victoria and square bandits. asked for Paris Hotel Central. Then Bolzan.
Mon	6	Queneau Hotel Central. then déjà. Paris delicious Tel. call around 11:00 to go K. then S.W. called. Bolz. then K. Left mental hospital.
Tues	7	L telephone calls. S.W. went out with K. saw Janine at her house. dinner with K. sent for S.W. The [ ] at Critérion.
Wed	8	lunch. La Roseraie in the morning. In the evening I am seeing S. at S.W.'s house.
Thurs	9	I am seeing S.W. at the departure [ ] of the text. Letter to Ch. P. first tel. Borel.[24]
Fri	10	re, cp, tre) Neuilly Ch. P. and S. deliver text. 2nd tel. call Borel
Sat	11	date and send text—go to Paris with Janine. Accident because following directions. Ch. P. [ ] S. seeing Janine
Sun	12	La Roseraie
Mon	13	La Roseraie. Call Borel and answer. Saw Danty Ambrosino, then Breton then Piel and Simone spending the night at their house
Tues	14	leave for Priva at 8:15. Saw Borel at 6:30.
Wed	15	Borel in the morning. German cyclist and [ ]. Lyon.
Thurs	16	return B.N. hist. Bartoul. evening La Roseraie. Letters Sylvia and M.L. D.A.

24. Trans. Adrien Borel, a psychoanalyst who also treated Bataille, Leiris, and Queneau.

Sat	18	received letter P. went rue J. d'au. Janine seeing L. Bad. Evil! Read Annabella
Sun	19	La Roseraie. Wrote to Ch. P. and to S. Sad about the third part.
Mon	20	2nd letter from Ch. P. telephone to Mademoiselle K. returned to La Roseraie. started *Fortuna* again.
Tues	21	Finished *Fortuna*. Tel. with the Dr.
Wed	22	received note from Jaqui telephone the letter that she received the night before from L. idea to invite C. —dinner Jacques Fl. and Peyrambut.
Thurs	23	J.L.'s return who telephoned at 9:00. Saw Ch. 3 to 5. B's return.
Fri	24	called J.L. 8:00. tried to call B. useless. P.S. A. go toward S [e] A. went 2M. idea 7:27. met Benstrom. had dinner with him. went home. then went out again. Wrote Rue.
Sat	25	went Biaritz. Wrote B. dinner with W. R. S. and G L. at the train station went Bayonne auto. basque. spoke to S. until 3:00 in the morning.
Sun	26	passport difficulty. looked for Duhamel. boat departure St. Sébastien lunch Miami drank Valdepi [ ] o'clock at the church. [ ] return Jean de Luz. saw Limbour again. olives café de Madrid. left S. at 2:00 and asked for address saw Cl. R.
Mon	27	sent telegram. went out. ate with L. and S. lunch café de Madrid. villa N. then pl. Miramar with Cl. R. last time. dinner with S. left café M. went Bayonne left S. and L. on the quay.
Tues	28	arr. P. received letter Borel. telephoned clinic. telephoned Jacques who saw B. saw Jacques at Neptos. saw Max at 2M; dinner slept Piel
Wed	29	received letter B.? dinner at Fl. J. and P. at Flo.'s. slept Piel.
Thurs	30	received tel. call S. clinic. answered B. slept Roseraie and Whisky
Fri	31	in the evening went home early letter Sylvia. slept Piel

September

Sat	1	Saw Dommangot. 5:00 and B. saw Ulmo. Evening la Roseraie. whisky.
Sun	2	morning boating. read

Mon	3	Limbour's return. Bayard. Tabarin. went back taxi
Tues	4	called J.L. was at P.K.
Wed	5	return the party tel. dinner Piel
Thurs	6	Borel is seeing L. Received tel. call Janine in the water etc. Jacques B. couscous
Fri	7	made appointment Dr. B. 5:00 saw G.L. at Francis's. dinner Piel
Sat	8	morning Diana Slip. 5:00 Simone B. 8:00 Viva Villa. Univers and Orangerie
Sun	9	10:00 2 Magots. daytime la Roseraie. drank. went home by Simone's side.
Mon	10	morning G. L. hairdresser Lénina 5:00 Borel. 7:00 J. and Fl. Saw War correspondent
Tues	11	morning clinic Frankel. lunch Muss. 5:00 Montmartre. met in moonlight. Went home Madame and Simone M.
Wed.	12	Began 9th part. Saw Ka her sister her mother and Zette. Met Denise.
Thurs	13	morning Limbour. Ke Boul Olivier Lunch etc. Bayard Went home then Tabarin then Sphinx then Dhôme OK—Sylvia telephone.
Fri	14	Limbour Madame Limbour Frankel
Sat	15	Red Braff.
Sun	16	Limbour dinner J. and Fl.
Mon	17	Boul dinner Mad and Pelly. (Borel, wrote Simone)
Tues	18	Dinner Chevalier (Divina)
Wed	19	Borel then Denise
Thurs	20	dinner P. K.
Fri	21	Borel appointment Petitjean. tel. Sylvia.
Sat	22	Concert Mayol[25] Maid Talbot the Catastrophe, received letter Denise
Sun	23	Went P [ ]. evening mischief the Naklès.
Mon	24	Borel. dinner Polly. tried to call Simone
Tues	25	dinner and Polly the am. saw Simone again
Wed	26	Borel. evening Leiris.

25. Trans. A nightclub that Bataille frequented.

Thurs 27 call from Odoïevtsova

Fri 28 Edith is no doubt coming for the first time to the library and asking for a paper

Sat 29

Sun 30 went to porte Maillot. stayed Paris rain Ct. Mayol P Ec. evening went to S.B.'s did not find Gernica meeting

October

Mon 1 J.B. came to the library met Edith at the door and at the Havas agency

Tues 2 dinner Chinese restaurant with B. Q. and J. Janine talked letter L. Meeting S.L. no one has seen Krakatoa again

Wed 3 tea Odoïevtsova. dinner with Fl. and B. saw Hollywood party Met Edith at 2:00 at [ ]

Thurs 4 looked for Edith at [ ]. L. at the library. I've gotten news from M.D. missed Edith at the Tuileries. saw Borel. evening Leiris. Thought of drinking etc. went home by rue Belle.

Fri 5 morning dentist at 2:00 PM Edith's note lunch with Edith at 2:00 at 5:00 Lac aux Dames 5:00 to 6:30 J. saw L. dinner round point. then drink then Madrid then Cuban cab.

Sat 6 saw Limbour. waited for Edith at 7:00 at the Univers. dinner Bayard. café Colisée. returned Issy around 5:00 S.W. had telephoned.

Sun 7 tel. P.K. morning Univers. Louvre. Univers. saw New York Miami drink dinner Bayard. met Fl. and J.

Mon 8 Tel. J. the taste of ashes. tel. S.W. then Odoïevtsova then P.K. Borel. then P.K. then 2M. etc. Simone. Edith C.F. night Florence

Tues 9 morning breakfast Univers. Saw Denise. Sh Kahme. Barrella assassination. dinner Chinese restaurant then 2M. then Fred P.[26]

Wed 10 2:00 bar aut. 5:00 Borel. 7:00 Edith Dupont dinner Poisson d'Or, returned Issy.

Sat 13 Sylvia coming back Coye then Chantilly. nightfall crossed the racecourse

26. Trans. Fred Payne: A nightclub.

Sun	14	Went out in the morning and made love in the woods afternoon after went out then tea then sunset above the racecourse oh! alot of madness.
Mon	15	found Sylvia at 8:00 left at 6:00 waited for Edith at the entrance of Com. fr. saw Ruy Blas
Thus	19	The Circle. S.W. Queneau and Ambrosino. I'm spending the evening with Edith.
Mon	24	Sylvia is coming back with Laurence.[27]
Thurs	25	Excluded from Ambrosino's circle.
Fri	26	Ambrosino love exclusion from Circle
Sun	28	gave up on trip to go Salon des Ind. Called Piel's. dinner Bayard. Slept at the hotel on bar des Fleurs street . . .
Mon	29	Edith expected at Balzar's at dinner, then rue Mouffetard. Dinner
Tues	30	Edith at 5:00 at library. Gare de l'Est then Rue [ ] Went Blvd. Haussmann. then Rue. Then Gare de l'Est.

November

Thurs	1	9:00 Thionville. 8:00 Trier. Hotel de Cologne breakfast then went Dom. Hotel. Lunch. Then Koukels bey. dinner at the hotel.
Fri	2	Shopping in the morning in Trier. then depart. 10:36 Moselle. 12:00 Koblenz lunch Eisbeim then café 3:45 PM the Rhine boat cemeteries stars and candles.[28] 6:00 PM Frankfurt Romer. dinner Börsenkeller. 5:52 Edith's departure for Heidelberg
4/1/35		Met Laure. Flore, then Fred P, then rue de Rennes.
5/9		Met Madeleine
5/16		

27. Trans. Bataille's wife and daughter.

28. Trans. Cf. Bataille's *Blue of Noon:* "We reached Trier . . . the first of November. [. . .] At one turning in the path, an empty space opened beneath us. Curiously, this empty space, at our feet, was no less infinite than a starry sky over our heads. Flickering in the wind, a multitude of little lights was filling the night with silent, indecipherable celebration. Those stars—those candles—were flaming by the hundred on the ground: ground where ranks of lighted graves were massed. We were fascinated by this chasm of funereal stars. [Dirty] drew closer to me. She kissed me at length on the mouth." pp. 141–143 (New York and London: Marion Boyars, 1988) trans. Harry Mathews.

5/17	dream sky upside down
27	Dorothé's return
6/13	Laure at Flo. then rue de Rennes. Flore. the Leirises and the Piels dinner Bayard. 12:00 Jean W cemetery. monocle. Fleurs. Kokô.
7/13	Madeleine met S.W. in front of the bar des Flano as Madeleine was telling me she saw Kiki.

Fragment of an autobiographical note, Bataille[29]

In 1935 Bataille founded a small political group called Contre-Attaque, which brought together former members of the Cercle Communiste and, after a clear reconciliation with André Breton, the whole of the surrealist group [. . .] Contre-Attaque dissolved in 1936, and Bataille immediately decided to form a "secret society" with the friends who had participated, among them [. . .] Pierre Klossowksi [. . .], which would turn its back on politics and envision only a *religious* (but anti-Christian, essentially Nietzschean) end [. . .] Its intentions were expressed in part in the journal *Acéphale*, four issues of which appeared from 1936 to 1939. The College of Sociology, founded in March 1937, was in a way the external activity of this "secret society" [. . .] Of the secret society itself, it is difficult to say anything, but it seems at least some of its members have retained an impression of "departure from this world" [. . .] A disagreement arose between Bataille and all of its members [. . .]

In 1938 a woman's death tore him apart.

29. Trans. "Notice autobiographique" in *Oeuvres Complètes,* Volume VII, Éditions Gallimard, 1976, p.461.

My Diagonal Mother
by Jérôme Peignot

My Diagonal Mother

I

This is not the first time I have felt this sensation of not being my mother and father's son, but rather my paternal aunt's and maternal uncle's. That I am the product of this altogether easy, total, and perfect transfer I sense today with great precision. This alone accounts for the peculiar awareness I have of life. The illuminating virtues of this sidelong glance are truly dizzying. In this chromosomal shambles, the effects of which I see in the smallest detail, I am suddenly revealed to myself as though from the angle of a transversal. Then not only can I explain my behavior but I can justify my attitudes and their interactions. It's as though I've caught myself red-handed being myself. At such moments I finally see myself as I am, and being aware of my peculiarities to this extent—the very ones that make me different from other people, and, therefore, someone—could lead me to the edges of insanity. Not enough awareness leads one astray, too much, in total clarity, makes one falter.

This shift at the origin of my birth gratifies me all the more in that it negates my father by replacing him with his opposite. I can imagine no one more different from him than his sister Colette. To the grandiloquent tower of her brother, she responded with such grace that her contours were tremulous with an exemplary light, with the exaltation of a poet as well as an authentic revolutionary. I have never dreamt of a more natural woman than my aunt. In her desire to attain ever greater authenticity, Colette, this dead woman (she died when I was twelve) spent her life merging into the transparency that envelopes us.

My real mother is exactly everything that my diagonal mother is not. My uncle—my mother's brother, my oblique father—was actually right-wing as well. A diplomat, he had a certain style, and even while he was alive, I felt I would not rest until I was certain I had inherited it. In my mind, it was a matter of putting his ways to the service of ideals the exact opposite of his. "Uncle Jean" was a stoic man. Having set off a mine at the end of the First World War, his right leg would hurt him constantly until his death in 1962. "You limp. Good start for a man seeking a career in foreign affairs," I told him. He smiled. Nothing pleased me so much as to dish up to my enemies what they offered me. This gratified me all the more since these relatives, despite the fact that I did not share their political opinions, were nevertheless courageous people. To divert the courage of one to the advantage of the conceptions of another gave me real pleasure.

Despite what I have just said, the relations between my mother and my diagonal mother were good. Indeed, Colette liked Suzanne because her presence alone helped her escape the stifling atmosphere of the Laporte family. To have been born in such a milieu made Colette's head reel. This Catholic and bourgeois family's ideas were so contrary to her she felt she had been denied by them even before her birth. The fact of enduring such contradiction blurred the purity of her features. When Laure, using her real name, Colette, writes for the first time to her sister-in-law Suzanne, who has just married her brother Jacques,[1] she is only eighteen years old. She lived with her sisters Catherine and Hélène at Dammarie, their mother's property in Seine-et-Marne. It is a pleasant place. In front of the house, a great lawn surrounded by stately chestnut trees slopes down to the Seine. One might think of Renoir or perhaps also Pissaro. Yet despite a church with a pointed steeple and cocks crowing at dawn, Dammarie is too close

[1] Trans. Charles Peignot

to Paris to be a true village. In fact, the houses—three or four at the most— that look out over the Seine beyond their gardens, almost parks, were family mansions. The "children" come there on weekends with their friends. Rather than the extravagant luminosity of the Impressionists, it would be more accurate to evoke the false bourgeois tranquility painted by Vuillard. There is something menacing at the bottom of this peacefulness: it was inevitable that someone pay for it. How, or rather at whose expense? When Madame Laporte, Laure's mother, greets her gardener, she gestures with two fingers. Into rifts such as these entire worlds are swallowed. Victor doesn't mow the lawn regularly: just a strip of land in front of the terrace, from time to time. Beyond, the grasses remain high. The smell of cut grass sharpens the mind. Laure does not need this scent in order to reason. She thinks too much, to the point of driving herself mad. The awareness she has of leading a comfortable life colors her thoughts with despair. The luxury in which she lives, whether excessive or not, does not allow her to escape herself. It would be best to leave it, no doubt, but how? A path has to be chosen, but which one? Gide already went through this: it is enough to have made a choice in order to tell oneself that one should have made another.

Laure's father, as well as her three uncles, died in the war of 1914. This made an impression. This is why in Paris today there is a street called rue des *Quatre frères* . . . Steeped in piety, Laure's mother chose to make the rest of her life seem a long, never-ending martyrology. Having given so much to the "fatherland," this woman was right. In the face of such pain, how could one not feel at fault by the mere act of living? But Laure lives. She has "an infinite thirst for life." Not that she allows herself to be swept away by the thought of "a dress or a box of powder." She aspires "to force things, to adapt life to her nature . . . enrich and embellish it herself." She is right. Happiness and ease are not gathered like the flowers she fills her house with: they are cultivated. "Life only gives in proportion to what you give it." Through indecision, Laure behaves in a way that contradicts her wishes: like young girls waiting for the perfect man. But is it possible to avoid this nonsense? "How can truly well-balanced young girls exist?" She is eager to be "delivered from this false, unreal state" in which she finds herself. She does not realize that it is precisely because she sees things all too clearly that she thinks she is unrealistic. Reality, made white-hot by the gaze resting on it, takes on a spectral aspect that inverts meaning.

But Laure is infinitely more of a realist than her sister-in-law, who, due to her insouciance as a rich and civilized woman, manages to avoid all of life's grave and difficult events without giving them a thought. Laure suspects this a bit, but after several outbursts says: "I'm the one spoiling what was your tenderness with the same atrocious habit I have of destroying what I desire." She admits she is being too stringent: ". . . Friendship, Affection, are only *words* when one cannot rise above differing ideas—we call ourselves 'broad-minded' but when we leave our sphere (our circle of friends) the heart does not follow—Affection is broader and more subtle than all this pettiness." That the two women do not understand each other is certain. Timidly at first, Laure begins to say to her sister-in-law that she feels as different "as a blond can be from a brunette." But she needs to be understood and is also so afraid of not being understood that, breathless and loveless, she expresses in a single, short appeal, her affection and anguish: "I'm afraid you don't understand me, my dear, I can't stand it anymore and I'm eager to be by the seaside." In fact, Laure is not so much speaking to Suzanne as she is attempting to make her share her solitude, what she feels in this silent garden "savoring the great nourishment that only solitude can give us; its brief joys are intense enough to dispel the tedium inseparable from isolation." But, in the end, there is no solution. That's how life would have it: "You can't imagine what wild joy I feel each second," she writes to her sister-in-law, "seeing my strength whole only since this summer, and I would like to exhaust my body in a thousand ways; I hate sleep, and I despair to see that by avoiding it in the morning you succumb to it earlier in the evening . . . we can break down every barrier, we are still *limited*." But as soon as she says this, she says she would like "not to know how to think" . . . not to have "reflected so much," to be something "precise," "defined." In fact, and Laure demonstrates this when she writes her first letters to Suzanne, a young girl who thinks is taking a fabulous risk. Because Laure does not accept being only what she is—a young girl from an affluent bourgeois background—she is, in fact, already a woman.

As a result of her contradictions, her startling about-faces, one deciphers her letters as one would hieroglyphics. And what if, in its pure state, thought was nothing other than these reflections of a young girl reduced to thinking when she is nothing but sensation, excitement? By beating too quickly her heart beats insufficiently, exactly as she writes, well. She is ready for anything but not yet for anyone. By thinking, it seems she has crossed the threshold she should not have transgressed. She writes letters and asks that they be sent back to her. She would all but prefer that they not be read. She is not crazy; she knows that perfectly well. To the extent that what Laure writes is merged with what she lives—or doesn't manage to live, as you like—her letters dazzlingly reveal certain facts about the nature of writing. I have, for example, picked out among many others, this sentence: "My heart wants to be one with someone." She does not specify "with one person." She's being honest. Laure writes the way one strips oneself . . . of writing. In truth, she is struggling with life and with words at the same time. In her letters, she cries, gets scratched on the brambles she collects on her writing path. There seem to be daggers fluttering above the lines of her handwriting. The more she speaks the truth, or, what amounts to the same, the more she struggles, she reduces what she is saying to what you can decode from it. It's a shame her letters cannot be reproduced in facsimile. Laure in her entirety is in her handwriting. For those who speak this way, language is a feverishness. And what if language was nothing but the occasion for drowning? "Do you see there are moments when everything crumbles and collapses and when there is nothing more than your tender clarity?" Although she does not stop proclaiming that her letters are "drafts," Laure knows how to write. You can see the scree. The tone of her letters assures us that the act of writing was both her salvation and her ruin. Her ruin because writing made her confront the untranslatable; her salvation because it enabled her to breathe again.

But why does she have to ask herself so many questions? Isn't it obvious that Suzanne's arrival is a godsend? Even so you have to "give yourself entirely, without ulterior motives. But why is it always her and other people, and her, and why so complicated?" She is always separated from others by a pane of glass. She signals to them but in the end does not reach them. Sometimes there is a light, a breakthrough; she finds a way to see things more simply and she exclaims, as in this undated note, which I found in her correspondence to Suzanne, written on her blue paper:

> And this does not prevent me from simplifying myself—
> Pardon me: you are part of the
> beauty of life; you and everything that surrounds you.

But then the sky clouds over again. Laure's letters have no sky. "I know I am so selfish," she writes, "that the most dreadful uncertainty is to love selfishly . . . to love because you like to love. Tell me, does one find the self there, too? Then nothing would be worth anything anymore. Do you understand, do you know what . . ." She does not finish her sentences, yet they speak, more than if they were finished. This language is full of precipices. It reveals all the more since it is apparently shapeless. If these letters have no punctuation they have something more: the empty spaces are Laure, who, without ever blinking, says what she feels through ellipses, bated breath. In one letter she asks her sister-in-law if she, who lives with particular grace, knows a way to love without allowing oneself to be intoxicated, without contradicting one's love by the self-love that it arouses. It is because we possess an ego that we are. Without an ego there is no love and yet this same ego kills love. Here, once again, Laure is grappling with the impossible. And yet this impossible is the real itself we face. Laure is asking the ultimate question here, the one that cannot be answered. And yet how can one not ask it? Does a line of reasoning always lead to an impasse? One must calm down, not get carried away and dramatize things. There must be some way out, the proof is that the skies are open. To the question, Suzanne answers with a formula: "marriage." Laure is more than disappointed: she is exasperated. In the end, Suzanne's answer will help her inasmuch as she sees quite clearly this time that she is forced to accept herself as she is. "Thank you, darling, it's thanks to you that I have been able to assert myself in contradiction."

If only to capture the horror that they quietly evoke, one should, in reading these letters, try to imagine the place where they were written for the most part: Dammarie, where on beautiful days, vacuous people trot along the estate's tennis courts and where this luxury is slowly killing her, all the more because she is able to take pleasure in it. Though she judges this ease the way she severely judges her brother Jacques, she knows that she needs it just as much as the brilliance of a sunny day. And yet she is painfully aware of lost time: ". . . submitting to an average and base life, taking no action, contenting myself with weak people, letting myself be dominated by apathy, banality . . . the vulgarity of others . . . the vulgarity of ideas, void of intelligence, beauty, the strength of love—I can't stand it anymore." She is right; vulgarity is the refusal to think. Here, the definition of a word is often that of the word next to it. Laure is given to these translations. Her writing is made of this mobility. Considering these deviations of meaning is the very sign of the mind. One summer, Suzanne, who is a singer, has her old friend Ricardo Viñes, the great Debussy pianist, come to Dammarie. For Laure this is a celebration. She prepares the house, has the piano tuned. Yet her letters from that time give the impression she is falling apart at the seams. Isn't the inexpressible "continuous and solitary pleasure" that she takes in such "perfection" a "sort of perversion"? In such conditions, it was inevitable that she write. She began, then, in her letters to her mother, by speaking of "this isolated self that I myself would like to feel through some kind of achievement." But her first efforts soon seem like a waste of time to her. "Pathetic, failed attempts," she says, "in which I immediately discovered the inherent emptiness of what I called reality." As I read her correspondence, I realized in spite of her anxieties and disillusionments, Laure was relentless. "To experience life with all our might, to the height of our potential," she wrote in a letter that alluded to her first efforts as a writer, "cannot destroy our richness to feel." And then, once again, she lost heart, torn by the need to start making choices, orientations that seemed to her like mutilations. She loved life, "wanted to live and not simply be a brain." Later, in one of the drafts of "Story of a Little Girl," she would write: "From this apparently calm, imperturbable day on, I began to hurl cries onto paper: I had a coffin for a cradle, and a shroud for a blanket. I had for love a vision of a lecherous priest or cynical jokes . . . I don't know where I'm going but what difference does it make because I know where I am: against everyone, as far from my sister as from my brother but there are four of us and there are four cardinal points, I'm in the east, why? Because the sun only rises and then I can see my cold sister so well in the north, my 'dissipated' brother in the south and the other ending . . . How idiotic. But since I am banal I have to go all the way with it. Will I ever be capable of leaving a trace of will in the real?"

Marly, Louveciennes, Garches: Laure is forced to play the piano in houses that the Laportes rent with their friends the Fleurets. At Louveciennes Laure meets Paul Rendier.[2] For some time already, she had spoken of spending her days at the low tide of "night fevers." All of a sudden it was not love at first sight—the expression has a romantic character inappropriate in this case—but heartbreaking love. Indeed, although there is scarcely any information on the exact nature of the relations between Laure and Paul Rendier, we do know that there was another woman in this man's life at the time, "a laundress," Suzanne told me with a knowing look that I refused to understand. That Laure immediately fell in love

2. Paul Rendier, [Trans. Jean Bernier], a friend of Georges Bataille, was one of the signatories of the tracts of the group Contre-Attaque in 1936.

with Rendier can be gauged in that she combines her confession of love with her disappointment as a writer. Because now that "the incommunicable in her is being shared," she considers her writing nothing but absurd attempts, "posturings," a source of "blunders," lies, and mistakes. But then, Suzanne was right: she *was* waiting for a man. No, that was not it, and Laure certainly foresaw this: "do you understand . . . he justifies the feeling that if everything that wanted to come to life in me, if all latent possibilites found their expression, it would be complete anguish, the height of anxiety—negation in exaltation." Besides, she adds: "Don't think anything is going on between Rendier and me—we had a simple conversation—maybe he likes me a little, barely—that's all I've wanted from him for a long time—" Nevertheless it is true that the encounter with Rendier marks a total change in Laure's relations with "her loved ones." "It is to her liaison with Rendier," writes Bataille, "that Laure owed her brutal break with her family." This is not quite accurate, since she continued to write to her sister-in-law from Corsica where she went to meet Paul Rendier, "one of the most difficult decisions of her life," Bataille points out, adding that "she got along with him rather badly" (this "rather," which says it all, being worse than "badly"). This is why, in this context, the three messages sent from Bastia and Ajaccio stand out in particular. No doubt, at first glance, they say more in what they do not say. Their tone is hardly that of a happy woman. The impression we get from reading these three letters is that if, indeed, Laure went to Corsica to be with Rendier, he was not there alone, and above all she was faced with herself. One can almost physically feel her solitude. She rests her gaze on the simplest things, and we know the exact weight of these looks. The disappointment of love makes it impossible to look at the world without giving it the weight of death.

No doubt we will never know the profound reasons for this failure: did their common political opinions prompt Laure not to rely romantically (or, conventionally) on her love? At the same time that she loves, does Laure intend to go beyond her feelings? Several months after the Rendier episode, she will indeed write to her sister-in-law: "it seems to me that if at thirty years of age one has not realized all the love that one has within oneself for desire, life, beauty (toward and against everyone) it just isn't worth it." Suzanne, through whom Laure met Rendier, would have wished for "something else entirely for her." Catherine, Laure's sister, feels the same. Thus what was bound to happen one day, happened violently. That evening, Catherine reproached Suzanne and Jacques, in Laure's presence, for introducing "that Rendier" to her sister. Wasn't he the one who "put all those revolutionary ideas in Colette's head?" After this argument, Colette flees. From Orléans, she writes to her sister-in-law the devastatingly lonely letter of a certain December 6, probably in 1926. Suzanne should have foreseen her reaction. Had Laure not written her: "everyone is content with a 'petty life' and abandons the ardor of living through fear of suffering. I like this, I don't know where I read it: 'Everyone needs intoxication whether it be passion, heroic action, wine or opium: a work of beauty is always an act of love for life even in the midst of despair and negation—there is never sin in love: the sinner is the one who abandons the ardor and grandeur of living.'" If she recopied this sentence, it is also because she feels vaguely alienated by what she is experiencing. She is already accusing herself of not being equal to what life has to offer. But, and one senses it with the first letters of this correspondence, Suzanne seems almost embarrassed by the too exuberant love that her sister-in-law has for her. Besides, if she had been more sensible, what should or could she have done?

For a long time, then, my mother followed with tenderness the fluctuations of this tormented mind, fluctuations all the more real because they were imperceptible. My mother's grace and common sense, which once meant everything to Laure, were of no use. These were the remarks of a young girl, one might say, of a child still trying to find herself while tearing herself apart. In fact, her anguish shows us that Laure had already reached the height of delirium. As an adult, she simply took her reflections as a sharp-edged young girl literally. Finally, her work shows that by trying to emerge from these impasses, she lived, until her last torments, the hell of reason. "Why when I see my thoughts through to the end do I get the impression of betraying what I love most in the world and of betraying myself without this betrayal being 'avoidable.' If you sensed all the anguish with which this *why* is charged, you would try to answer, but there is no possible answer. We bear within us the most dangerous opposition."

There is a central event in Laure's correspondence with my mother, which, from the fact that I did not mention it in the preface to *Écrits de Laure*[3] seems a serious ommission: Laure's suicide attempt. One evening as they were getting ready to go to the Opera, Jacques and Suzanne received an urgent telephone call

3. Éditions J.-J. Pauvert, 1971.

telling them to go to Laure immediately. Something serious had happened. She was living in a small, wrenchingly sad hotel on Avenue d'Orléans. They found her lying on a bed, splayed like a mannequin, bathed in her own blood. It was later learned that the bullet Laure had intended for her heart had ricocheted off a rib. One can imagine the scene: Suzanne in her evening gown, Jacques in a tailcoat. How can one not feel, even in spirit, the extravagantly lurid reality of this scene, the rawness. Laure's first words, that mustered whatever remaining strength she had, were to absolve Rendier and make it clear that she did not kill herself over him. Then, she begged to be brought to a hospital and not to a private clinic. In her brush with death, this was not a small detail. By this gesture, she meant to redress the error of her birth: to be born in surroundings in which she felt foreign. Her brother, fearing a scandal, agreed to do as she wished. She was determined to settle her debt; the clinic demonstrates the fact that she considered her failed suicide yet another luxury.

So, by taking Laure for a mother, I did not betray my real mother except with my father's better. In fact, far from betraying her, I was only doing justice to her dreams as a woman in love.

Yet, despite this harmony between the two women of my account, I will not have accomplished my goal unless each line that I write is seen as a cross. I am trying to evoke a being: me, going back in time endlessly, through ever altered courses, until spinning in an age-old void.

Let us return to Laure. Shortly after I first formulated the idea of this transfer at my birth, I received a letter from Georges Bataille. His work exerted a fascination over me that was all the greater because it dealt with eroticism and its author had been my aunt's lover for more than four years. Besides, what brought my agitation to a peak was the fact of knowing that Bataille was genuinely, passionately in love with Laure. Seeing this love from two perspectives conferred on it a singular depth.

Because they had each discussed this at length, I knew that in embracing each other, Laure and Bataille had had a certain apprehension about death. That Laure was dead allowed me to participate in the experience that had been theirs.

I was able to reread all of Bataille's work and find something of his mad love for Laure behind each of his pages. The two volumes of *l'Expérience Intérieure* and, especially, *Guilty* were reduced, for me, to the utterance of the passion-inspired grammar of their author. Behind these paragraphs, just beneath the surface,

Laure's face stood out with the terrible force of an incantation. In fact, I tried to interpret Bataille's entire work in light of his desire for Laure. So, as I progressed through *Eroticism,* I felt I was retracing my own exploration of pleasure. Finally there was *Blue of Noon*. Its boundlessness both clearly and impalpably restored Laure's image to me with all the power and enchantment of the evident.

My agitation in receiving a letter from Bataille might be understood all the more given that, if I had made Laure *my diagonal mother*—my dead woman, my endless obsession, my true love—she was as much for Bataille if not more. What fascinated me about her was that the excesses of her lucidity had formed the flowers of her madness. I knew that seeing the world all too clearly and listening to the pulse of its transparency had imparted to Laure all her beauty.

Once again, I could not help imagining Laure and Bataille's embraces. I imagined their passionate fury and nameless tenderness ensnare their relationship in a series of laws that made their madness natural. I even saw Georges, like a good theoretician of pleasure, justify their love until it had all the elements of an implacable logic. For a long time, I made Bataille a father, too, not a sire but a mental father. That Laure was dead, that she was my aunt and that I had loved her passionately without ever having been able to touch her, reduced me to a wounded state, alive enough to suffer from love, and given the violence done to me, not alive enough. I have not ceased to feel this silent, infinitely deep burning. It has reduced me today to embers that continue to consume me. All of this explains why I did not so much read Bataille's works as scrutinize them, seeking in his writings, given our common love, something of the throbbing of my blood.

What contributed even more to shadowing both the happiness of having found my Laure again and the anguish of having to admit that I had lost her forever, was a book by Bataille which announced Laure's presence in his life more than the others: *l'Abbé C.* After World War I, suddenly aware that, in the euphoria of victory, the middle class was likely to become estranged from the Christian faith, the Church had placed priests in Parisian families. Thus, before the worker-priests in World War II France, there were "bourgeois priests." One of them came to live with my family, which had lost men in the war. My three great-uncles and my grandfather had died in the space of several weeks, and my father had enlisted in 1917 and had been sent to the combat zone. The opportunity was too good to let go: a priest moved in. His name was l'abbé D.

My grandmother was a person steeped in piety and stifling Catholicism. She had three daughters. As one may well imagine, the abbé took advantage of the situation to fondle my aunts. I never found out the real story behind it all. Each time I mentioned the presence of this priest at my parents' house, I saw their mouths pinch. The Laportes, including and especially my father, are actors, people who have mastered the art not only of dividing themselves, but of no longer even knowing where they stand, having assumed so many affected expressions. Even very recently, I tried to find out what really happened; I found only puppets, broken robots.

Reduced to calculations that have since become part of my fantasies, I have come to imagine Laure hiding in an attic, confiding to a notebook (which was not quite, and, at the same time, much more than a young girl's diary) the secrets of the partially successful manoeuvres of her mother's priest.

Finally, and this played no small part in dooming to silence all that concerned her, Laure had been a "communist." In the family, the word was uttered with restrained intonation fraught with meaning, causing such discomfort that it threw into question those who tremblingly *alluded* to it. In fact, Laure's revolutionary fervor answered for what she understood to be evident. For her, to be a militant revolutionary was only to expose the transparency that was hers, to express it completely. No more than Bataille had radically opposed the USSR,[4] did Laure follow any precept to the letter. She had gone to the Soviet Union in the '30s where her pure-heartedness had made inevitable her fascination for the nascent cause of socialism. She had brought back from this blood-soaked country the best of its flame and had nourished it as much with her love for Bataille as with her profound political convictions. Deep down, I knew the tumult of her courage, which occupied her not only in the time of her political engagement, but throughout her existence. Her entire being was the Revolution. The latter is never anything but truth manifesting itself. True to her nature, Laure was so filled with holy rage that her whole being radiated the almost imperceptible trembling of light vibrating at the edge of a fire.

So I separated Laure's revolutionary convictions from the rest of her life only artificially. Her love, the Revolution, and her poems formed but a triangle in which she lived, enclosed, a sign that was found again at the place of her sex, on her face and in the palms of her hands; a triangle that she constantly shattered the better to reconstruct it.

4. Cf. *La part maudite* (Éditions de Minuit). *[The Accursed Share]*

It was February 1936. Because of the political events, minds were "overexcited," to use Suzanne's expression. Yet Laure's calmness and serenity were assured. The Popular Front was in power, no doubt a source of great joy for Laure, but also a source of greater strength.

When Laure arrived at rue du Ranelagh that day, she immediately noticed a tricolor flag which her nephews had made from rags and hung in the window. "You let them put that filth on the balcony," she said. "The French flag is not filth," replied Suzanne, outraged. If Suzanne realized then what 1936 represented for Laure, she obviously did not or could no longer imagine what the flag evoked for her. Not so much the death of her father as everything her mother had forced her and her sisters to experience, the sorrow that would become the substance of *Story of a Little Girl,* her autobiographical narrative. And yet, Suzanne could have remembered. In a letter of August 1922, hadn't Laure already said to her: "Mama is certainly very much mistaken"? It's true that this was a euphemism—that's the least we can say—true, also, that Laure was all "ferocious propriety" and, finally, that it was more than ten years ago that this little sentence had escaped her lips. And then, in spite of everything, Laure had never ceased to show compassion toward her mother.

But if Suzanne could not ignore everything her sister-in-law had gone through—her familial and amorous dramas as well as her trip to Russia—she does not even think about it. This is because Suzanne's "grace," which Laure appreciates and admires so, is essentially obliviousness. In Paris, a rumor circulated about Léon Blum, launched by a right-wing journalist to discredit the man who then headed the Popular Front: "Léon Blum's name is Karfunkel and he has silver dishes." Suzanne had invited a few friends over. They were at the table discussing the events—scarcely anything else was talked about—when Suzanne mentioned Léon Blum's alleged name and his "silver dishes." "Do you have proof?" Laure asked her calmly. "Well, really, it's something everyone knows," Suzanne replied. Laure immediately got up, threw her napkin on the table, and left. A half an hour later the telephone rang. It was Mr. Bluwal, head of Blum's cabinet: "Madame, a moment ago, you said that Léon Blum's name was Karfunkel and that he had silver dishes. What do you mean by that and do you have proof to support what you are suggesting?" Suzanne hung up without answering. Her friends, to whom she immediately related the conversation, frightened her by telling her that she was "ready for the next tumbril." After this, Suzanne would never again see the person who had borne her so much love. Something in this rupture tells us that, although she was its architect—at least at first glance—Laure not only suffered more from it than Suzanne but she suffered physically from it. Laure lived her ideas so uncompromisingly that she felt affected by them in her whole being. She sensed perfectly what it cost her to wage this internal battle. So she could have not been unaware of the price she paid for losing what was more than a friendship, and almost a love.

Numerous rumors about my aunt's death spread in the family, where, usually, stories rarely circulate. First (and I have every reason to believe this, after all I learned about the abbé), while Laure was in her agony, my grandmother insisted they send for a priest. Still conscious, Laure objected to this with all her remaining strength. Moreover, I was told that my grandmother met Bataille when Laure was placed in her coffin. How many times have I imagined this scene. I envisioned my grandmother recognizing Bataille over Laure's body, her kissing him (and each time, I had the impression of knowing very precisely the calculated pressure of her old lips on Bataille's cheek) and, finally, Bataille having said that "this time Laure was his," these two people fighting jealously over the corpse.[5]

In a letter, Bataille told me that he had "just seen my name in a journal." I knew he was referring to a publication that had reproduced part of the book I was publishing at the time. Now, there is not a single a work of mine in which, attempting to give back to Laure the presence that she deserved, I have not mentioned her name. For so long, and today still, her name is like a muffled cry to me, beyond death, that real life need only let out to prove its permanence. Bataille immediately pointed out that "it was shameful not to have written for so long or, rather, to have been radically incapable of writing." He then mentioned that "this coincided with the fact that he was finally coming back to live in Paris." He gave me his future address, his telephone number, the times I could reach him and added: "If we can simply see each other in Paris the obstacle we have encountered will be overcome." Finally—and to reread this very simple closing written in his hand still moves me—he assured me of his "deep affection." If he had had such difficulty writing me, it was because it was in his nature to erect artificial

5. On Laure's death, see the article by Moré in the appendix.

obstacles. Without even knowing me yet, he was trying through me to forbid himself from rejoining Laure, nevertheless lost forever.

When I arrived at the Pont-Royal bar, there was a man with gray hair waiting for me. What we said to each other then is not important. What is, on the other hand, were the tears I saw rolling down his cheeks.

Since in light of their political choices I challenged both of them, I am neither entirely my mother's son, nor my father's; since I am neither that of Laure whom I loved and still love passionately, nor, even less that of Bataille, I have gradually come to feel like no one's bastard. Under these conditions (who would not feel it?) there is nothing to hold on to. Worse, or perhaps better, I no longer engage in any reality, I live in a landscape that slips beneath my feet, a country of shimmering ripples that, ultimately, never existed.

II

Each time I recall Laure's face, I rediscover a sort of harmony, my emotional life organizes itself, rids itself of the slag that weighs it down. This woman and the love I have for her purifies everything. My passion restores my authenticity. Reading Laure's writings verified this, and also helped to confirm my blood ties to her. As it was, I felt I was experiencing with my father the same thing that Laure had with her mother. With a generation's distance, the same family, of opposite sex, we are in fact the same two lost children. By finally reading "Story of a Little Girl" and "The Sacred," it seemed to me that I changed sexes and found myself in hers. I exchanged our texts as well. I felt what Laure had written, down to the last comma, the last breath. And what if all my work were reduced to making Laure's known? I have perhaps written only to meet the men who could let me read these texts and help me publish them. Once again I remember the moments of this first reading:

I read slowly, in all this light. These texts are so beautiful they splash in my eyes.

A desire to transform each of my women into Laure. I want to force them to be what she was, what she still is for me: not my aunt but "my diagonal mother."

Laure, a woman rid of all family, alone in order to be increasingly more open to pleasure and, therefore, to death.

In her writings, I see that Laure spoke of her first bullfight. In these few pages, she said that "next to her the sight of blood made a man have an erection like a stag." This man, as soon as I read these lines, was me, ravaged with desire for her: Laure.

In *Blue of Noon,* Bataille recounted a trip to Barcelona and I learned that Laure had gone there. He had entitled another book *L'Abbé C.* and I knew what role a certain abbé D. had played in Laure's life.

But Laure was not present in either of these books any more than she was absent from them. The paths I followed intersected, broke off, but a little further I found them intact again. Laure was undoubtedly present in the strongest places in Bataille's books. How had I not thought of it earlier? I was so convinced of it I ended up recognizing Laure's presence in books that Bataille had written before Laure had even come into his life.

Laure managed to make work what some call a failing (and what I call the desire to give back words all their meaning), making her way toward ever more purity. "In conversation," Leiris explained to me, "you had to be careful. There were things you couldn't say without exposing yourself to an implacable reprimand. With her you got the feeling of being on the edge of a blade." Laure had an edge, I feel it. Her judgments on certain things, those pertaining to her political opinions, for example, were absolute. "I cannot stand banality in others any more than in myself, saying things for the sake of saying them," she repeatedly states in her writings. I imagined her in conversation with "other people" and could not help thinking that she must have exacted constant rigor. This was because, for her, what approached truth touched on "the sacred." From the family fights she experienced, she had acquired this sense of "the sacred" that marks all her work. For those who know Bataille's work, it is easy to conclude that, from earliest childhood, Laure already responded to the most beautiful and most authentic of the writer's aspirations. She made this relentless strength, which she used to defend her sensibility, the very principle of her sex.

I feel I am explaining Laure through nerves or, rather, through blood, identical to hers. To understand Laure in this way is, for lack of embracing her, to identify with her in moments of agitation bordering on love. At such instants, I have the sensation of making love not so much with this dead woman as with the very air in which she exists, the air that, because it intoxicates me, explains me in return.

Curious all the same that the man who links me to the woman I love *éperdument* (and in this word there is *perdu*)[6] is so undeniably the opposite of what we, Laure and I, are, or were. At the same time, and this explains the violence of my passion for her, I love my aunt *against my father.*

In her texts, Laure does not show herself to be as vindictive toward her brother. Somewhere, she compares him to a cat or something of the sort: "Jacques set off, his gait supple (it looked as though he spent all his time on a tennis court while the others moved through the house as though on a carpet leading to the holy altar)." Elsewhere, she points out again: "Only my brother pulled us from the malaise with an offhandedness that brought forth those sacriligious bursts of laughter that must be contained in the drawing room or in church." But later her reservations are expressed when she admits that he was scarcely more for her than

6. Trans. Éperdument = desperately; perdu = lost.

a false breath of air. Bataille recognized that my father was surrounded by a certain aura of scandal. For this reason, he accorded him a certain respect. But my father's posturings were just that. His sexual freedom did not go beyond the confines of the bourgeois, conventional proprieties in which he was determined finally to remain.

For Laure, each person had the duty to live the purest of himself. The bullfight seemed to her the quintessential moment of pathos. It was under my aunt's influence, or rather in thinking of her and the issues she raised, perhaps to help her, that Leiris admitted to me having written *Miroir de la Tauromachie* [Paris: G.L. Mano, 1938]. On the flyleaf of this little book illustrated with André Masson's drawings which he sent to me, he had written: "Dear Jérôme Peignot, here is the little book I told you about. I hope I will be able to explain to you one of these days its exact link to the woman who (unable to name her) it was necessary to baptize 'Laure.' " Even though Michel's book was illustrated with Masson's sumptuous, erotic drawings, I felt invested with the right and even charged with the duty to vigorously underline the passages that touched me most deeply each time I felt the need. It did not take long to realize that these lines were those behind which I recognized the presence, even better, the face of Laure. "The thrust—to the matador's flowery hilt—disappears in the top of the withers, like the red rose that a girl with a tight blouse plants between her breasts." "A lunge to the chest: place it between the breasts." "Everything can be summed up perhaps in a piece of red fabric nailed to a whitewashed wall: a rag of blood burning against the prison of bones." To tell the truth, if these quotations bring me back to Laure, for those not in on the secret, they allude only to the love life of anyone provided it was passionate. Like a splinter, Laure became embedded in the very feeling I had of the life whose highest moments she sustained with all the fever of her truth.

When I finished reading it, I was seized by the desire to add commentaries that Leiris's words suggested to me. Laure was at the origin of this text; I was in a position to finish it. Thus, in line with a theme of Leiris's, who brilliantly established these links that united and even merged the gestures of the bullfight with those of love, I spoke, in the margin of his book, of "the virginity of the bull in the face of death." Didn't man, too, die in love? I took so much pleasure in Leiris's story I wanted to appropriate it. Through blood, wasn't it mine a little bit already? One can see, from whatever way I took this affair, I multiplied the to-ings and fro-ings: through the intermediary of *Miroir de la Tauromachie* I found my Laure again. Through this book, Laure and I melded our same, irresistable need to write, our same desire to confuse love and writing.

Finally, shortly after my meeting with Michel, I realized he had sent me *Miroir* twice. My agitation was great when I read on the flyleaf of the second copy these few words: "To the memory of Colette. . . ." To read my aunt's name there, or rather mine placed beside hers, was undeniably moving. The letters of this name surrounded a mirage. I felt then that Michel had sealed our union, Laure's and mine, this union that I could not designate. For lack of something better, I spoke of my "diagonal mother." The expression is only worth something if one grasps that the term "mother" here does not exclude that of lover.

To be honest, I must also say that "The Autobiographer as *Torero*" (Leiris's preface to *Manhood*) has always served as a beacon. As an autobiographer, the supreme rules that must guide me are found here. From a mental point of view at least, I saw "Miroir de la tauromachie" precede "De la littérature considérée comme une tauromachie" [The Autobiographer as Torero] and, as a result, decree the laws of my work. Laure was indeed at the source of my strongest requirements in terms of writing or, at least, I knew that she had to be there. The very idea of placing her before me, like a light in the darkness of her death, charged with bringing the best of myself safely to port, intoxicated me. Looking at things this way, I was no longer prevented from thinking of my cries as merged with those she no longer uttered but to which, in their remotest vibrations, the air still bore witness.

It was at this same time that Jean-Pierre Faye reminded me that Laure appeared throughout *Fourbis*.[7] I had read it, but no longer remembered it. Was it that, despite myself, I had until then censored everything concerning Laure? If I was not to deceive myself, I saw only one reason for my behavior: it was to make my aunt, even though she was dead, ever more inaccessible, like a lover inflicts on himself the delightful torment of being separated from his beloved. I bring up this text, *Fourbis,* again with the confused happiness that one might imagine. Traces of Laure appeared in Leiris's book, sweet and human traces that transformed everything attached to her name into love:

7. P. 214 of the Gallimard edition, as well as pp. 213, 225, and 239, noted by Marie-Odile Faye in 1970.

"To say good-bye to her corpse, so young despite the illness that for so long gnawed at her lungs, I placed my hand for several seconds on the cold forehead of a woman of my century and of my climate in whom I had placed the best of my friendship, I who, without being a homosexual, regard friendship as a sort of love and am probably—whatever disgust I have for the sublimity of platonic love—a man of feminine friendships rather than a man of passion. I discovered later that this last gesture, addressed to a creature who for years maintained with the Angel of death such familiar relations that she seemed to have borrowed from him a bit of his marble impenetrability, had only been the mechanical but tender reproduction of an earlier gesture, made when she was still more or less healthy. One evening we were lolling about the bars of Montmartre and she had gotten drunk, as she often did when she could no longer sustain the effort necessary to safeguard an equilibrium always hanging by a thread, suspended as she was between ice and fire by her rigor and her passion, her disgust for life, her social messianism and her incapacity to suffer any constraint. I had placed my hand on her forehead to help her to relieve herself of her nausea by vomiting, a single caress, which my right palm—on which this heavy head leaned, heaving as much because of the alcohol as the implacable antinomies of which she was eternally the prey—has never forgotten. As the pages she wrote and has left testify, this friend had chosen, in order to depict herself, the touching first name of 'Laure,' a medieval emerald combining a slightly catlike incandescence with the vaguely parochial sweetness of a stem of angelica."

Shortly before I made the discoveries I have just described, I was invited by Dominique Aury to come to la Boissise-la-Bertrand, where Paulhan had lived and where, while he was alive, I had been invited to one of these memorable croquet games which sharpened his malice and increased his joy. Paulhan was not unaware of the existence of Laure and when I had brought him my first essays at N.R.F., he immediately said to me: "It runs in the family!" Then we had brought up the existence of Laure's texts. From this moment on, Paulhan would incite me to approach my father to convince him to authorize the publication of his sister's work. When some time later I went to see my father, whom I hadn't seen for several years, with this goal, I heard him reply to me:

"Paulhan likes nothing but scandal."

"But Leiris," I said, "says the same thing."

"I've never understood a single line of anything he's written."

"And didn't Bataille say that Colette's work is admirable?"

"Bataille hurt Colette very much."

These answers, dilatory as they were, were all that I obtained. For me, who had made these three men my masters of thought, I was overwhelmed. As it was, the fact alone that he gave so little credit to Laure's work stupefied me. It was possible nevertheless to formulate another, far more pertinent critique with regard to my father. "Why do you want to stir all this up again?" he was essentially saying. He was forgetting that it was a matter of a brilliant woman's work and that such writing to remain unpublished was like the cadaver Antigone so fiercely refused to allow to remain without a grave: they haunt the consciences of those who are responsible for them and who, by their neglect or refusal, deprive the world of a cry that it needs. My father argued that these texts were scandalous, that it was useless to divulge them and thereby allow them to upset people, particularly the children of my other aunt, Laure's older sister. Was it only Laure that they wouldn't be able to understand? Couldn't they bear what we, their cousins, understood well? It was nevertheless ages ago that all these brats had reached so-called adulthood. Was it because they had, in reality, sunk into the woolly dialectic of bourgeois reasonings, social conventions, and above all a Christianity at once aggressive and deceitful? Compared with the splendor of Laure's writings, such arguments do not hold up, and the shadow my father has attempted to cast on Laure's work, by his refusal to publish it, darkens only him. His attitude alone in this matter would be enough to justify my separation from him, which has already lasted over fifteen years.

I had barely left Paulhan's house when I decided to go to Dammarie, the little village where, as children, my brother, sister, and I spent vacations during the month of September, at our grandmother's. The house, just two kilometers from Paulhan's house, had not changed a bit. The pink of its walls still clashed with the very white stones that surrounded the building like a trunk with leather-reinforced corners. Two men were playing tennis under a dazzling sun. Was it because I only saw them from a distance that the heat seemed to make their tennis balls heavier? The barge on the Seine was the same. The backs of the gray fish were still transparent, like the backs of combs. What sweetness in this place that, for Laure, had been so troubled! I followed in Laure's footsteps. It was here that I, too, learned to know nature. These intersections made me uneasy. I moved forward slowly. Each emotion this walk aroused in me had to be felt, one by one, pulled from the skein in which it was entangled. I was struck by a vague nausea. Nevertheless, all this was attached to a past time. Why did I want to wrest it from the past? Because of this feeling that at the end of my days was the woman of my dreams, the one who haunted my blood's hallucinations.

For me, in fact, Dammarie must have been the bourgeois paradise of her hell. One by one, I took up my remaining threads again, the ones that could help me find my Laure. I remembered the last time I'd seen her; I was twelve years old. It was on the boulevard Lannes where she had a small apartment, "maids' rooms" end to end. I remember: my brother was her nephew, and, already, I suffered from the fact that her tenderness was thus deployed to my disadvantage.

The face of love is close to that of death. Laure had that face. Though not skinny, one felt her bones beneath her skin, these same bones one must have touched when one made love to her. I kept the memory of a tall and blond Laure, blond like women who know what it means to love, hypernervous and sensitive the way true poets are, and at the same time, at once abrupt and fragile the way many men are not. In spite of reality, children pull the whole world and the people who surround them into their dreams. I was all the more prompted to do so with Laure since I already loved her. Upon inquiry, I found out she was of medium height and brown-haired. Who cares, after all. What counts is that Laure was capable of reaching utter abjection. I feel that conjuring her image in my mind, I am conforming most closely to what she would have wanted to be. Now—and I am sure of this—her aspirations were so strong that with all her being she transformed herself into a single stridency. Her desire for authenticity was such that she drew from it the essential of her beauty. Understandably, this goes to my head when I remember it. Then, identified as I am with my abberations, I no longer recognize even myself.

But let me go back to Laure's writings which I have never disassociated from her beauty. They nourished it, in effect, like a flame feeds off another. The one leads to the other and vice versa. It is from the beauty of her poems that for me, Laure had this transparency that flowed over her face. The violence of her poetry answered to the power of her eyes, at once burning and icy. There is no feminine beauty that does not start from this central fire of the soul and that, for this reason, cannot be reduced to consumption. The moment of Laure's beauty is eternal. It remains fixed in my mind like the beacon of all my certainties.

All of Laure's work is autobiographical to such an extent that she becomes it, she is rocked by it, in the most obvious of poetries. I do not know anyone who, by the same path, reached the crystal which is the mark of Laure's work. In her writings, Laure so reveals herself she seems to offer herself, transfixed.

In looking at these writings a bit more closely, their perfection is in their economy. I spoke of Laure's bones visible beneath her skin and of what those who loved her must have felt. Beneath the simplicity of her sentences you feel the skeleton of her words. Thus, to read a poem by her is to merge with the life that, in a breath, gave birth to them. Because of her suffering, for all the reasons that I mentioned, we know that, in the end, Laure must have been nothing but skin and bones. She died of tuberculosis at thirty-five, on the eve of the war, as though eroded by a mental evil that finally cut off her last breath. Her last writings also vibrate with fragility. It's as if the words that compose them retain, instead of dispersing, the tension that impels them.

Having mingled my existence with hers for so long, I no longer see why (if I ever saw why since I became aware of them) I would accept the idea that Laure's texts could not also be mine. Considering my love for her, I will go even further and assert that they are everyone's for all eternity. All my father's arguments on this subject seem ridiculous to me. By taking such an attitude I am only stating the obvious. To wrest these writings from the hands of those who attempt to stifle them: I could not have a better way, in the precincts of death where sounds are at once deadened and eternally resonant, to cry out my love.

Not only had the family blacklisted Laure's writings, but they tried to blot out her memory. These people who were not worthy of her sought, once she was dead, to extinguish her name. In the end, however, I did not wish to know where Laure had been buried either, but for different reasons. This way I knew that her beauty and her truth would always haunt me. Contrary to Antigone's attitude which I spoke of earlier, this desire to remain unaware of my aunt's burial place gave her all the life that deep down, without always knowing it, she had never ceased to have for me.

I have not yet sufficiently emphasized Laure's political opinions. They were joined to her beauty as much as to her poetry. If, on this point, my information is fragmentary, I know enough to assert that she maintained links of friendship for a long time with a French militant in the first Communist party, Léon Bourénine,[8] who, in his time, must have known Lenin and Trotsky. Did Laure

8. Trans. Boris Souvarine.

decide to go to the Soviet Union alone or did she in fact make the trip accompanied by this man with whom she returned to France? So many questions remain unanswered.

If Laure indeed wanted to demonstrate to herself that she was capable of not falling into the trap of marriage and of living her sensuality without hypocrisy, by giving herself entirely and even more (this is the episode of her life in Berlin which Bataille mentions in "Laure's Life"), she was also persuaded that to lead a dissolute life was not enough to consider herself a revolutionary. To convince herself of this, it sufficed to look at her brother's behavior: "her name conjured for me her brother's Parisian orgies," Bataille would later write. The attitude is very precisely the opposite of what Laure aspired to. She is purity itself and it is in this way that she meant to exhaust herself. From now on, she wants to give herself in another way, more completely still. She wants to be identified with love itself. "She wanted to become a militant revolutionary," writes Bataille, "yet her agitation was vain and feverish. She learned Russian at the École des Langues Orientales and left for Russia. She lived at first in poverty and solitude, eating in miserable restaurants and only rarely setting foot in the opulent hotels for foreigners. Then she met writers. She was the mistress of Boris Pilniak, of whom she kept bad memories, but whom she nevertheless saw again later in Paris. She stayed in Leningrad but mostly in Moscow. Weary of everything, she wanted to know and even share the life of Russian peasants. In the middle of winter, she insisted on being taken to a family of poor mujiks in an isolated village. She withstood this excessively hard trial poorly. She was hospitalized in Moscow, gravely ill." From this trip to Russia, Suzanne kept a letter that expresses the sadness and solitude that Laure experiences feeling powerless to this extent; a postcard in which she brings up an idea for work in Moscow for her brother, as good a way as any to latch onto a buoy or to call for help; and, finally, a note scrawled in faded pencil. If Laure had always disdained punctuation, at least the dashes of her letters created a rhythm. This time, the tension of her handwriting had been replaced by the sinuous lines of a drowning woman's writing. Things were so distended here that a single word sometimes stretched across the entire width of the paper. Laure demonstrates here that the summit of writing is a move toward writing's underside.

"Her brother came to fetch her and brought her back in a sleeping car," Bataille goes on. "She came back to Paris: she lived on rue Blomet then.

Disgusted, she would sometimes seduce vulgar men and make love to them, even in the bathroom of a train. But she did not take pleasure in it." There is a point on which I have not expanded, that is, Laure's illness, her consumption. But is this even useful? Through the quotations I have already cited, doesn't Laure's writing, at once labored and desperate, alone already express all the fragility of her life? If these episodes in the trains bring me back to Laure's illness, it is because Suzanne alludes to it when she speaks of "the sensuality peculiar to the tubercular." If, by this, she wanted to evoke some sort of inevitability of a physiological nature, she is mistaken. Laure was such that we can be sure she gave herself heart and soul to each of her casual lovers. The opposite happened: it was not the illness that prompted her to pleasure but it was her will to look love in the face that killed her. Each embrace conferred on her the false ardor of a flame being extinguished.

On her return, Laure is, on account of her political opinions, a plague to her family. In fact, no one even talks about it. They keep quiet, which is worse. Actually, with these appeals for help from Russia the correspondence with my mother stops. This silence alone is significant. But it does not say everything. At her most frail, Laure is alone, forced to recognize her failure to enact her convictions—a trial that sustained her physically. She is no longer reduced only to her intransigence. But no doubt it was always this way. In fact, looking back on this correspondence as a whole, Laure does not so much write to her sister-in-law as talk to herself in front of her, abandoning herself to a delirious threnody. With her letters, Laure proves that we reveal the truth only when torn apart.

Under these conditions Laure lives with Léon Bourénine. "He tries hard to save her," writes Bataille, "treats her like an invalid, a child, was more a father for her than a lover." If one is forced to repeat Bataille's formulations, it is because he is the only one able to clarify things. Indeed, at the time, the ties between Laure and Suzanne have greatly slackened. Besides the political reasons that one can guess, Suzanne and Jacques are in the process of a divorce. Not that Laure ceases for all that to preserve a real attachment to her ex–sister-in-law—the two women continue to see each other until 1936—but, in spite of her physical weakness, which betrays a certain lifelessness in her relations with her family, Laure is from now on no longer sure of what she thinks, and thus capable of solitude. Moreover, she lives increasingly in a circle of intellectuals, which is not the circle her brother moves in. From the dandy that is Drieu La Rochelle, a friend of Jacques Laporte whom Laure meets at his house, to Bourénine, and especially to Georges Bataille, there is a world of difference. Jacques will no doubt make the acquaintance of Bourénine, but he will not meet Bataille. Already this difference says everything.

Finally, in the notes added to one of the two little books by Laure that Georges Bataille and Michel Leiris would publish at her death, signed with the pseudonym Laure,[9] I found this on the subject of Laure's political convictions: "Rebelling early against a bourgeois and Catholic upbringing, she had become totally devoted, after a prolonged stay in Russia, to opposition communism as the solution to give her life meaning. Events having led her to reject political activity as devoid of value, she had to pick herself back up, as she would say, 'from this great earthquake that is loss of faith.' Without ceasing to know moments of distress—as well as happiness or caprice—she came to find again 'a more total state of consciousness than ever,' the highest ambition someone could achieve when *integrity of being* occupied, in the scale of values, the privileged place." What I am certain of is that Laure would never cease to reveal an authentic spirit of revolt. I see this confirmed first in her separation with Bourénine and, second, paradoxical though it might seem, in her love for Bataille which followed. To go from the first of these men to the second was to slip from a too dry wit to the never excessive ardor of the heart (or, if one prefers, the senses). In actual fact, what can one say of a political choice that is not supported by the madness of one's love? Laure showed more authentic communist conviction by living with Bataille than by going to the Soviet Union, even though it was in 1930. Then, she joined her love for Bataille with her love for humanity. Revolt to her was not hate but love. Laure had no hate in her, not even for "her own" (indeed, the horror of this expression when it designates people one has not chosen!). Even though, by their presence alone, her family denied her, Laure was inhabited only by love that engulfed her features, that submerged them in such tenderness that you discerned only the outline of a face.

To read Laure's letters dating from the first months of her passion for Bataille, it seems that in love, not having attained happiness and precisely in the name of her love, she demanded the impossible. It seemed, under the pretext of not considering herself worthy, she obstructed this heaven before having reached it . . .

9. Two small works published underground in 1942 in a limited printing, given to friends of Laure.

Something of this habit she had inherited from her childhood—always considering herself at fault—still impeded the expression of her affection. Moreover, we know enough about it to guess that her life with Bataille was not an ordinary liaison. She did not ultimately find peace any more than she lived a tragedy. To define this period of her life, one can evoke not a hell but its opposite, which is not happiness either but rather an analyzed joy, examined to the point of anguish. Finally, her moments of jealousy were the gauge of her truth: they tore her apart and at the same time revealed her to herself. We are right to wonder if, precisely because he loved her, Bataille was not inclined to push her to her extremes.

I have experienced the story of my encounter with Laure's manuscripts and that of their publication as a novel. This narrative confirms my own existence. The least strange in all this is not that it was necessary for me to reach the age of forty-four to be able finally to read these texts once again. The succession of events convinced me that it had to be this way. So many prohibitions weighed on these papers that, had they been at my disposal earlier, I would not have been able to extract from this reading the conclusions that are imperative.

To read them was, in fact, to commit to publishing them. How could I have done that earlier? One evening—it was during the war—my father had in fact read a few carefully selected pages to my brother and me, and then, his conscience no doubt appeased, though at small cost, had once again locked everything up in a little cabinet in the library that I would later find. Since then, I kept in mind a certain passage in which Laure spoke of "seventh heaven." More than twenty years later, what Laure said made my head spin slightly again. Such clarity was almost sickening in its subtlety. And then, attracted by the scandalous character that remained attached to her writings, writings that my father had promised to read to us later (but when?), I managed, one evening, to break open the lock of the small cabinet. Yet, in my feverishness, I hardly discovered anything more than what I already knew. The sound of the elevator would too quickly force me to put everything back in place.

But in all honesty, I must say that supposing I had managed to spirit away and read these documents in their entirety, I surely could not have found the strength to rebel against my father's wishes. However murky they seemed, the arguments he used to justify his prohibition of divulging the whole were unalterable. Besides, who would I have spoken to? Before I had even become fully aware of it, the splendor of Laure's writings had already left me defenseless.

Thus, when thanks to my friend Bernard Noël I discovered that the journal *Ephémère* had published texts by Laure ("Story of a Little Girl"), what I read was not entirely foreign to me. Once again, needless to say, I felt the little vertigo I spoke of. To observe that at the heart of all this darkness, this infinite sky was still there, brought my agitation to its height. But reading these writings, I found still more things, among others the confirmation of what I felt vaguely, namely that Laure and I had something in common in the way we expressed ourselves. This so struck me that I felt as if Laure had essentially written my autobiography. If only in this superimposing, there was already something to confuse me. Had I really written my life through the intermediary of Colette? Where did I leave off, where was I? Was I even still alive? For a moment, I thought I was losing my mind. Already of Laure's blood, I was thus of the same ink. Yet it was nevertheless true that in comparison to her writings, mine seemed like babblings. Hers resonated in a great profound space, something black, eternal, with almost metallic sonorities. There was no case in which Laure did not attain myth. If this is true for "Story of a Little Girl," it is even more so for "The Sacred," the second small volume by Laure (which Bataille titled). But I will go even further: after Laure had written in my place, I had only one desire, now that she was no longer there: to write in hers.

The most touching moment for me was when Louis René des Forêts, to whom Leiris had sent them, sent me Laure's papers. Discovering these documents, I felt not so much that I was taking possession again of traces of a past that concerned me as I felt faced with the framework of time itself. In fact, though unable to explain it to myself very clearly, to read these lines, between each of them, was to decipher this buzzing grayness of which duration is composed. A great disorder reigned in this file of thin yellow sheets. Immediately, Laure's handwriting surprised me. Of course, almost all her letters were detached, her writing was larger than I had imagined it to be, and some of the loops that Laure had formed ended with a real bluntness. Also there were some enraged strokes above the t's, accents that seemed like billhooks. Had I been wrong to see Laure only as a diaphanous being? Indeed, I had not considered the fact that for her, her writing could not fail to be the locus of her confrontation with herself.

Louis René des Forêts deemed that, all things considered, there was not much more to use in this collection of papers than what had already been published in the two small books I mentioned. I took it upon myself to ascertain this for myself. In leafing through the ensemble of these documents, I was initially struck by the fact that they had been written in many different places. There were letterheads from a hotel in Lyons-la-Forêt, others from Avignon, a letter of employment from l'Agence Opéra Mundi, sentences scrawled in the margins of torn newspapers.

I had to go back in time to these trifles, especially to them. Soon it seemed to me that all these texts, in one way or another, revealed a singular intimacy with death. "You turn away, hide, renounce in vain . . ." she wrote in the rough drafts of "Story of a Little Girl," "you are part of the family, said the dead, adding: and you will be with us this evening. They held forth, tender, amiable and sardonic or else in the image of Christ, the eternally humiliated one, they held out their arms." And yet, in spite of the bourgeois horror that Laure described, an undeniable sweetness inhabited the background of her stories.

"The question was this: is it possible to communicate?" Everywhere in these papers, I found this sentence again. Laure had asked herself this question in an anguished way, as though breathless. It seemed very clear that all she had written could be confused with a panting, a gasping for breath. Knowing that she died of tuberculosis, one is struck by the observation that her writings at once recreate her physical life and announce its end. It seemed the words she formed on paper in the intention of writing letters she didn't send, were reduced to traces. These were no longer but the last signs of a life. By living her life without concession, Laure no longer had the energy to live the reprieve that had been accorded her. "You can have several beings within you and struggle ferociously and even debase yourself (in the eyes of others, this *does not matter,* but for yourself, it's atrocious). There are times you can grind your teeth until you've broken your jaw." It was not until the last dizzying spells of fatigue that she was able to evoke perfectly: "But I remain here, mute, as though nothing were the matter, strangled and in my depths I find a magnificent party and then this changes, it's vulgar and intoxicating like a carnival or else I see with my eyes closed and I am completely covered in a fine rain of sweat and ash."

In her lassitude, Laure used a strategem that consisted of using ready-made phrases, diverting them from their sense to give them a singularly acute, deviated, or if you like, distorted meaning. Steeped in an atmosphere of pretense and affectation her whole childhood, she had come to writing false words that proved more capable than true ones of translating the truth she sought to transmit, what she had experienced that was most horrible. In this way, Laure reconstructed this upside-down world of syrupy sweetness in which we find ourselves mired with great luxury of detail. It seemed that with the meticulousness of a scholar, she wanted to give an account of all the harshness of a cry. Is language itself, the one Laure used, ours, an enormous rhetorical figure? Was this, then, the task of poets: to force language to confess what it is hiding, to turn it inside out like the finger of a glove?

As I gradually read through this file, in which I recognized other handwritings besides Laure's, I had the impression that she had passed along to those who had copied out her poems a sort of treasure which she alone had been unable to haul up into the light. I immediately recognized Michel Leiris's handwriting and, on these famous yellow sheets (it seemed time had left its mark here), very firm and very round, that of Georges Bataille. It corresponded rather well to what I knew of him. He had an engineer's handwriting, where a glint of light seemed to take on the appearance of a mirage. Indeed, something about Bataille's handwriting in recopying Laure's texts made the whole of it shimmer with an intensity that was sometimes unbearable. "Others: they play with life, play with crime, with suffering, misery." Because I sometimes fell upon the double of a poem that I had already read, I often had the sensation of a refrain, a haunting. All of this manuscript, Laure's work in its entirety seemed to me to be musically organized, orchestrated in this quasi-miraculous beauty that is attached to the writings denouncing the horror of weakness and sentimentality. Sometimes I saw that Laure had first, or perhaps *also,* given poetic form to certain passages of her "Story of a Little Girl." I was not surprised by this, because reading Laure's "Story," poised as it is on the beam of a pair of scales, it's hard to say whether these paragraphs are not more poetic than her poems.

The intertwining of her different styles gave her work many dimensions. Yet what was distressing in reading these admirable texts was to sense that writing them did not manage to free Laure from her anguish. On the contrary, it seemed that this work, because she was never satisfied with it, contributed to giving her mental pain the intensity of a furnace. Instead of allowing her to breathe a little easier, her poems were ultimately mirrors where this obligation she felt to live was stirred up, and which she, more than anyone else, denounced. After thirty years of waiting, in finally reading these texts, I found myself denounced as well, to the very depths of my being . . .

Concerning the notes that Laure had written on envelopes or bistro napkins, what they revealed with great clarity was how much it was necessary to inhabit words entirely, if they were to mean something. It seemed as though, afraid of not nourishing them enough by underlining them, she sought not only to give them all the power of their meaning but to confer upon them the obsessive buzzing of reverberating sounds. "*Do not accept* what lessens you," "make up for things by being interesting," "which, finally, becomes artificial." It was beautiful to see her reduce her poem to nothing like this: a simple line sometimes beneath an adverb. What was also striking was to find again in these scrawled notes, these drafts of letters, the skeleton of poems that I had read in the two small books that Leiris had sent to me. I said that from the point of view of language, Laure's writings revealed an exceptional economy of means. This time, I found myself in the presence of the life itself that had served to elaborate these texts. Without a doubt, the most powerful episode of all those that could be divined was a scene between Laure and Bataille. For someone who knows Laure as I know her: beyond death and by heart and by blood, to think of the loneliness she must have felt, retrospectively, gave you the sensation of seeing the ground disappear from under your feet. What was most impressive was to discover Laure's determination. To see a sick woman as weak as she was display such resolution troubled me to my bones.

But Laure would not leave Bataille. No doubt, she would always remain capable of mockery. Yet Bataille's turn of mind which incited her to elevate every debate (to the level of the *sacred*, precisely), his knowledge of pleasure, would not only keep her by his side but would bring her back there, as though fascinated. It was impossible to get angry with Bataille, because he was so able to drown his opponents' reasoning in the hell of his too beautiful lucidity.

What Laure was reaching toward was total harmony. She imagined her love as the crucible in which the truths she believed in would attain a furnacelike intensity. Now she suffered down to her flesh from the least divergence, to the point that her life consisted only of heartbreaks. Thus, in spite of the fact that she would never be able to find the means to give shape to her political aspirations, it was impossible for her to continue living with a man whose points of view she did not share: resolve she had to prove during her separation with Bourénine. She points out, however, in her papers that she was only conforming to the laws of nature. For her, the reasons for a separation were expressed as a syllogism. She wrote of the components as small fragments flying in all directions on a page like so many flashes of lightning: "Both of us have to know where we are going, what is happening"; "There are days we can stand each other, days we can't"; "There has to be profound agreement between oneself and *all* the moments of one's life"; "To be strong is to be alone"; "to be able is to dare"; "to have a strong back"; "to want in the nothingness is nothing. To want? With great powerless cries?"; "We have to be perverse enough, libertine enough, so that nothing matters." Though she stated that she was only conforming to nature, there was also no doubt that she was striving to attain the serenity of perfect solitude. From her attitude in these matters I came to the conclusion that everything she had done in her sentimental life (the word does not suit her) was to come to conclusions that were imperative to her after so many years spent in her family's oppressive world of duplicity. Even physically, she was no longer able to endure hypocrisy.

At one given moment, Laure spoke of these notes she kept and she said: "In fleeting moments note the essential of one's life. 'Note' them, why not live them?" No doubt there is not a single "note" in Laure's notebooks behind which one cannot decipher a scrap of her life, a suffering, or else a revolt. Yet she did indeed describe this life, precisely thanks to her notes. In the end, reading her work gives one the feeling Laure lived her whole life divided between the need to devote herself to life and, if only to catch her breath, her wish to codify in her writings that which at the same time kept her alive and killed her:

> You cannot catch yourself on paper
> Like a drowning man clinging to a rock
> the sheet is smooth, smooth, smooth
> Paper is milksop
> dried paste, words worn thin.

In fact, the pleasure of a certain literature or, rather, of detecting something like an evil smile between her words, incited Laure to start over. For a person as proud as she was, there was already something very remarkable about that. It is true also that she got herself out of the embarassing situation in which she had placed herself, precisely through a detachment that was hers alone. Laure marked this distance from her words, by the intermediary of formulas that she used: "One can always speak but to speak truthfully the way others speak German or English . . ."

But her goal was not to express her solitude or her confusion. Ceaselessly, she sought to dissolve these moments of intense anguish in the suffering of others, of those for whom "the fear of the next day cancels out the day itself." If she did not cease to wish to meld her pain to the sorrow of these beings with crushed lives, she also felt this desire was an insult to their poverty. Thus, her great sorrow was reduced to choking back her luck. How could one not *keep quiet* at least? "There are two worlds and rare are those who in one are truly aware of the daily reality of the other. Each has its dwelling place and hours and what they bring to each existence. There are lives that have no hours. The dawn of the desperate . . ." And further on, on another sheet with a completely different handwriting, she resumed:

In seeing the charm, the grace, the disdain
One is surprised that there are not incidents
More often . . . on a daily basis
Fits of anger. Why does this remain
An act of the mad
Then I try to hope
That anger hides away
in working-class neighborhoods
Confines itself there
To better arm itself
To spring forth in control
And attain its goal
More certainly
All will come one day in a great solid mass
To inflict the lesson.

But Laure was not content to denounce injustices. I think it was knowing herself to be on the side of the oppressors, and not being able to do anything concrete to dissociate herself from them, that killed her. No doubt she could have told herself that the will alone to distance herself from her family was already an act to attribute to the Revolution. The important thing was that she did not see things in this manner: "What is an unproven conviction? A certainty that is not supported by facts? A verbal solidarity? . . . Thought hinders gesture and you remain there, stuck. Thought? While one thinks, facts remain, history, men and their antinomic languages. Ultimately you stand there with your hands clean before a totally blank page?" There is not a single successive version of this where one does not get the impression that each word counts. And yet, Laure started over, crossed out, started over again . . . For her each of her passages became a torment, the siren wail of a sinking ship. Elsewhere, several times, I found here and there, in trembling capital letters, calls for HELP.

Each time I thought I could finally give Laure the chance to speak, I fell back into the well of her jottings, her corrections, and her repetitions. Of course, even these had interest for me. I followed her thought down to her least jolt. But, supposing I managed to copy out and organize everything, would the rhythm of this halted breath be perceived by others? I no doubt allowed some beautiful aphorisms to slip away. Nevertheless: I still took the position of conforming essentially to the work that Bataille and Leiris had done and more or less presenting to the public the fruits of their labor. What they had done had been done well. After all, they knew Laure better than I, and most of all, they loved her. For me, this love responded first of all to the quality of their task. And then I felt that, in the last analysis, it was in the state of flares and flashes, almost incomprehensible as they were, that these little cobblestones of text found all their strength. After going through these papers, the writings of Laure finally published seemed to me like wild flowers, poisonous because true.

But this was not counting the contribution of her correspondence which, all things considered, is an integral part of her poetic work. One will see that it holds a capital place in this volume. In fact, there is still a point I would like to stress, and that is the fact that, little by little, while I thought I saw in her only a person lost in pain and solitude at the heart of a family that, having scarcely given birth to her, stifled her, I was forced to recognized that Laure had acquired for me the dimension of a master of thought, better still, a master of behavior. Indeed it seemed everything had happened in her life as though, at the end of her fragility, she had intuited certain solutions: "Laure had found God again," she wrote. "He was not a human being, she made him a hero, a saint. In his arms, then, she wanted him to hurt her. She imagined being beaten, thrashed, wounded, a victim, ridiculed, held in contempt, scorned and then, once again, adored and sanctified."

Still emerging no doubt from the religious obscurantism that had brought her to the brink of exhaustion, had Laure caught even a glimpse of these spots of brightness? She nevertheless codified them with obstinacy. However flickering they were, as soon as I saw them I decided to make these lights my sole beacon. These laws that Laure had suddenly begun to decree were proclaimed in a particular atmosphere, one her suffering had helped define: the atmosphere of the sacred. No doubt, this atmosphere was not unrelated to that which Bataille had made the subject of his analyses. What I would submit is that Laure had provided him with his privileged theme of reflection. Without her, his work would have remained entirely based on philosophical concepts. Yet Bataille is both a poet and a philosopher, and it is the imbrication in him of these two contradictory beings that, ultimately, make the books of the second part of his life poems. "... Poetic work is sacred," wrote Laure, "in that it is creation of a topical event, communication experienced as *nakedness*. It is self-violation, a stripping, communication with others of reasons for living ..." Under Laure's very pen, I could not find a stronger injunction. It was when I read this that I decided not simply to "publish her work" (Bataille's dedication in *Le Coupable* had already had the effect on me of an order[9]) but to allow this work to be read in its entirety, which meant including the passages that my father considered scandalous. Indeed, it seemed precisely through those passages above all that these texts attained the *sacred*.

At her death, Laure "made up for," as she says herself, all the weaknesses she had accused herself of all her life. She did not cease to denounce "the blackmail of weakness," which her mother used and abused. She, on the contrary, intended to show herself to be proud in death. Her last writings left no doubt on this point. From the sanatorium where she stayed for two months, she wrote to friends: "... Know this, I am horrified by pity and—*even now*—I don't feel pitiful in the least and *even now* it is impossible for me to envy anyone else in the world. I envy one thing perhaps, a state, health—that, yes—And still! *My illness is so profoundly linked to my life*[10] that it could not be separated from all that I have experienced. So? Perhaps it is still one of those misfortunes that turn into luck ..." Shortly after, in a letter that she did not send, she wrote:

10. "To Jérôme Peignot, with the very faithful friendship of Georges Bataille and with plans to see him again very soon in view of the publication of a new edition of the works of Laure. Please excuse me for this long silence, due to a state bordering on illness."

11. My emphasis (J.P.)

"Well, if this is death.

Will I lack the courage to love death[12]

I am afraid that something is broken in me: a broken back?

To be weak to that extent.

Don't obsessions replace the fear of God?

Isn't it intolerable to have come to that point?

I want to talk about "loving death" because this means loving life without *restriction*, to love it to that extent, death included. Not to be terrified by death any more than by life. On this condition, I feel myself becoming . . . noble again."

And, before, always in the proximity of this death that she announced so lucidly: "The idea of death, when one follows it to the end . . . to the point of putrefaction, has always relieved me and that day more than ever. I thought about various forms of 'accidental death' in detail and all of them seemed enviable and delicious to me. I became calm and even cheerful."

Finally, during her trip to Spain, Laure had read William Blake's *Proverbs of Hell* and had discovered this sentence which I found several times in her papers: "Drive your cart and your plow over the bones of the dead." This very sentence was the last she would write before dying. It testifies to her wish to see the last traces of her life totally erased from the minds of those who loved her. It is nonetheless true (Michel Leiris confirmed it) that she wanted the cries of her unfathomable distress to be heard, be it beyond her death.

In their notes, Bataille and Leiris expressed themselves plainly on this subject: "Before dying she formally indicated her wish that her testimony not remain uncommunicated, asserting that one must not isolate onself, as only that which exists for others can have meaning. But the misery inherent in all that is literature horrified her: for she had the greatest conceivable concern not to confide what seemed heartrending to her to those who cannot be moved."

On this point, relating to Laure's wish to see her writings published, several remarks come to mind. Whether she read him under the influence of Bataille or not, the fact remains that several times I found references to Nietzsche in Laure's manuscripts or drafts, particularly to *Ecce Homo*. Nietzsche spoke precisely of this desire which, admitted or not, those who write always have—to bring the fruit

12. "What an old maid I am getting to be, lacking the courage to be in love with death" (Arthur Rimbaud, *A Season in Hell*, "Bad Blood").

of their work to the attention of "other beings." Why would they have troubled themselves, he says, essentially, if this were not the point? The successive versions of "Story of a Little Girl" and of each of the poems in the collection *The Sacred* would seem to confirm Nietzsche's words.

I do not know anyone who has died with such calm, such clear-sightedness. To the simplicity and courage Laure showed during her last moments her family responded with the most shameless outbursts, too horrible not to mask a genuine lack of love.

In truth, by dying before him, Laure justified Bataille's books which, in all the tangle of their words, cry out this implication of death in love. No doubt by dying she placed true death between them, but she was already there in the fact alone that they loved each other.

In *Fourbis,* speaking of Laure's name, Leiris evokes an "emerald linking to its catlike incandescence the vaguely parochial sweetness of a stem of angelica." And here Bernard Noël brings me a collection of Bataille's poems for which he wrote the preface and I note that he titles it *l'Archangélique.* Is there a secret link here, a code I cannot break? These poems, in any case, have something of the simplicity of Laure's. Thus, undoubtedly, here again, the signs match up:

I find you in the star
I find you in death
You are the frost in my mouth
You have the odor of a deadwoman
Your breasts open like an animal
And laugh at me from beyond
Your two long thighs are delirious
Your stomach is naked like a death rattle
You are beautiful like fear
You are mad like a deadwoman.

Laure despised literature and everything connected with it. I've said that she hurled cries onto paper only in order to be able to breathe. Unformulated, would these "cries" have been truer? By way of expression, we find ourselves at the edge of the unspoken and at the same time at the height of exactness. More cannot be said: with her "Story of a Little Girl" as with her poems, Laure coincides with language itself. Confronted with such perfect harmony between that which an author meant to signify and the manner in which she has gone about trying to achieve it, we may be prompted to be affected viscerally.

My task accomplished, I feel I have rummaged through the womb of darkness, the darkness with which Laure identified. By writing this I have lived in a certain intimacy with death and because of that I was able to extract from these shadows—which, at times, I was able to detach from one other perfectly—this image. For me, it glitters in an upside-down firmament. Upside-down because it is to the horror of the world in which she lived that Laure owes being who she is. There are no terrible truths. They can be talked about simply because they are what they are.

A time bomb explodes in the future. The one whose fuse I am aware of lighting, by publishing the writings of Laure, will explode in the past. And yet, amidst the debris that it will scatter, there will be some that belongs to the present. The reason is that since Laure died, some of the situations she faced have reappeared. Worse: Whether it has to do with bourgeois sectarism or a so-called "revolutionary" intransigence, isn't obscurantism more stifling today than after the Revolution of 1917?

Finally, by ending this preface,[13] I feel I am sealing my union with death. To have written this, to publish the writings of Laure, installs death into my life. By "sealing my union with death," I mean knotting my relationship with Laure, which, by definition, can only be interrupted by my life, and perhaps not even then . . .

13. Trans. "My Diagonal Mother" was the preface to the French edition.

CITY LIGHTS PUBLICATIONS

Acosta, Juvenal, ed. LIGHT FROM A NEARBY WINDOW:
Contemporary Mexican Poetry
Alberti, Rafael. CONCERNING THE ANGELS
Allen, Roberta. AMAZON DREAM
Angulo de, Jaime. INDIANS IN OVERALLS
Angulo de, G. & J. JAIME IN TAOS
Artaud, Antonin. ARTAUD ANTHOLOGY
Bataille, Georges. EROTISM: Death and Sensuality
Bataille, Georges. THE IMPOSSIBLE
Bataille, Georges. STORY OF THE EYE
Bataille, Georges. THE TEARS OF EROS
Baudelaire, Charles. INTIMATE JOURNALS
Baudelaire, Charles. TWENTY PROSE POEMS
Blake, N., Rinder, L., & A. Scholder. IN A DIFFERENT LIGHT:
Visual Culture, Sexual Culture, Queer Practice
Bowles, Paul. A HUNDRED CAMELS IN THE COURTYARD
Bramly, Serge. MACUMBA: The Teachings of Maria-José, Mother of the Gods
Brook, J. & Iain A. Boal. RESISTING THE VIRTUAL LIFE:
Culture and Politics of Information
Broughton, James. COMING UNBUTTONED
Broughton, James. MAKING LIGHT OF IT
Brown, Rebecca. ANNIE OAKLEY'S GIRL
Brown, Rebecca. THE TERRIBLE GIRLS
Bukowski, Charles. THE MOST BEAUTIFUL WOMAN IN TOWN
Bukowski, Charles. NOTES OF A DIRTY OLD MAN
Bukowski, Charles. TALES OF ORDINARY MADNESS
Burroughs, William S. THE BURROUGHS FILE
Burroughs, William S. THE YAGE LETTERS
Cassady, Neal. THE FIRST THIRD
Choukri, Mohamed. FOR BREAD ALONE
CITY LIGHTS REVIEW #2: AIDS & the Arts
CITY LIGHTS REVIEW #3: Media and Propaganda
CITY LIGHTS REVIEW #4: Literature / Politics / Ecology
Cocteau, Jean. THE WHITE BOOK (LE LIVRE BLANC)
Cornford, Adam. ANIMATIONS
Corso, Gregory. GASOLINE
Cuadros, Gil. CITY OF GOD
Daumal, René. THE POWERS OF THE WORD
David-Neel, Alexandra. SECRET ORAL TEACHINGS IN TIBETAN
BUDDHIST SECTS
Deleuze, Gilles. SPINOZA: Practical Philosophy
Dick, Leslie. KICKING
Dick, Leslie. WITHOUT FALLING
di Prima, Diane. PIECES OF A SONG: Selected Poems
Doolittle, Hilda (H.D.). NOTES ON THOUGHT & VISION
Ducornet, Rikki. ENTERING FIRE

Duras, Marguerite. DURAS BY DURAS
Eberhardt, Isabelle. DEPARTURES: Selected Writings
Eberhardt, Isabelle. THE OBLIVION SEEKERS
Eidus, Janice. VITO LOVES GERALDINE
Fenollosa, Ernest. CHINESE WRITTEN CHARACTER AS A MEDIUM FOR POETRY
Ferlinghetti, Lawrence. PICTURES OF THE GONE WORLD (Enlarged 1995 edition)
Ferlinghetti, L., ed. ENDS & BEGINNINGS (City Lights Review #6)
Finley, Karen. SHOCK TREATMENT
Ford, Charles Henri. OUT OF THE LABYRINTH: Selected Poems
Franzen, Cola, transl. POEMS OF ARAB ANDALUSIA
García Lorca, Federico. BARBAROUS NIGHTS: Legends & Plays
García Lorca, Federico. ODE TO WALT WHITMAN & OTHER POEMS
García Lorca, Federico. POEM OF THE DEEP SONG
Gil de Biedma, Jaime. LONGING: SELECTED POEMS
Ginsberg, Allen. THE FALL OF AMERICA
Ginsberg, Allen. HOWL & OTHER POEMS
Ginsberg, Allen. KADDISH & OTHER POEMS
Ginsberg, Allen. MIND BREATHS
Ginsberg, Allen. PLANET NEWS
Ginsberg, Allen. PLUTONIAN ODE
Ginsberg, Allen. REALITY SANDWICHES
Goethe, J. W. von. TALES FOR TRANSFORMATION
Harryman, Carla. THERE NEVER WAS A ROSE WITHOUT A THORN
Hayton-Keeva, Sally, ed. VALIANT WOMEN IN WAR AND EXILE
Heider, Ulrike. ANARCHISM: Left Right & Green
Herron, Don. THE DASHIELL HAMMETT TOUR: A Guidebook
Herron, Don. THE LITERARY WORLD OF SAN FRANCISCO
Higman, Perry, tr. LOVE POEMS FROM SPAIN AND SPANISH AMERICA
Jaffe, Harold. EROS: ANTI-EROS
Jenkins, Edith. AGAINST A FIELD SINISTER
Katzenberger, Elaine, ed. FIRST WORLD, HA HA HA!
Kerouac, Jack. BOOK OF DREAMS
Kerouac, Jack. POMES ALL SIZES
Kerouac, Jack. SCATTERED POEMS
Kerouac, Jack. SCRIPTURE OF THE GOLDEN ETERNITY
Lacarrière, Jacques. THE GNOSTICS
La Duke, Betty. COMPAÑERAS
La Loca. ADVENTURES ON THE ISLE OF ADOLESCENCE
Lamantia, Philip. MEADOWLARK WEST
Laughlin, James. SELECTED POEMS: 1935–1985
Le Brun, Annie. SADE: On the Brink of the Abyss
Lowry, Malcolm. SELECTED POEMS
Mackey, Nathaniel. SCHOOL OF UDHRA
Marcelin, Philippe-Thoby. THE BEAST OF THE HAITIAN HILLS
Masereel, Frans. PASSIONATE JOURNEY
Mayakovsky, Vladimir. LISTEN! EARLY POEMS
Mrabet, Mohammed. THE BOY WHO SET THE FIRE

Mrabet, Mohammed. THE LEMON
Mrabet, Mohammed. LOVE WITH A FEW HAIRS
Mrabet, Mohammed. M'HASHISH
Murguía, A. & B. Paschke, eds. VOLCAN: Poems from Central America
Murillo, Rosario. ANGEL IN THE DELUGE
Parenti, Michael. AGAINST EMPIRE
Paschke, B. & D. Volpendesta, eds. CLAMOR OF INNOCENCE
Pasolini, Pier Paolo. ROMAN POEMS
Pessoa, Fernando. ALWAYS ASTONISHED
Peters, Nancy J., ed. WAR AFTER WAR (City Lights Review #5)
Poe, Edgar Allan. THE UNKNOWN POE
Porta, Antonio. KISSES FROM ANOTHER DREAM
Prévert, Jacques. PAROLES
Purdy, James. THE CANDLES OF YOUR EYES
Purdy, James. GARMENTS THE LIVING WEAR
Purdy, James. IN A SHALLOW GRAVE
Purdy, James. OUT WITH THE STARS
Rachlin, Nahid. MARRIED TO A STRANGER
Rachlin, Nahid. VEILS: SHORT STORIES
Reed, Jeremy. DELIRIUM: An Interpretation of Arthur Rimbaud
Reed, Jeremy. RED-HAIRED ANDROID
Rey Rosa, Rodrigo. THE BEGGAR'S KNIFE
Rey Rosa, Rodrigo. DUST ON HER TONGUE
Rigaud, Milo. SECRETS OF VOODOO
Ruy Sánchez, Alberto. MOGADOR
Saadawi, Nawal El. MEMOIRS OF A WOMAN DOCTOR
Sawyer-Lauçanno, Christopher, transl. THE DESTRUCTION OF THE JAGUAR
Scholder, Amy, ed. CRITICAL CONDITION: Women on the Edge of Violence
Sclauzero, Mariarosa. MARLENE
Serge, Victor. RESISTANCE
Shepard, Sam. MOTEL CHRONICLES
Shepard, Sam. FOOL FOR LOVE & THE SAD LAMENT OF PECOS BILL
Smith, Michael. IT A COME
Snyder, Gary. THE OLD WAYS
Solnit, Rebecca. SECRET EXHIBITION: Six California Artists
Sussler, Betsy, ed. BOMB: INTERVIEWS
Takahashi, Mutsuo. SLEEPING SINNING FALLING
Turyn, Anne, ed. TOP TOP STORIES
Tutuola, Amos. FEATHER WOMAN OF THE JUNGLE
Tutuola, Amos. SIMBI & THE SATYR OF THE DARK JUNGLE
Valaoritis, Nanos. MY AFTERLIFE GUARANTEED
Veltri, George. NICE BOY
Wilson, Colin. POETRY AND MYSTICISM
Wilson, Peter Lamborn. SACRED DRIFT
Wynne, John. THE OTHER WORLD
Zamora, Daisy. RIVERBED OF MEMORY

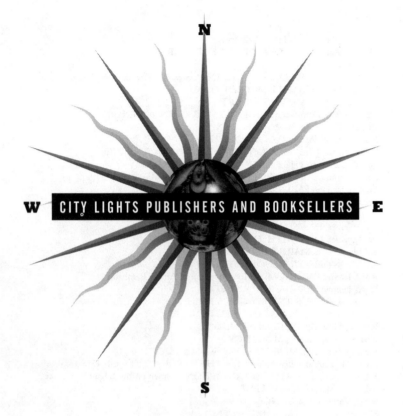